NEW YORK EMPIRES SERIES

GOING ALL IN
ICING THE PUCK

ICING THE PUCK

New York Empires

ISABO KELLY
STACEY AGDERN
KENZIE MACLIR

T&D
PUBLISHING

ICING THE PUCK

CONTENTS

ICING THE PUCK

New York Empires

ISABO KELLY
STACEY AGDERN
KENZIE MACLIR

LIGHT THE LAMP

Isabo Kelly

CHAPTER ONE

D r. Ann Bell stared at the woman across the open workout room of the physical therapy center. She was a pretty, tall brunette who held herself with a natural confidence Ann envied. And though Ann looked for a resemblance, she didn't see any.

Well, she'd known Nathalie looked more like her father than like their mother anyway.

Ann nibbled her lip as Nathalie laughed and talked with the man laid out on a message table while she worked on his knee. Ann wasn't sure she could go through with this. Already her heartbeat was thumping hard and her palms were starting to heat. That was dangerous.

All emotion was dangerous.

Pulling in a deep breath, she let the scents of medicinal rubs, cleaning products, and a faint tang of sweat pull her focus so she could settle herself. Attention to details beyond her body always helped her calm down.

Calm, logical, emotionless. That was her only choice.

But all her techniques were starting to fail. She needed help. Soon.

3

Or someone would get hurt.

She pulled herself in, centered and focused, and started across the large room, making a beeline for the only person who might be able to save her.

She was so intent on reaching Nathalie, she forgot to pay attention to her surroundings and plowed into someone. Hard.

Strong hands gripped her upper arms and held her as she got her feet under her. She looked up...and up some more, to see the hulking man she'd just barreled into.

He was huge. How had she missed him?

"You OK?" he asked with a crooked grin.

"I'm sorry. I didn't see you." She stepped back, adjusting her coat over her arm and pushing her purse strap back up over her shoulder.

"Obviously. Unless you bumped into me on purpose to get my attention."

"Um. No."

He chuckled. "Too bad. The people normally trying to run me down aren't nearly so cute."

"Cute?" She frowned. No one ever referred to her as "cute," not even as a child.

His grin grew, showing off a surprisingly attractive dimple on his right cheek. "We don't know each other well enough for me to leap to the stunning and beautiful compliments yet."

"Are you...OK?" People didn't talked to her this way. She wasn't sure she could trust the man's sanity.

"Not a hockey fan are you?" He laughed.

"No. Why?"

"Where were you going before our collision?"

She blinked. She wasn't good at social interactions, and this man was obviously a master. Better to get away as fast as possible. She glanced toward Nathalie again.

"You looking for Nat or Alex?" he asked.

"Who's Alex?"

"The guy on the table. Alex Semenov. Goalie for the New York Empires. Nathalie's fiancé."

"Oh. Nathalie is engaged to a hockey player?" She knew so little about the woman. Maybe this was a bad idea.

"Well, they'll be engaged if she ever says yes to one of Alex's many proposals."

"OK." Nibbling her lip, she glanced at Nathalie again.

"Since you had no idea who Alex was, I assume you're here for Nathalie. You need treatment." He looked her over. "No obvious injuries. Unless bumping into me caused one?"

"No." She blinked again. Managing a conversation with this man was like maneuvering through a maze. She had no idea where she was going.

He laughed again. He did that a lot. A part of her sighed over the punch of jealousy she felt. It must be nice to release emotion so easily, without worrying about torching the surroundings.

"I'm teasing you," he said. "You're very serious. It's kind of hard to resist."

"I'm not sure how to respond to that."

"Which is the reason you're so much fun to tease."

"You don't even know me."

"We can change that. Go out with me. Tomorrow night."

Her head spun. "You don't know my name and you're asking me out on a date? Are you sure you're OK…mentally?"

"Probably not. Too many hits to the head."

He tapped a rather large fist against his skull, a move that drew her attention to his thick, shaggy mop of brown hair. Her fingers twitched and she pushed down the little needy desire to run her hands through all that glorious brown.

How strange. She didn't normally notice a man's hair.

"But I do still want to take you out," he said.

"Why?"

"Like I said, you're cute. And fun to tease."

"I could be a psychotic killer."

He shrugged. "Then I won't ask you on a second date."

She was so confused she was close to being charmed. Tilting her head to one side, she considered him. "Are you seriously asking me out, or is this a joke I don't understand?"

"I'm seriously asking you out. But maybe I should introduce myself first. I'm Brody Evans. I'm a defensemen for the Empires."

"Hockey." Realization sunk in. "You know Nathalie's…boyfriend well?"

"As well as anyone knows Semenov. Why? He's taken. You can't go out with him."

She shook her head. "I have a very hard time following you."

"Wait till you see me on the ice."

"I…" She paused, no longer even sure why she was part of this conversation. "Excuse me. I need to…" She glanced back at Nathalie.

"Want me to walk you over there? You seem a little hesitant now."

"No. Thank you. I'll be fine."

"How do you know Nathalie anyway?"

She flattened her lips and straightened her shoulders. "She's my sister."

"I didn't know Nat had a sister?"

"She doesn't know either."

With that she left Brody the Defensemen and started toward her goal.

Nathalie was the only person Ann knew of who might understand what she was going through. She needed to find out how to control this curse, because shutting down her emotions and refusing to feel anything was no longer working.

Without help, she was afraid she'd kill someone with the fire.

Brody watched the woman walk away, admiring the view. She was a lot more than cute. Despite her bland pant suit and the tight bun holding her dark blond hair, she was a truly stunning woman. Sexy soft features, blue eyes, perfect heart-shaped lips. Very kissable lips.

She seemed a little stressed, a little uptight. Rather than turning him off, that just encouraged him to find a way to loosen her up. Maybe help her release some of that stress.

He never had been able to resist a challenge.

He was still admiring her ass when he realized he'd never gotten her name. And she hadn't agreed to go out with him.

But she hadn't said no either.

With a grin, he headed toward the locker room. If she was Nathalie's sister, he was sure he'd be seeing her again. Time to make a plan of attack. The uptight woman with the kissable lips was a challenge he intended to accept.

CHAPTER TWO

Despite her trepidation, Ann marched up to her half sister, extended her hand and said, "Nathalie Mendez. I'm Dr. Ann Bell."

Nathalie smiled, but a furrow formed between her brows. She held up her hands, and Ann realized they were covered in oil.

"Sorry, or I'd shake. What can I help you with, Dr. Bell?" Her voice was deeper and huskier than Ann would have guessed.

Her use of Ann's title helped Ann continue. "I'm not sure how to say this easily so I'm going to be blunt."

"Is my father OK? My grandmother?"

Nathalie's sudden panic had Ann backpedaling. "I'm sorry. I gave you the wrong impression. The 'doctor' comes from my Ph.D. in genetics."

Nathalie let out a low breath and settled her hand on the man—Alex's—knee. He sat up and gripped her hand in return, but his gaze settled on Ann. Ann worked very hard not to fidget or flinch under the intensity of his stare.

Before things could go further downhill, she said, "I'm your sister. Half sister. Your mother's oldest from her second marriage."

Nathalie's eyebrows jumped up as she glanced at Alex then back at Ann. Then she frowned. "You're a scientist?"

"Yes."

"And related to my mother and her evangelical preacher husband?"

Ann shrugged. "I understand your confusion. It's a rather complicated story."

"You don't have a Texas accent."

Should she be surprised that Nathalie knew where her mother had settled and that she had a new family? "I've worked hard to cultivate a neutral American accent."

She worked hard to ensure everything about her was as neutral and unassuming as possible. The less people noticed her, the less possible chance of conflict, the less chance she'd lose control.

"Story there," Alex muttered.

His comment made Nathalie blink and she gave herself a little shake. "Sorry. This is Alex Semenov."

He did shake Ann's hand when she extended it. His grip was firm and dry, his gaze intent but not threatening. She gave him the firm but undemanding handshake she used with other faculty at Columbia, the university where she worked as a research assistant.

"I'm sorry to bother you at work," Ann said, trying to stay focused. "I didn't know how else to contact you."

"How did you know where I worked?"

"I knew you were here in New York when I moved here. It was one of the very few things Mother ever said about her previous family. But I…" She trailed off because she was getting off topic again. Nathalie didn't care that Ann had specifically moved to New York in order to eventually meet her. They could have that conversation later. "I saw you on a sports news program that mentioned your work place."

She hadn't paid much attention to the report, or she might have realized Nathalie was dating a hockey player. She'd been too surprised at the time, hearing her half sister's name on TV. She'd had just enough presence of mind to make note of the physical therapy center where Nathalie worked, and that was all.

"Why are you here?" Nathalie asked.

The million dollar question. "I need help. I don't know who else to go to. Because of things my mother said about you and your father…I think you might understand." She hoped so anyway. "It's to do with… fire."

Nathalie's frown deepened as she glanced at Alex again. Then she picked up a towel and rubbed the oil off her hands. "I have a feeling this is a private conversation."

"Yes." Ann glanced around. "Can you take a break now? Or should we arrange to meet at a later time?"

"Later would be better. I have an apartment in Queens."

"You can meet at my house," Alex said, his voice quiet.

Nathalie rolled her eyes. "He keeps trying to talk me into moving in with him."

Ann just nodded. She had no idea how to respond to that. "Whatever is most comfortable for you. I can meet you where you like. I just need help."

"Are you in danger?"

"I will be soon. But I'm more concerned with…others."

Nathalie's dark eyes narrowed and she pursed her lips. "Huh. OK. My place it is then. Eight tonight." She gave Ann an address in Forest Hills. "Do you need me to write it down?"

"No. I have a very good memory." She sighed as relief she was afraid to feel loosened her shoulder muscles. "I'll see you then."

She left the Center with more hope than she'd had coming in. Maybe she could survive this. Maybe she wouldn't end up killing anyone.

Maybe her mother was wrong.

Brody spotted the cute blonde just outside the Center as he was heading to his car. She'd put on her coat, a mid-thigh black wool thing, and tightened a belt around it, which did much better things for her waist than her suit jacket had. He took a minute to admire her figure before sauntering up to her.

"You need a ride?" he asked.

She startled before facing him. "No." And, as if it were an afterthought, she added, "Thank you."

"I promise to be on my best behavior." He put his hand to his heart and grinned because that confused little crease between her brows was beyond adorable. How did she expect him to resist her? If he didn't know better, he'd think she was putting on an act just to get to him.

But this woman was obviously not a puck bunny.

"You expecting someone?" he asked. "A boyfriend, maybe?"

"Taxi. I live in the city."

"Tell you what. I'm on my way into Manhattan. I'll save you the taxi fare."

"The taxi was only taking me as far as the train station."

"Oh, I like trains. How about I ride in with you?"

"What? Why? You have a car." She looked around, as if hunting for the vehicle in question.

"I do. I can get back to it."

"You don't make any sense to me."

He laughed. "Dinner. Tonight. Public place, so you'll be perfectly safe." He remembered her comment about being a potential killer and said, "I'll be safe, too."

"Are you always like this?"

"Yes. Dinner?"

"I'm meeting Nathalie at eight."

"Lunch then." He paused when he remembered it was after two o'clock. He shrugged. "Late lunch."

She shook her head, but before he could argue his cause more, she said, "If I eat a meal with you, will you leave me alone?"

"Depends on how the meal goes." He didn't point out that, because he had yet to get her name, he'd have a lot harder time pestering her if she left without agreeing to lunch.

"If it's awful and uncomfortable?" she asked.

"I'm rarely uncomfortable."

"I could have guessed that. But I'm awkward. Which means lunch may be."

"Can't wait. I love a challenge. It's why I play hockey."

"You're used to getting your way, aren't you?"

"I'm not nearly as bad as my brother."

"There's another one of you?"

"Oh, it's worse than that. He's my twin."

"Good God."

Her wide-eyed shock made him want to laugh again. Though he got that reaction a lot when people heard he was a twin.

"Don't worry," he said. "I'm the easygoing one. I promise to keep the conversation light."

"Of course." She looked around, like she might panic and run.

He resisted the urge to step closer because he didn't want to spook her, but he desperately wanted to reach out and smooth that crease between her brows.

"You are so damned cute," he muttered.

"I…" Her mouth hung open for a few beats, before she finally sighed. "One lunch. I am hungry. You pay."

"Absolutely. What do you eat?"

"Everything."

"I think I'm in love."

She snorted, just shy of an outright laugh. He couldn't wait to make her laugh for real. He had a feeling he'd enjoy that sound.

Before he could make good on that goal, a taxi pulled up to the curb. He opened the door for her and she slid in easily. He took a moment to regret that she wasn't wearing a skirt, then slipped in beside her, using the excuse of his bulk to sit just a little too close. She smelled wonderful, a little spicy like cinnamon and something hotter. The scent went right to his head. If he weren't sure she'd balk, he'd lean even closer to tease out all the delicious nuances of her smell.

The train station was a relatively short drive from the PT center, so he didn't push conversation. He'd have an entire train ride for that.

"This was an excellent idea," he said as he handed her out of the taxi at the Tarrytown station.

"What idea?"

"Taking the train. I never do this anymore, but the Hudson line has great views of the river."

She blinked up at him. "I loved the view, too. This was my first time coming this direction."

"Were do you live?"

"Brooklyn."

"So trendy of you."

"I'm subletting from a colleague."

"Man or woman?"

"Who?"

She preceded him into the station and through to the platform, heading toward the stairs leading up to the walkway over the tracks to the Manhattan-bound side.

"Your colleague," he said. "Man or woman? Are they still in the city?"

"Why do you care?"

"I want to know if I have competition."

"In what?"

"For you," he said, in an exaggeratedly self-evident tone. "What else would I be talking about?"

"I really have no idea. I can't follow your line of thinking at all."

"Probably a good thing." He leaned in close at the top of the stairs down to the platform, putting his arm on the handrail just in front of hers so she had to stop. "I'm trying not to scare you off. And my thoughts are not exactly…innocent right now."

She narrowed her gaze at him over her shoulder, and his heart picked up speed. Jesus that look went right to his cock.

Oh, this was going to be fun.

"I am not going to fuck you," she said.

Definitely going to be fun.

"Not this afternoon," he said. "I promised to be on my best behavior. Though I could be persuaded…" Her eyes narrowed more dangerously this time, and he grinned. "But now is just about getting to know each other." He risked her wrath and leaned in close enough to set his face right near hers, working not to get distracted by her heat and scent. "You still haven't even told me your name."

"You haven't asked." She turned and continued down the stairs with a little swish of her hips.

Leaving him grinning, and more than a little turned on.

CHAPTER THREE

Ann flexed her fingers, opening and closing her hands until the tingling and heat dissipated. Letting him get too close had been a mistake. God, he smelled good. Should a hockey player smell so good? Like soap and musk and male, but not cologne or anything too strong. Just deliciously sexy. She'd wanted to put her face against his neck and absorb his scent.

And that had been an incredibly dangerous desire.

She shouldn't have let his flirtations get to her. She shouldn't have allowed herself to feel the attraction that was so obviously there. She didn't want to be charmed or intrigued, and she definitely didn't want to be excited.

Her irritation didn't help.

He was too much for her—too much energy, too much enthusiasm. Too male.

So very very male.

Her stomach tightened a little and the heat in her palms increased again. She didn't dare touch the stairway banister for fear of heating it up—which would be very noticeable to others on the stairs given the chilly October day.

Taking slow, deliberate breaths, she stepped onto the concrete platform and checked the board displaying train times. They had a ten minute wait. Damn. At least if they kept moving, she could mostly ignore him.

But she'd agreed to eat a meal with him. She couldn't very well ignore him through lunch. Not that he'd let her. Not that ignoring a man of his size and…attractiveness was even possible.

She glanced at him from the corner of her eye. He stood a little too close, hands in his jacket pockets, looking perfectly at ease and maybe a little bit smug. The rebellious part of her—the part she usually kept ruthlessly suppressed—wanted to do something about that smug expression. Knock him off his game. Confuse him as he'd been confusing her.

That wasn't going to happen. She was having enough trouble keeping her emotions in check around him. She didn't even need her own coat at the moment because her skin was so warm. Engaging him in anything but casual, meaningless conversation was out of the question.

Eight o'clock tonight couldn't come soon enough.

They were on the platform for less than three minutes before a man with a wooly hat displaying some sports team's logo on it walked up to Brody and extended a hand.

"Great season so far," the man said. "You guys are looking really good. Great third period in Friday's game. Love the way you made that asshole eat ice."

Brody laughed, shaking the man's hand in a friendly, quick jerk of motion. "Thanks. Gotta protect my teammates."

"How's The Wall's knee?"

"Good now. Wasn't a serious injury."

"That's a relief. I'm really hoping to see you guys holding up that cup again this year."

"So are we."

"Looking forward to the Classic, too. Don't suppose you have any spare tickets?" The man winked.

"Wish I did. Keep checking. We want as much support as we can get."

"You got it."

"Thanks, man." Brody clapped the stranger on the back of his shoulder before the man wandered off with a passing glance at Ann.

"Who was that?" she asked when the stranger was far enough away not to overhear.

"No idea. A team supporter. They're great. They keep us energized. I love when they take the time to say hi."

"Doesn't it get a little intrusive?"

"Mostly, no. I'm pretty new to the National League, though. This is only my second year with the Empires. I was in the minors before that. So I'm still enjoying all the attention. Maybe when I get to be an old man like Semenov I'll start hiding from it all."

"How old are you?" Nathalie's boyfriend didn't look particularly old, though he did seem more reserved than Brody.

"What's your name?"

Her cheeks heated at the reminder she hadn't been particularly polite with him so far. Not that he deserved it, the way he threw her so off balance. But still…

"Dr. Ann Bell."

"It's a pleasure to meet you, Dr. Ann Bell. Very melodious name."

She frowned. "Thank you. I think."

"Doctor of medicine or philosophy?"

17

"Ph.D."

"In?" He waved a hand in a small circle to encourage further explanation.

"Genetics."

She braced herself, sure he'd make some asinine comment. She was used to that from her family. Why genetics? Did she think she could interfere with God's creations? How did she think she could possibly understand the inner workings of God's plan?

She didn't actually believe in God, at least not the one her fanatical parents espoused—the vengeful and hypocritical one her family professed was the One True God. If God did exist, she wanted to see that deity as a lot kinder than the one she'd grown up with.

Before Brody could disappoint her with some crack about genetics being the work of the devil, though, the deep rumbling approach of the train diverted them. She turned to watch the Metro North whoosh into the station, blowing cold air on her face.

As they boarded, he put a hand on the small of her back, helping her over the gap between train and platform, then guided her to open seats. She thought to dissuade him from the gentlemanly—and very unnecessary—behavior, but the rebellious part of her thrilled at having his hand on her.

Dangerous, that tingling of excitement.

All the way down the narrow aisle, random people high-fived Brody or commented on something to do with his team. He took all the comments and gestures good-naturedly, greeting the attention with a deep laugh and an infectious smile.

How could anyone be that happy all the time? It was contrary to everything she'd experienced in her life. And was so diametrically opposed to how she had to live.

She slid into a seat near a window on the side of the train that would be closest to the river, and Brody settled next to her, once again too close for a perfect stranger and yet somehow not really crowding her. His huge body took up so much room, though, she wondered in passing if he even fit in airplane seats.

Then the train jerked into motion and he leaned closer to look out the window. His nearness set her nerves tingling again. He smelled entirely too good. She could surround herself with his scent and live in it.

She swallowed hard and looked away from the side of his face, trying to ignore the way his nearness made her stomach dance. Their thighs touching didn't help her ignore him.

"Genetics, huh?" he said as he sat back. "Research?"

"Yes." She lifted her chin and straightened her shoulders. Defensive, but she couldn't seem to stop herself. It was a knee-jerk reaction now, thanks to her family.

"What specifically are you looking at?"

"You wouldn't understand."

"Try me."

"My lab is studying the connection between telomere degradation and mutation rates in relation to age-specific disease progression."

"Are you working on the cancer tie-ins as well or just studying the mechanisms of telomere degradation and how to prevent it?"

"Our lab is researching the relationship to cancer as well." She frowned.

"That's good research. If scientists find a way to prevent telomeres from getting too short, we'd have some good information for helping fight against aging and cancer. What do you think of the whole CRISPR/Cas9 technology? Ethically? Will it lead to designer babies or is it just a great new technique for studying the genome and repairing faulty gene sequences?"

She blinked a few times. "How on earth do you know about CRISPR?"

"I read. A lot."

"On genetics?" That seemed hugely coincidental.

"On everything. Of the sciences, my particular cake is genetics and cosmology."

"Why?"

"Aliens," he said in that matter-of-fact, isn't-it-obvious way.

"You believe in aliens?" That was worse than her parents.

"Don't you? I mean, it seems pretty arrogant to assume of all the planets in all the galaxies in a vast universe that we've only got the barest understanding of that there's not some other life somewhere. Even if it doesn't look anything like what we think of as life. In fact, I'd be more surprised if we didn't at least find microbes on other planets and moons than if we did."

Her mouth dropped open a little and she had to snap it shut. Then she leaned back against the window to see him better. "This isn't the conversation I was expecting from a hockey player."

"Snob." But he said it with a grin.

"Maybe," she admitted. "You're more enlightened than my family."

"Tell that to my brother. He thinks I'm a lunatic. Wait, I take that back. I don't want you to meet him. Not yet. You might like him better than me, and then I'd have to kick his ass."

She huffed an unexpected half-laugh, then pressed her lips together, surprised by her amusement.

His gaze dipped to her mouth, just long enough for her to feel the look like an actual touch.

"One of these days," he said, "I'm going to get a full blown laugh out of you. And that will be a glorious day."

"What if I snort when I laugh?"

"Even better."

"You're a very strange man, Mr. Evans."

"We're on a date. Call me Brody or you'll hurt my feelings."

"I find that hard to believe."

"Tough. Brody. Say it."

"Brody." She frowned. "We're on a date already?"

"Of course. What do you think this is?"

"Getting back into town. Then lunch."

"Which is what we here in New York call a date."

She scowled at the slight condescension. But since she probably deserved it, she let it pass. "Are you from New York originally?"

"Nope. Northern California. Nevada City. We got out as soon as possible."

"We?"

"Connor, my brother, and I. Nevada City is a great little town, but we're both more big city boys."

"Why didn't you move to San Francisco?"

"We did for a few years—college. But Connor needed to be here for work."

"What does your brother do?"

"He's a financial genius. Billionaire."

He said the billionaire part so casually, as if it was something people managed to achieve all the time. "So young?"

"You assume we're young?"

"Your comment about Alex earlier," she reminded him.

He grinned. "Caught. He's pretty young to be a billionaire, I guess. No gray ties, though."

"What do gray ties have to do with anything?"

"Don't read a lot of fiction, do you?"

"Not really. I prefer nonfiction."

"Probably best you don't get that reference. We don't know each other well enough for conversations about kinky sex."

"What kind of books do you read?" Her head spun, and she had to grip the armrest to get her balance.

"I told you. I read everything."

"OK."

The heated look in his gaze sent a hot little spark of desire through her gut. She had no idea what they were talking about, but she suspected this line of conversation would get her even deeper into trouble, so she went back to something she hoped was safe.

"Your brother must be very good at what he does."

"Oh, he is. And you definitely can't meet him now."

"Why is now different?"

"You're showing interest in him. You'd probably like him. Which means I'm not introducing you two any time soon."

She wasn't even remotely sure how to respond to him. Especially because his pretend jealousy and possessiveness pleased her. She didn't understand that reaction. It didn't make sense. But very little about her encounter with Brody did.

"What brought you to New York?" she asked, scrambling for something like solid ground in this conversation. "Did you move with your brother?"

"No. I was in Connecticut first, with my AHL team. Then New York when the Empires brought me up."

"So you and your brother are here coincidentally?"

"Mostly. He could move if he wanted to, but he likes me too much."

"Are you sure?"

He laughed, loudly. Again. The sound attracted the attention of other passengers, but Brody didn't seem to notice.

"He has to," he said. "He's my twin. But you need to stop talking about him now. Get back to talking about me."

She was close enough to laughing at his over-the-top arrogance, she did change the subject. "Where are we going to eat?" she asked.

"Steak house in midtown. Fantastic food. You'll love it. You do like steak, right?"

"I like all food." It was one of the few indulgences she could manage without risking the fire, which meant she didn't deny herself the pleasures of good food often. Fortunately, her metabolism was high. She was curvy but managed to maintain her weight without extreme dieting.

Which was good because she wasn't sure she could face denying herself anything else that was supposed to be natural and enjoyable to humans.

She'd already had to shut off too much.

CHAPTER FOUR

The ride into Grand Central Station went a lot quicker than Ann expected. Brody kept up a steady conversation that, while it knocked her off balance, never seemed awkward or forced. She really envied his easygoing nature.

Once on the street, he hailed a taxi. They reached the restaurant in only ten minutes, and when she offered to pay for the ride, Brody refused her money.

"I'm old fashioned. The man pays when he takes a woman out. Besides, I'm trying to impress you." He got out of the taxi and then reached back, offering his hand to help her out.

She risked touching him because she wanted to more than she needed help.

"I'm still not entirely sure why you'd want to impress me," she said as the taxi eased back into traffic.

He tilted his head and gave her a quizzical look.

The Midtown sidewalk was crowded with people rushing about, women and men in suits hurrying to some business, tourists in their casual clothes stopping in the middle of the pedestrian traffic to stare at a building, a few extremely well-dressed and tall women Ann assumed were models, delivery workers pushing carts piled with boxes. The area smelled like New York to Ann, from the nearby cart selling kebabs, to the scent of exhaust from heavy traffic, a few undercurrents of things less pleasant, and a faint hint of heated concrete, despite the cool, late afternoon air.

She knew she and Brody were causing a block in the flow of pedestrian movement, but he didn't seem to notice. He just stared at her as the crowd parted around them, the noise of car horns and people talking wafting past.

"You don't have any idea how attractive you are, do you?" he asked quietly, and more seriously than almost anything else he'd said to this point.

She glanced away, making a study of the front of the restaurant. His attention, his stare left her uncomfortable on levels she didn't care to think about.

She nodded at the restaurant and forced a casual smile, but couldn't quite meet his gaze. "Shall we go in?"

Lunch was delicious and, to her surprise, a lot of fun. True to his word, he was never awkward and because of that she managed to relax, too. The staff at the restaurant knew him and treated him like an honored guest, but he took it so easily and with such good humor, it didn't come across as obnoxious.

She wasn't sure what to think of the looks she got from the staff, or the wink from the head chef when he'd come out to say hi to Brody. She spent so much of her time trying to avoid attention, it was more than a little disconcerting to have so much focused on them.

Yet Brody managed to spin it all into a fun and casual atmosphere. By the time he forced a dessert on her—which didn't take a lot of convincing—she'd forgotten to worry about her emotions, or the fire, or much of anything else. She lost herself in the moment, smiling more than she could remember ever doing in her life.

She was so caught up in his charm and humor, so distracted by the sexy tug at one corner of his mouth when he watched her eat, and the way he filled out his long sleeved shirt, giving her a spectacular view of thick, tempting muscles, she didn't notice the warmth in her palms or the tingling along her fingers. She didn't feel the subtle heat building, or the warning flutter of sensation down her arms.

Until she glanced at the water glass she held in one hand. The water was just starting to boil.

Gasping, Ann pushed back from the table.

"I…I'm sorry."

She darted out of the restaurant so fast, she forgot her coat and purse. In her panic, she didn't even care. She had to get outside, into the cool October air, away from Brody's scent and presence. She had to get herself under control.

He joined her on the sidewalk, where she stood with her hands fisted, taking long, slow breaths. It was early evening now and lights were winking on along the street and in the nearby buildings. She focused on the cold air, the approaching night, the sounds of people and cars. She tried not to feel Brody step up close behind her.

"What happened?" he asked. "Are you OK?"

He settled one of his large hands on her shoulder and she flinched, then shifted away.

"Please. I need just a few minutes. I can't…"

She felt like a fool. How could she explain? She knew her departure from the restaurant made no sense. But she could still feel the heat in her palms, the pulse of the fire in her fingertips. Her skin was so warm, even the sharp bite of the evening wind didn't touch her.

She'd spent her entire life suppressing emotion to keep her fire under control. Why had she dropped her guard? She knew better. She had to get away from Brody Evans.

Before she killed someone.

Without really paying attention to where she was going, she turned down the street. Foot traffic was still heavy as business people hurrying home flooded the sidewalks. She wove through the crowds, working hard to avoid touching anyone. Something in her expression must have given warning, because most people moved out of her way.

She was aware of Brody following her, but she didn't turn to look at him.

"We didn't dine and dash just now, did we?" she asked over her shoulder.

"I paid before I followed you. Can we talk about what happened?"

"No."

When she felt his fingers brush her arm, she jerked away again. "Please, don't touch me right now."

"Ann. Damn it, stop walking and talk to me. I thought we were having a nice time."

"We were. Too nice. I need to go." She reached for a purse that wasn't there and finally stopped. When she faced him, he was holding her bag and coat out to her, a little crease between his brows.

She was sure she'd ruined whatever good feelings he had for her, and she regretted that. She'd never met a man who made her feel so at ease and charmed all at once. But better he think her a bitch than she hurt him with the flames.

She took her bag from him, careful not to touch him.

"Aren't you cold?" he asked.

"No." She couldn't bring herself to be completely rude. "I *am* sorry. I had a very nice lunch. I just have to go."

He held up her coat then and she acquiesced, turning so he could help her into it. The gesture put him too close, his hands brushing her shoulders as she shrugged into her coat. She stepped away quickly so he wouldn't notice how warm she was.

"Did I do something wrong?" he asked. "Say something to insult you?"

"Of course not. You're perfect. But I'm…" Damaged. Dangerous. Broken.

The Devil's spawn.

She forced that last label from her head. That was her parents talking, and she refused to let their fanaticism define her. But she was damaged. And she was very dangerous.

He took a step closer, too close again, and yet somehow still not crowding her. "I really had a good time today. I'd like to see you again."

"I don't think that's a good idea." She had to crane her neck back to look him in the eyes. The angle made her feel vulnerable because all she could think was how easy it would be to kiss him. He'd just have to lean down a little bit, she could ease up onto her toes…

She realized she was staring at his mouth when one corner quirked up a little in a half-smile.

"I think seeing you again would be an excellent idea," he said.

He leaned down, and she did go up onto her toes, until she could feel the warmth of his breath against her lips. The faintest touch of his mouth to hers, a brief brush of temptation…

And the heat in her palms intensified.

She hurried back a step. "I need to go. Thank you for lunch." She spun and flagged an approaching taxi before he could object.

Maybe it was her desperation, or maybe she just got lucky, but the cab stopped. She climbed in, leaving Brody staring after her, that little crease between his brows deep.

Her guilt and fear settled like a hard ball in her gut all the way to Forest Hills, ruining what had been an excellent meal. She had to talk to Nathalie. She was too early for their appointment, but Ann would wait as long as necessary.

She couldn't go on like this anymore.

CHAPTER FIVE

At exactly eight o'clock, Ann went up to Nathalie's apartment. She hadn't seen Nathalie enter the building, but she knew from her own building there could be another entrance. She'd waited until the appointed time on a low brick wall across the street from the main door. The night was chilly so she'd huddled in her coat, her skin finally cool enough she felt the autumn weather, but she hadn't dare go anywhere more pubic.

She could still feel the warning tingles in her palms.

As she knocked on Nathalie's door, she tried not to let worry overtake her. Worry was as bad as any other emotion. She focused on her breathing, counting slowly each time she breathed in, then reversing the order as she breathed out.

When the door opened, she released a relieved sigh.

"Thank you for meeting me," she said to the stranger who was her sister.

Nathalie nodded and motioned her inside. She gestured to a small, comfortable couch, waited for Ann to sit, then settled in a beautiful wooden rocking chair.

Ann took a moment to study the apartment. It wasn't very big, but it was cozy and neat, with clean wooden floors, a few rugs scattered around the living room, and a very interesting set up of candles and incense holders on a low table against one wall. From the couch, Ann couldn't see into the kitchen, except that a door near the table with the candles led into one, but from this angle it looked like a reasonable sized space for New York. Everything looked so homey and lived in. It was nice.

"So," Nathalie said without preamble. "I assume you're a firestarter."

Ann blinked a few times, her mouth dropping open as she stared at Nathalie.

"Pyrokinesis. Am I wrong? That reference to fire was pretty pointed. You know that's the reason our mother left my father."

"What? No. What?"

Nathalie frowned. "OK, maybe we need to backtrack a little. Did I guess right about the pyrokinesis, or is this a more mundane problem?"

Very slowly, Ann said, "You guessed right. But how…?"

"You came to me because you assumed I'd understand, because of things your mother has said."

"She called you and your father Devil's spawn."

Nathalie snorted. "Yeah, heard that before. But she didn't tell you why exactly she called us that?"

"She said you and your father were devil worshiping pagans."

Nathalie rolled her eyes. "What a load of crap. I am a solitary green witch. I don't even believe in her devil."

The admission took Ann by surprise. "You think you're a witch?"

Nathalie dropped her chin and gave Ann a deadpan stare. "You've heard of the Wiccan religion, right?"

"Well, yes, but…"

31

"Like that only a little different. It's my religion. A type of philosophy, if that helps."

"But you knew what a firestarter was? You believe in…"

Nathalie stared at Ann a moment, then raised her hand. A ball of blue fire burst into life in the center of Nathalie's palm. She glanced at it a moment, then closed her fist and the fire vanished.

When she meet Ann's gaze again, she raised a brow. "I understand that particular gift. Though, I'd always assumed it came from my dad's side of the family. He's going to get a kick out of knowing it came from my mother."

"Why do you say that it came from our mother?"

"How else? That's our only blood tie."

Ann closed her eyes and shook her head. She felt like an idiot. She was the geneticist. Of course if they shared this trait, it must be inherited from their linked genetics. Ann had gone into the field specifically to look for a genetic cause for her curse…

She paused at that word and looked up at Nathalie again. "You called it a gift. I've always considered it a curse."

"You said you're in trouble. No one has taught you how to control the fire, have they? That's why you came to me."

"You're very astute."

Nathalie ignored the compliment. "My grandmother trained me. I was four the first time fire sparked out of my hands. It's the reason your mother finally abandoned us, why she calls us what she does. She saw the fire and saw Satan and Hell. My grandmother, though Catholic, was a pagan at her core, and saw the fire as just another skill."

"Did she have it?" Ann was genuinely curious. For the first time in her life, she felt free to discuss things she'd never dared talk about openly before for fear someone would stick her in a psychiatric hospital—or worse, her family would bring in some weird fanatic preacher to try and "beat or burn" the demon out of her. She shivered.

"You OK?" Nathalie asked.

"Yes. Sorry. I've just never been able to discuss this without worrying about the reaction. My family... Well, you know. The reaction would have been bad."

Nathalie snorted a laugh. "Yes. How did you manage to keep it from them?"

"The first time it happened, I was alone. I was almost four and had snuck out of church to play with rocks in the parking lot. I accidentally incinerated a section of dry grass at the edge of the lot. The whole thing scared me so much I ran back into church thinking I was possessed. But crossing into the sacred space didn't change anything."

"You're not possessed. Or cursed. Or any of the other stupid things your mother might have put into your head. It's just a skill. Like any other skill. Less typical, obviously, but just a talent."

"A biological impossibility according to all known science."

"And science knows everything right now? You know as well as I do that a hundred years from now everything we take as fact at the moment will be wrong."

Ann smiled a little. "You sound more the scientist right now than I do."

"What science?"

"Genetics."

"Apropos."

"Is that why your grandmother could train you? Why you thought the...skill came from your father's side?"

"No, *Yaya* wasn't a firestarter. She was just old enough to have learned a lot. And her mind was wide open to a very grand world, so nothing really surprised her. Plus, she has visions like I do, so there's that."

"Wait, you have visions, too?" Ann felt a little lightheaded. She leaned back in the couch. This couldn't be a real conversation. And yet this was exactly why she'd come to Nathalie.

Nathalie waved that away. "Off topic. Sorry. Back to the fire. Does yours get harder to control when your emotions swing?"

"Yes," Ann breathed. "A lot worse. I shut down emotions not long after discovering what I could do. I was afraid."

"Of course you were. Shutting down your emotions won't help long term, though."

"I've noticed."

"Starting to slip already? Not surprised. OK, let's start."

"Wait." Ann slid to the edge of the couch. "What do you mean, let's start?"

"You need to learn control. I can teach you. Then everyone will be safe, and you can start feeling things again."

"Do we need to go somewhere special?"

"We'll start with the basics here, then I'll take you to my father's house for the real control tests. He's got a cement basement, designed for me, so I wouldn't burn his house down."

"He won't mind? I'm his ex-wife's child from another man."

Nathalie rocked gently in her chair. "He'll see what I see. A young woman in a lot of trouble who needs our help. He's big on helping those in need."

"He sounds like a good man. Not what I expected."

"Yeah, well." She shrugged. "You need to talk more or do you want to learn how to keep the fire under your control?"

"Control. We can talk later."

Nathalie smiled. "Good. Let's go sit on the floor." She motioned to the low table with candles on it, set against the wall, and with a simple rug on the floor in front of it. "That particular rug is fire proof."

Ann followed, a strange combination of confusion and relief making her knees wobble. As they settled on the floor for her first lessons, she acknowledged how very grateful she was to have a "Devil's spawn" half sister. It seemed she didn't have to hide from every member of her family after all.

CHAPTER SIX

Brody wasted no time finding Nathalie the next day after his date with Ann. He had morning practice to get through first, and ended up with his face in the ice a few times because he was distracted—Jahr, Karpov, and Sandberg would never let him live that down. As soon as practice ended, he went right to the physical therapy center.

He had no idea what had happened with Ann, why she'd run away from what he'd thought was a really good date. He'd gone over the conversation again and again. He hadn't said anything offensive—in fact, there'd been a lull in the conversation just before she'd bolted.

Whatever had happened, he knew he couldn't let things just end the way they had. He wanted to see her again.

He'd never met anyone quite like Dr. Ann Bell. She was smart, clever, and incredibly interesting. Though she did give him funny looks when he jumped topics, she went with the flow of his conversation better than most people. She even had a lot to say about a lot of the things he brought up. Which was such a nice change of pace. Most people he knew had no interest in all the various things he was interested in. Even his own twin didn't care to discuss some of the stuff Brody liked to talk about. But Ann was curious and easily discussed everything.

The fact that all that smart curiosity was wrapped up in a sexy little body and adorable face was like frosting on a beautiful cake. And that mouth of hers... So damned kissable.

The thought of her mouth reminded him sharply of their almost kiss, a moment more erotic than any full-on liplock he'd ever experienced. So close, so enticingly close...

Then she'd run.

But for that one instant, he knew she wanted him as much as he did her, and that meant he had a chance with her.

The only problem was she hadn't given him a way to contact her. He knew she studied genetics at one of the universities in the city, but not which one because he never got back around to asking. Or else she'd avoided telling him, and he hadn't noticed. Though even if he knew, he had a feeling he wouldn't win any favors stalking her at work.

Nathalie came out of a back office onto the main therapy floor while he was hunting for her. He made a beeline to her.

"Do you have Ann's phone number?"

"Huh?" Nathalie looked up at him, blinking in confusion.

He got that a lot. "Ann Bell. She was here yesterday looking for you. Said she was your sister. I need to get in touch with her."

Nathalie's eyes narrowed. "Why?"

"Do you have her phone number?"

"Again, I ask, why?"

"So I can call her." He gave her a what-else-would-I-want-it-for look.

"Why, Brody?"

"We had a date yesterday, a date that I thought went very well, but she ran off at the end."

"What did you do?"

"Nothing that I can figure out." He gave a huff of frustration. "And I've thought about it a lot." He frowned a little. "Actually, she ran off twice. Once from the restaurant when we weren't even talking."

"And the second time?"

He grunted. "When I almost kissed her."

"Hmm."

"Hey, I wasn't forcing anything. I didn't even get a chance to kiss her, but she *was* leaning into me."

The crease between Nathalie's brows deepened, but her focus was on a wall not him. He tried to wait her out.

His effort lasted all of forty seconds before he said, "Well? Do you have her number?"

"I do. I want to get her permission first before I give it to you."

He bit back a growl because he understood why she was hesitating. His frustration was hard to hold in check though. He glanced around the therapy room, looking for a way to work off the irritation at having to wait.

"Tell you what," he said, "I'll go for a run. Will that give you time enough to contact her?"

Nathalie snorted. "You are severely lacking in patience, Evans. Fine, I'll call her while you go for a run. But…" She raised a hand, stopping him when he turned away. "She's probably at work, so don't get your hopes up. It might be hours before she calls back."

"I'll just keep running, then. I can wait."

"Right." Nathalie shook her head and turned to the massage table where an older woman was waiting for a session.

Brody hit the Tarrytown streets, trying hard not to let the impatience in his stomach get the best of him.

By the time he return to the Center an hour later, he was sweating, breathing hard, and still so impatient he couldn't stand still. What the hell was it about Ann that scattered his focus?

He was going to get his ass cut if he kept up like this.

His team needed him. He wasn't a superstar player, like Semenov or Emmerson or Jahr, but he was a grinder and a good defenseman. He was also one hell of a fighter. Because of that, it was his job to make sure the other team played nice and when they didn't, he took care of the problem. It meant a lot of time in the penalty box, but he was happy to do it for his teammates. During his brief time in the NHL, he'd built a reputation for aggression on the ice, and it meant his team was safer.

That aggression came from focus and a very solid sense of justice. But without the focus, he wouldn't do his team any good.

During the long, hard run, he recognized he was more...invested in what happened with Ann than he should be after one date. Women were a wonderful part of his life and he enjoyed their company, but they never interfered with his work or his concentration. No one had ever distracted him during a practice session before, or set him this much on edge just because he couldn't be instantly in contact with them.

That should have been enough to push him in the opposite direction from the good Dr. Bell.

It wasn't. Which meant somewhere during their train ride and lunch, he'd grown a lot more attached to her than he'd expected. And he had to see where that took him, no matter what.

His brother was going to get a huge laugh out of this.

Nathalie found him when he emerged from the locker room where he'd gone to shower so he didn't offend her with his stench.

"She's agreed I can give you her number."

He breathed out in relief and grinned.

"But she's asked that you not call her for at least a week."

So much for relief. "Why?"

"She has some things to do first."

"Like?"

"Like none of your business."

"I knew it. She does have a boyfriend, doesn't she?"

"Not that I know of."

"Then what?"

"If she wants you to know, she'll tell you. In the meantime, leave her alone if you don't want to drive her off."

He grunted. If not for that last jab, he probably still would have called before the week was out. Now he *had* to wait.

"Fine." He considered Nathalie a moment. "She's your sister, but you two don't look a lot alike."

"Same mother different fathers. I took after my father—fortunately."

"Ah. That bad, huh?"

"None of your business, either."

He made a face. Nathalie and Semenov were notorious for protecting their privacy. Even though he played on the same team with Semenov, he didn't really know The Wall very well.

"So are you and Ann close?" he asked.

"So nosey. No. Not at the moment."

"But you might be?"

"Brody, if you want to know more about Ann, you're going to have to ask her yourself. Next week. When she's ready to talk to you."

"But you know why she wants to wait?"

"I do."

"Is there any way at all I can bribe you into telling me? Food? Jewelry? A good book?"

"That's a wide range of bribes—all of which are nice offers, though Alex will kick your ass if you give me jewelry."

"I'd risk it."

"I can't be bribed. Be patient with her. She's going through things that will require time. You're not going to be able to rush her."

"I hate waiting," he said with groan.

She patted him on the arm. "I know." Then she handed him a folded piece of paper and went back to work.

He stared at the paper. He wasn't known for his patience. But Ann was worth it. He'd just have to find things to do to keep occupied.

Training. Training would keep him busy. Lots and lots of training.

Chapter Seven

As the Empires hit the locker room after another win, Semenov stopped Brody just inside the door, out of the way of any milling reporters. The bright, blue room smelled of sweat, soap, and melting ice—Brody's favorite scents. At least before he'd met Ann.

The clanking crash of dropping gear and loud conversation made Brody smile. He loved winning. He loved the way the locker room felt after a win.

"What's up?" he asked his goalie.

"Great game. Little rough on that winger."

"He shouldn't have taken Dobrynin out. Poor bastard might be out for weeks with that injury."

"I didn't say it wasn't deserved. Glad you did it. But you were a little more…aggressive than usual. Even for you. Anything you want to talk about?"

He frowned. "What's Nathalie told you?"

"You're interested in her sister."

"Is this the part where you try and scare me off?"

"Why would I do that?"

"She's your fiancée's sister."

"Whom I've only met once. If Nathalie tells me to drop kick you to New Jersey for hurting her sister, I will. But otherwise, I don't care who you date." He leveled a hard look on Brody, his blue eyes as sharp as ice chips. "Unless it interferes with your performance on the ice."

"Are you saying it did tonight?" He was starting to get a little pissed off—which didn't happen often off the ice.

"No. You played great tonight. Just more intense than usual."

"I take the game seriously." But he flinched, knowing he was bullshitting Semenov. "Fine. I've been distracting myself with work. She made me wait the week before I could call her."

"Nathalie's sister?"

He grunted a yes.

"When are you allowed to call?"

"Tonight."

Semenov nodded at one of their teammates when he shouted something rude at him. "Better get on the phone, then," he said and smacked Brody on the arm before heading to his locker.

Brody grinned and glanced at the clock. He should probably shower first, but a week of keeping his impatience in check had been more than enough time. He snatched his cell from his locker and went back out into the echoing corridor, still in full gear, moving away from the reporters hovering around the entrance.

She answered after only two rings.

"I saw you play tonight," she said without waiting for him to tell her who was calling.

That made him grin wider. She'd been expecting his call and knew it was him. For some reason, that was as thrilling as their win.

"What'd you think?" he asked, leaning against the hard concrete wall.

"You're very…dangerous."

He chuckled. "Only to other hockey players. Not my teammates."

She made a non-committal kind of humming sound that wasn't exactly agreement. "Is that one player going to be OK?"

Dobrynin took a serious enough hit, he'd had to be carried off the ice. Brody ensured retribution was paid to the opposing player and had spent five minutes in the box for it.

"He'll be out for a few weeks," Brody said. "Maybe longer. But he'll be OK."

"I'm sorry." She paused.

He wanted to say something into the silence, but instinct had him waiting her out.

"I didn't realize how…violent hockey was."

Brody frowned. His gut tightened with just a hint of worry. "Does it bother you?" She sounded like she wasn't saying something.

"No. Just, you were so easygoing last week. I wasn't expecting you to be so…mean, I guess."

"Mean? I wasn't mean. I was just doing my part for the team."

"You slammed that man into the glass pretty hard. And then punched him. A lot."

"He hurt my teammate. It's what I do."

"He made you angry?"

"Well, yeah."

"Are you still mad?"

"No."

"Why not?"

He ran a hand through his hair. "I don't know. Because I hit him back, and then everything was even."

"Do you get angry like that…when you're not playing?"

Ah. He was starting to understand. Maybe. "The me you met last week is the man I really am. I only beat people up on the ice—and

44

only when it's justified by something they've done."

"You threatened to kick your own twin's ass."

"Well. He's my brother. That doesn't count. We've spent our lives beating each other up."

She fell silent.

"Hey, I'm not violent by nature," he said, wondering if she heard the edge of panic in his voice. "I promise."

More silence. Then, quieter, "Did you get hurt?"

"No." He glanced at his swollen knuckles and shrugged. She didn't need to know about that. "Were you worried about me?"

"Maybe a little."

He let his shoulders relax. "Good. I have hope for us."

"Why did you want to call me?"

He pulled the phone back to frown at it before answering. "Because I like you. And I didn't like how things ended after our date."

"I told you I wasn't going to sleep with you."

He chuckled. "That wasn't what I was talking about and you know it. Give me another chance?"

"Meaning?"

"Go out with me again. Tonight."

"I can't. I have work tomorrow. Early."

"Fine. Saturday night, then."

"Don't you have a game on Sunday afternoon?"

"I still have to eat Saturday night. Dinner. You like food. I like feeding you." When she didn't answer for a long moment, he said, "Please. I'd really like to see you again."

Her resigned sigh was loud enough he grinned.

"OK. Dinner. Saturday. I'll meet you. Where are we going?"

"You like Mexican?"

"I'm from Texas. I was bottle fed Mexican food."

He gave her an address in the Village. "You'll love this place. Excellent guacamole."

"Sounds good."

Her voice softened, and he pretended he'd made her smile.

"Have a good night," she murmured and disconnected before he could say more.

Didn't matter. He was going to see her on Saturday. That was enough hope to keep him happy for the rest of the week.

CHAPTER EIGHT

Ann tried not to fidget as she waited in front of the restaurant. Cold air kissed her cheeks, probably turning her nose red, while the scents of the restaurant behind her made her mouth water. The Village was bustling, with people laughing and shouting as they passed, hands in pockets against the chilly wind.

Staying close to the restaurant wall, she let the waves of people flow by as she practiced her breathing. Nerves jumped around her belly, a sign of potential trouble if she didn't concentrate. But the week of working with Nathalie and her father, Mr. Mendez, had helped. She felt a little more in control—at least, she didn't feel like she might burn something down at any moment.

She spotted Brody easily as he sauntered toward her. He was hard to miss at 6'7". As usual, a few people stopped him and shook his hand. But most of his attention was on her as he approached, an intensity that had her stomach muscles tightening in anticipation.

He was criminally handsome. Really, no one should be that good looking in real life. Even in New York where movie stars and super models walked the streets. Despite telling herself to take a step back from the emotions battering her, she couldn't take her eyes off him. And the closer he got, the more her excitement and anticipation built.

Flexing her hands, she pushed away from the wall to greet him, unable to resist smiling back at his grin.

"You showed," he said.

"You were worried?"

"Hell, yeah. You didn't sound entirely sure about this on the phone."

"I wasn't. But I wouldn't have left you standing here without calling."

His grin softened. "I knew I liked you." He motioned to the glass door entrance. "Shall we?"

He held the door for her, and then held her seat when they were shown a table in a private corner of the restaurant. The place was comfortable without being too large, with a casual ambiance of Tex-Mex kitsch, quiet Spanish music in the background, and all of it highlighted by a delicious spicy scent. The light level was low enough to feel intimate, without being so low she couldn't see her menu.

"Very nice," she said.

"Glad you approve. The food is fantastic. Best I've had in New York. So far."

"So far?"

"I'm working my way through as many restaurants as possible while I'm here. Don't want to miss anything."

She sighed. "That sounds like the best way to experience New York I've ever heard."

"You're more than welcome to join me on my odyssey. In fact, I'd love to have you with me."

He held her gaze, no longer smiling, his expression too serious for a second date.

"You still don't make any sense to me," she murmured, focusing on her menu.

"What's bothering you now?"

He sounded casual enough, almost amused, as if she'd mentioned a joke. So she wasn't sure if he actually cared about her answer or not. She risked a glance up. He was also studying his menu.

She released a breath. "You're very scary on the ice. Vicious."

"I get paid well to play that way."

"But off the ice, you're so...easy."

"I am not easy."

She smiled at his mock-offense. "I meant easygoing. You chat with perfect strangers. You smile a lot. You joke a lot. How can you be so aggressive one moment and so laid back the next? I don't get it."

"I don't know. I've never given it much thought. Hockey is just a game—I mean it's my job and I'm very serious about my job. I take the games seriously. I play hard. I want to win and I want to take care of my teammates. But when I'm off the ice, it's not like I feel the need to go around hitting people."

"But how do you separate those parts of yourself?" She looked up then, really wanting to know.

She felt so split down the middle. All the time. Most of her numb so she wouldn't hurt anyone, but a part of her chafing at those restrictions and wanting to throw caution to the wind. She'd never dared before. Being out with Brody a second time was the closest she'd come to this kind of risk. So how did he contain the violence he showed during a game and not let it spill into his ordinary life?

He shrugged. "I don't separate anything. All of that is just who I am. The game is the game. Life outside the game is life." He frowned at little. "I don't know how to explain it any other way."

"You make it sound easy." She wished she could do that. Allow her fire to just be part of her without taking over her life.

She shook off the worry. She was learning, had learned a lot already. She felt more in control than she had in her entire life—though that wasn't saying much since she'd never felt in control of her curse at all before now. With practice and patience, she hoped to go on and have a normal sort of life where the fire didn't overwhelm everything.

And she realized as she studied Brody's handsome face, she'd like to spend more time with him without fear.

"What are you ordering?" she asked, shifting to an easier subject.

As promised the food was wonderful. Brody's company was even better. He awed her with his ability to keep her comfortable. Had anyone in her entire life made her feel so at ease? She wasn't even this relaxed around her own family.

She smiled a lot as they chatted about things that weren't scary or weird, things that normal people discussed. And not once, during the entire meal, did she boil her water on accident. At one point, she did have to excuse herself to the bathroom to do some slow breathing and cool her hands down, but she hadn't felt like she might catch the restaurant on fire at any moment. She hadn't really felt out of control. When the warning signs hit, she remained calm—as she'd been learning—and practiced the techniques she'd been taught.

It was, by far, the most freeing date night she'd ever experienced.

As they left the restaurant for a stroll through the still crowded, well-lit streets, she started to hope she could do this, go on dates with handsome men and enjoy herself.

She glanced up at Brody. Not dates with handsome men, plural. Dates with this particular handsome man. She'd never known anyone quite like him, and as far as she was concerned, that made him even better.

"What?" he asked when he caught her staring.

"I'm having a really good time. Thank you for taking a chance on me again."

He took her arm, tugging her closer to his side. "It's my absolute pleasure, Ann. Thank you for taking a chance on me."

They window shopped through the quirky stores that lined the narrow streets, and he pointed out a few of the restaurants he hadn't tried yet but wanted to. She agreed to meet him for a third date at the Moroccan place once he got back to town after some away games. He didn't even bother to hide his pleasure at her acceptance.

And though she could have carried on that way for hours more, the cold eventually drove her to say, "I'd better get home."

"We could go for a drink first. Just one."

She smiled, thrilled more than she would admit that he wasn't in a hurry to get rid of her.

"Come on." He bumped gently against her arm. "It's Saturday night. You're not working tomorrow, right?"

"You said you had an early start. Packing for your trip before the afternoon game."

He waved that away. "I've been waiting to see you for almost two weeks. I am happy to sacrifice sleep so I can stay in your company longer."

"I still have no idea why."

"What does it matter? I like you. Have a drink with me. Then I'll take you home."

"You'll be going out of your way." He had an apartment near Battery Park. Brooklyn was not on his way home from here.

"It's an excuse to spend more time with you. I won't be able to see you for another week now. I need all the excuses I can get."

She shook her head but gave in. She didn't really want to say goodnight yet either.

51

The little Irish sports bar was quiet enough for them to talk, and though the bartender knew Brody immediately, he gave them privacy after exchanging a few words about the upcoming Winter Classic.

Once settled in a booth with a pint of beer for him and a glass of wine for her—a risk as she rarely drank alcohol—she finally admitted something she'd been shying away from all night.

"I know nothing about hockey. At all. I had no idea what was going on in the game I watched. But it looks very exciting. I don't suppose you could teach me a little about it? So I understand what people are saying to you when they talk about your team and the games."

His expression went through several emotions she couldn't read before settling into a huge grin.

"I'd love to. Where should I start?"

"The basics. The very basics."

For the next hour, he explained the game to her, in enough detail she thought she might understand a little more, and from there they moved on to talking about other sports, then her work, before circling back to their mutual passion for food.

Before she knew it, it was two in the morning, and she'd managed the entire night without losing control of her fire while still thoroughly enjoying herself.

Her pulse beat a steady, heady thrum every time she caught Brody's scent, or he leaned in close enough for her to feel his heat. For once, her hands tingled with a need to touch rather than as a warning of potential disaster. And whenever he touched her, she felt it all the way to her toes.

She was in trouble with this man. A lot of trouble. In serious danger of losing her heart. She couldn't explain how it had happened since they'd only just met, this was only their second date, and she never lost her heart to anyone. But as she rose from the booth and he set a hand against her lower back to guide her out of the bar, her stomach danced in delicious excitement.

She could fall for Brody. Hard.

The thought was both thrilling and terrifying.

So much so, she didn't argue when he flagged down a taxi then climbed in with her to take her home.

By the time they reached her building—a narrow, four-story place, wedged between brownstones, with two apartments on each level— she finally started to feel the awkwardness that usually accompanied her dates. It got worse when he followed her to the front door after waving the taxi away.

She hesitated on the stoop, part of her wanting to invite him up for a coffee, but the rest of her knowing if she did, he'd stay the night and she wasn't even close to ready for that yet. She fidgeted with her keys, the silence between them making her feel even more awkward.

Finally, he spoke and she nearly groaned aloud in relief.

"The special events for the Winter Classic start after we get back," he said. "There's something going on in each borough during the build-up. A few formal parties after exhibition games. Stuff like that."

"When is it?"

"The Classic is played January first, at the Queens Bank Stadium in Queens."

"It's a big deal, right?"

He grinned. "Pretty big deal. Do you ice skate?"

"Never even tried."

"Can I bribe you into trying?"

"What do you mean?"

"I'd like you to come with me to the event in Bryant Park."

"Is this before or after you take me for Moroccan food?"

His grin grew. "After."

"So you're planning two dates ahead? You're very confident we'll have fun on our third date."

"Absolutely. What do you say? Music, ice skating, a concert that night by the Philharmonia. Our team captain, Chris Emmerson, his sister Kayleigh plays with the orchestra. I've heard they're excellent. I'll have to do some media stuff, and sit with the team at the concert, but I'll still have time to just enjoy the event. I'd like you to be there."

"Do I have to ice skate?"

"I won't let you fall. I promise."

"Impossible promise. What's my bribe for agreeing to make a fool of myself in front of you and half of New York?"

His expression went very serious and he took a step closer. She sucked in a breath, his nearness overwhelming and exciting all at once. He leaned close, putting his mouth by her ear. The brush of his hot breath sent her heartbeat thumping hard.

Quietly, he murmured, "I'll give you the one thing I know you want more than anything else."

She closed her eyes, thoughts of what he might be offering making it impossible for her to talk.

He leaned even closer, his big body almost touching hers, and said, "More Mexican food."

His offer was so different from what she'd been expecting, and at the same time such a perfect bribe, an unexpected bubble of laughter popped out. She pressed a hand to her mouth, but she couldn't contain her chuckle.

"Tease," she said through her amusement. "But that's a very worthy bribe."

She looked up at him, still grinning at his joke, only to get caught in his intent gaze.

"I've been waiting for that sound since we met," he said. "Worth every minute."

He cradled her face in his big hands, his heat seeping into her skin an instant before he kissed her.

She held very still for a split second, then opened for him, sinking into him, savoring the feel and taste of his mouth on hers. No almost-kiss for them this time. His lips were firm and soft at once, both gentle and intense. She set her hands against his chest, only a little amazed she could feel all his thick muscles even through coat and shirt. He was so large and solid, so tempting. She clenched her fingers into his coat to keep him near and rose up on her toes to deepen the kiss.

He moved his hands from her face to wrap his arms around her, pulling her flush against him. Exactly where she wanted to be, her body tight to his. She tunneled her fingers through his hair and surrendered to simply feeling, letting the excitement build, the anticipation of more making her giddy.

And then she felt the dreaded tingling in her hands, the warning that she'd let her control slip too far.

Dropping her hold, she stepped back, breathing hard, surprised at how bereft she felt once out of his arms. The heat in her palms built dangerously high before she could calm herself enough to control it.

She realized she'd dropped her keys during the kiss and used that as her excuse not to meet his gaze immediately. Very deliberately, she worked through the calming, control exercises she'd spent the week practicing, centering and breathing away the fire. She picked her keys up carefully, holding the leather keychain until she was sure she wouldn't melt the metal. Then she stood to face Brody, bracing herself for... She wasn't sure. His disappointment maybe?

But he surprised her. Again.

"Can I call you while I'm on the road?" he asked.

No pressure to invite him in. No frown at her abrupt end to the kiss. No accusations of her being a tease. Just a simple request to stay in touch.

She swallowed hard and nodded. "If you have time."

"I'll make time." He brushed his thumb over her cheek. "Sleep well," he murmured.

He waited for her to unlock the building door and step into the narrow lobby. "Goodnight, Ann," he said with a small, sexy smile.

"Goodnight." She watched long enough to see him reach the sidewalk before closing the solid wood door.

Her skin still tingled as she started up the marble stairs to her third floor apartment. But for the first time in her life, she was more worried about the state of her heart than the fire.

CHAPTER NINE

B rody hunted the crowds outside the concert hall, then grinned when he spotted Ann walking toward him. She was wearing heals under her long black pants. He loved the way she walked in heals.

He left his teammates to great her.

"You look lovely," he said when he reached her, charmed by her blush.

"You can't see what I'm wearing yet," she said.

"I wasn't talking about your clothes. I'm glad you could make the concert. How's your head?"

She'd called that morning to back out of the ice skating, claiming a headache, but she had agreed to show for the concert, so he let his disappointment go. Seeing her now, he forgot all about it anyway.

"Much better, thank you." She scanned the crowds in the lobby of the concert hall. "This is exciting. I've never heard the Philharmonia play before."

"They're doing a bunch of crossover stuff with the Classic events thanks to Emmerson's sister playing with them."

"How nice." She looked past him to the rest of the team. "I don't want to keep you. I know you said you'd have to sit with them."

"I'm sorry we can't sit together. But Nathalie is here. She'll keep you company. And as promised, Mexican food after."

She frowned a little. "My stomach will be growling all the way through the concert now."

"Then I'll know where you are."

She rolled her eyes but smiled, and his heart thumped a little harder. He stayed with her, chatting as long as he could, then left her with Nathalie to rejoin his team.

The concert was excellent, as he'd expected, though he would have preferred sitting with Ann. Fortunately, the new kid on the team, Max St. Laurent, the defensemen they'd brought up to fill in for Dobrynin, provided a good deal of entertainment by spending the concert drooling over Emmerson's sister. Brody warned the kid that Emmerson would kick his ass, but the look on St. Laurent's face said he wasn't listening.

That would make for a fun fight sometime down the road.

As soon as he was able after the concert, Brody extracted himself from his teammates to find Ann. She was hovering at the back of the room with Nathalie, frowning slightly as Nat patted her arm in what looked like a reassuring gesture. The exchange worried him just enough that he almost missed the pained expression on St. Laurent's face. He looked around in time to see the viola player from the Philharmonia baring down on them.

"What's wrong?" he asked his new defense partner.

"This man...the viola player. I have been told to...avoid him. He is...not believing that an athlete that is...can speak two languages."

"Ah. He looks pretty intent on talking to you." He patted the kid's shoulder. "Leave it to me. Duck and hide. I'll take care of him."

Brody headed the viola player off and went into a short ramble about violas and their position in an orchestra, followed by a brief discussion of the way classic violas were made, and a few random questions about the music the group had performed that evening. As usual, his conversation partner stared up at him with a slightly confused expression, lost in the flow of Brody's subject-changing interest. Since he'd hoped for that reaction, he didn't take it personally. When he was sure St. Laurent was away and safe, he patted the dumbfounded viola player on the back and excused himself, making a beeline for Ann.

"How did you enjoy the music?" He stepped close and brushed her cheek with a brief kiss, the contact not nearly as satisfying as pulling her into his arms. But it would have to do in the full room with Nathalie standing there watching them.

"It was wonderful."

She smiled up at him, no signs of the frown he'd seen earlier. He hunted her expression, just to be sure, but she seemed OK now.

"Thank you for inviting me," she said.

"Thank you for coming. You ready to eat?"

"Always."

Nathalie patted her arm again. "Have fun tonight. And don't worry. Everything will be fine."

Ann sighed and nodded without saying more.

Brody raised his brows in question, but neither woman elaborated and Semenov chose that moment to join them.

They said their goodnights, then made their way to the street for a taxi.

On their way to the restaurant, Brody debated bringing up the exchange between Ann and Nathalie. She'd looked upset, though as they talked on the way to the restaurant, she seemed comfortable and relaxed. He didn't want to ruin that mood, but concern nagged at him.

By the time they got to the restaurant—a different Mexican place with the second best food in the city that he'd tried so far—he'd mostly convinced himself to let it go and just enjoy the meal with her. If she wanted to tell him about it, she would.

Watching her eat was almost as seductive as kissing her. He suspected there was something wrong with him, that he enjoyed the pleasure she took from food so much. He didn't care. Ann Bell smiling was the best thing ever. Ann smiling and sighing over her food, better than that.

"You and Nat seem to be getting closer," he commented as he savored his chicken mole. "Must be interesting having a new sister you didn't grow up with?"

"She's fantastic. I'm really glad we're getting to know each other finally. My parents wouldn't approve, but…" She made a little gesture with her fork before diving back into her fajita salad.

"Why wouldn't they approve?" he asked.

She hadn't told him a lot about her parents yet. The basics—her mother was a stay-at-home mom, her father a preacher, both very involved in the church. But he knew there was a lot more there after the vague hint Nat had dropped about being glad she didn't look like her mother.

"My mother left Nathalie's father," Ann said quietly. "She didn't… She didn't approve of their religion."

Ah. That explained the tension. It was common knowledge that Nathalie was a green witch, though he'd never had a chance to discuss her religion with her, as she was so private. He was curious and would have loved that conversation. But not everyone understood the neo-pagan religions. Too many people assumed devil worship even though Wiccans and other neo-pagans didn't even believe in that devil. Since Ann's mother had gone on to marry an evangelical preacher, Brody had to assume Mrs. Bell was one of those who saw the devil where there was none.

"So she thought Nat would be a bad influence on you?" he asked.

Ann shrugged, her gaze focused on her food. "I'm not sure she even considered that I'd want to know Nathalie." She drew a small circle in her rice with her fork. "I don't have another sister, just two younger brothers. And they're more like my parents."

"How so?"

"Religious. Extremely religious."

He frowned a little. "How extreme is extreme?"

"*Extreme*. Fanatical." She shook her head and scooped up some guacamole on a chip. "They don't understand why I want to study genetics."

"Because it's a cool field of science," he said, making sure to use the matter-of-fact tone that amused her. He was rewarded for his efforts with her soft smile.

"I'm glad you think so. It's nice talking with someone outside work who actually understands."

"I love that you entertain my alien genetics questions."

She chuckled, the sound making his muscle tense and his heart pound. God he loved when she laughed. And because he loved it so much, he steered the conversation away from her family and back to easier topics.

"I'm sorry you missed the ice skating today," he said. "It was a great event."

"I would have spent most of it on my backside anyway."

"I like your backside. I'd never let you damage it."

She blushed, and it was all he could do not to pull her across the table for a kiss.

"How about a rain check on the skating," he said. "I'd still like to teach you." Mostly because it would be an excellent excuse to keep his hands on her.

"It could be hazardous." She smiled when she said it, but the smile dropped away suddenly, and she looked back at her plate.

"I'll take my chances." Brody frowned at her sudden mood shift.

She made a noncommittal noise and shoveled food into her mouth.

"I promise to take care of you on the ice," he said seriously.

She nodded but didn't meet his gaze.

Worry tightened in his stomach again, worry he couldn't explain, but it kept coming back to poke at him. Something there...something she wasn't saying. The fact that she was keeping something from him, something that kept putting that distressed expression in her eyes, bothered him a lot. Every competitive, curious bone in his body wanted to push her for answers.

But another part of him just wanted to see her smile again.

That part won out. He moved on to a topic he knew would keep the grin on her face. Food. To his relief, she relaxed again, and he breathed a little easier.

Once the main course dishes were whisked away, they ordered coffees and one dessert to share.

"You're in training," she said primly.

Which made him chuckle. "That has never been a reason to give up dessert."

"I'm having a lot of fun tonight, Brody. Thanks."

"Told you I was fun."

She smiled. "Good thing I turned out not to be a psychotic killer, huh?"

He chuckled. But the reference to their first meeting was yet another reminder that she was hiding something. He tried to ignore his nagging curiosity. Every time they veered toward the subject, she shut down on him. He wanted to keep things easy and light. He wanted her relaxed.

Yet concern that whatever she was keeping from him might be serious, and could affect their growing relationship, was like a spur in his heal. He couldn't seem to let it go.

"Can I ask a question?" he said, then wanted to bite his tongue.

"Sure."

He took a deep breath and dived in. "Why did I have to wait a week to call you after our first date? You told Nathalie she could give me your number, but then you asked me wait. Why?"

Her face closed up instantly, and that little crease between her brows reappeared. He cursed silently and with a lot of feeling. Damn it. He'd known that would happen. He shouldn't have brought it up. But he couldn't take it back now either.

"What did Nathalie tell you about that?" she asked.

"Nothing. She said I should ask you. Although, judging by your reaction, I'm not sure that was such a hot idea."

She forced a half-smile, but it fell away quickly. "I can't...I don't want to talk about it."

"Boyfriend? Ex-husband? Ex-girlfriend? Stalker? Current husband? IRS? Mob?"

Her frown turned to the adorably confused expression he loved. That felt like a minor win.

She shook off his list of possibilities. "Nothing like that. It's personal, though."

He desperately wanted to know the truth, to ask the next logical question. But watching her face close up was worse than not knowing. His knee-jerk reaction was to make a joke of the whole thing and move on, as he'd been doing all evening.

It still bothered him, though. He had a feeling whatever had happened in that week was important enough to get between him and Ann.

"Personal…in that you don't want to talk to me about it yet?" he asked, trying to balance his curiosity against caution.

"We've been on exactly four dates. We met less than a month ago. We're nowhere near the stage where I can tell you everything about me." She looked down at the table, toying with her coffee cup. "Not sure I'll ever be at that stage."

She murmured the last so quietly, he wasn't sure she was talking to him anymore. His heart hurt at her desolate tone. He could practically feel the loneliness in it, and that tore at him because she didn't have to be lonely. Even if things didn't work out between them, she was too wonderful to be alone.

"Well, I have secrets, too, you know," he said, defaulting to light humor, hoping to erase the sadness in her expression. He just couldn't take it anymore. "Deep, dark secrets."

Her lips quirked up. "You? I find that hard to believe."

"Why?"

"You put everything out on the surface. I'm not sure you could keep a secret if you wanted to."

"That's not true." He purposely infused his voice with exaggerated offense. "I have a big secret."

"Really? And that would be?"

He leaned across the table, looking left and right before focusing on her. "I have an extensive collection of romantic comedy movies," he whispered.

Her laughter bubbled out in a short burst. The sound settled his nerves and sent a wave a pleasure through him.

She shook her head. "First of all, I'm not sure why that's a secret."

"I'm a big, mean hockey player. I can't be caught with a rom-com collection."

Truthfully, he didn't care, and he was pretty sure she realized that since they talked about his romance novel collection all the time. But he liked that the humor had returned to her expression. He was willing to say whatever it took to keep it there.

She snorted. "Second of all," she said, "you've just confirmed you're terrible at keeping secrets."

"OK. You got me. But I can keep one if necessary. I mean, you should hear the stuff I know about my brother."

She laughed. "If you tell me, will he be upset?"

"Hell, yeah. It'll tarnish your view of him before you've even met him. Wait, I like that idea. OK, so this one time, when we were six years old…" He went on to tell her some of the most embarrassing stories he could remember about his twin—one of which was actually his own embarrassing moment, but he wasn't about to admit that.

By the time he was finished, she was grinning, chuckling, and a few times had laughed heartily. He made a mental note not to ask about that first week again. At least not until he was more sure of their relationship.

Realizing he wanted a relationship with Ann wasn't particularly shocking. He'd barely been able to think of anything else since meeting her. He *liked* Ann. A lot. And not just because he found her adorable and sexy. He enjoyed spending time with her and wanted more. As much as she'd give him.

But that first week, the mystery around it, felt like a threat hanging over their heads, just waiting to destroy the good thing they had going.

And there didn't seem to be a damned thing he could do about it.

CHAPTER TEN

Ann waved her arms about trying to catch her balance, teetering precariously on the thin line of steel that was supposed to be holding her upright. She flailed, backpedaled, and would have dropped hard onto the ice, but Brody's strong arms caught her around the waist.

Cheerful music blared through the air as skaters with significantly better skills than she had swirled past. The Bryant Park open air rink was full of people laughing and shouting, gliding and spinning over the ice. The November air was brisk, but the day was bright and sunny. Around the rink, adorable wooden house stalls that made up the holiday market lined the park's stone paths.

The atmosphere was cheerful, the air filled with scents of delicious sweets, cinnamon, and the exquisite meals being served at the open-air, two-story restaurant set up at the corner of the rink. On the opposite side, the long, white tent where the skates were stored and people waited for their session on the ice glowed as brightly in the sun as the ice itself.

Ann glared down at her skates as she clung onto Brody for dear life. This would be a lot more fun if they were sitting outside the rink, drinking hot chocolate, and watching other people fall on their asses.

"This is impossible," she said.

Brody laughed. "You'll get the hang of it. You just need more practice."

She made a face. "Right."

Despite her worry about melting the rink, she had agreed to let Brody try teaching her how to ice skate. Her "headache" excuse last time had had nothing to do with a headache and everything to do with the terrible training session she'd had the day before with Nathalie's father, Mr. Mendez.

They were trying to teach her how to start the fire on purpose and control it, an effort that went against everything she'd spent her life trying to do. She'd failed miserably. And repeatedly. The session had gone so badly, she'd been sure if she went to the ice rink the next day, she'd turn it into a swimming pool. And then hurt Brody when he tried to help her. The thought of hurting him—or having him see her fire and turn away from her like she was cursed—was too much to take.

But she'd known she'd disappointed him by not showing up. She hated doing that. Hated that the fire kept interfering. So when he'd declared their next date would be ice skating, she'd given in.

In truth, she wanted to prove to herself she could manage it. And she'd worked her ass off during the week in between their last date and this one to ensure she could keep her hands cool.

Starting the fire on purpose, controlling it to that degree... Well, she still had a lot of work to do there. But for now, she was determined to have this date, this experience without hurting anyone.

Or ending up in a swimming pool instead of an ice rink.

She hadn't realized how hard the actual skating would be, though.

Her legs wobbled again, even though she wasn't moving, and she tightened her grip on Brody.

"Didn't you ever try this as a kid?" he asked.

"I grew up in Texas. When would I have bothered with ice skating?"

He eased her away from the support of his big body so she had to stand on the skates again. Her ankles felt like rubber as she tried to find a way to balance.

"That's no excuse," he said. "There are rinks all over Texas."

She didn't release her death grip on his arms but did try to stay upright. She stood that way for exactly two seconds before her feet, of their own accord and through no effort on her part, flew out from under her. Brody caught her full weight again, holding her close as she growled in irritation.

His chuckle didn't help her embarrassment, but the fact that his arms were around her went a long way toward making her feel okay about her inability to stand on her own. In fact, she rather liked the excuse to have his arms around her. She leaned into him, savoring the solid strength of his big body, even though doing so was risky.

"How did you learn to skate?" she asked as they adjusted their stance.

He shifted to holding her with one arm around her waist, keeping her tight to his side but with enough room for her to stand mostly on her own. Her ankles wobbling, she made an attempt at a step forward. When she didn't fall, she tried another step. Not exactly skating, but at least she was staying on her feet this time. Sort of. With a lot of help from Brody.

"My dad took us to the rink," he said as they slowly made their way across the smooth, glossy surface. "First time when we were ten. We'd been getting into a few too many dust ups with other kids, and he was trying to find us a sport to channel our energies."

"You were fighting even as a child?" She wasn't entirely sure how to feel about that. He was so full of emotion, it still amazed her.

He held her a little tighter as she wobbled again. When she didn't fall, she grinned up at him in triumph. His answering look sent tingles of awareness across her skin. She looked away quickly to concentrate on her breathing and on keeping her hands cool.

"We got picked on a lot," he said, his tone easy and relaxed.

"You got picked on? Who would be stupid enough to do that?"

She smiled at his bark of laughter. She might worry about the intensity of his emotions, but she did love hearing him laugh.

"Connor and I were pretty gangly and awkward when we were kids—growing so fast our bodies had trouble adjusting and staying coordinated. There were a lot of clumsy moments. And Connor was… He wasn't as outgoing as I was. The bullies tended to go after him first."

"And you jumped in to defend him," she guessed. So he'd been like this his entire life, the one to jump into a fight to save a brother. The story explained a lot about him. "What happened?"

He shrugged, as if it weren't a bad memory. "We got into a lot of fights. Ridiculous fights that rarely resulted in anything worse than bloody noses, but it happened so often my parents knew they had to do something about it. Connor and I were so much bigger than the other kids, my parents were afraid we'd end up really hurting someone."

"But you were the ones being picked on! Why didn't anyone stop the bullies?"

"Oh, they worked on that part, too. Lot of suspensions from school handed out, that kind of thing." He waved away the bullies as if they were nothing. "But as far as my parents were concerned, what Connor and I really needed was an outlet for our energy. And maybe something that would help us adjust to our lanky bodies. My dad thought skating, and hockey, might do the trick. Give us a team sport, a safe place to go, and a way to train some coordination into us."

She wanted to comfort the little boy that had to fight to defend himself and his twin brother. Before she could consider how to do that, though, the balance she'd managed to maintain for a full five minutes abandoned her and she slipped again.

She clung to Brody like a life line as he wrapped her up in arms, pulling her up flush against his chest. This close thoughts of kid bullies fled. All she could think about was how good he smelled, how near he was, how easy it would be to kiss him.

A group of teenagers skated past just then, hooting and whistling. "Kiss her! Kiss her, dude!"

She winced and felt her cheeks heating. Brody just smiled as he helped her regain her footing.

But before she could put any distance between them, he leaned in close and said, "I think those kids had a good idea."

He kissed her softly, just a gentle brush of lips, but she felt the contact all the way through her body, tingling along her nerves, sparking very dangerous heat.

She resisted the urge to melt against him, to take the kiss deeper, only because her hands inside her gloves were feeling a little too warm. The reminder that she still hadn't mastered control of her fire had her easing away, reluctantly.

They made their way in slow, shuffling increments to the exit when the announcement came up that their session on the ice was coming to an end. She continued to cling to him around the edge of the rink. For balance she told herself. Not because she desperately wanted to stay in his arms.

As they laughed and stumbled to the break in the wall—and freedom from the demon ice skates—Ann realized she was in deep with Brody now. She liked him. A lot. And it was getting harder and harder to resist doing something about those feelings.

She still couldn't invite him up to her apartment, though. She wasn't ready for sex, despite being more than a little desperate to take Brody to bed. Their goodnight kisses left her reeling, almost drunk with need, and she wanted him more than any other man she'd ever met.

She'd only risked sex twice in her life, and both times had been bad because she'd had to suppress her emotions and reactions to keep from catching the sheets on fire. She didn't want that with Brody, not when she was so sure they could be good together. Every time he kissed her only confirmed that.

Until she was more sure of her control, though, she didn't dare relax. And if she couldn't relax fully, she'd only disappoint them both.

He helped her remove her skates, a process which had her entire body tingling. He knelt on one knee on the padded ground in front of the bench where she sat, unlacing her boots, his big fingers working the skate loose with ease. Her breathing sped up. God, having his hands on her legs was like a kind of torture. Having him remove even something as innocuous as footwear felt like a seduction, a promise of what could be. When he looked up at her from his position, his lips lifted in that knowing smile, she felt the look all the way to her core.

She held her hands in her lap, her grip tight, and concentrated on her breathing so she didn't start a fire she still didn't know how to stop. Her leg muscles were aching, her ankles sore from attempting something she'd never done before. The November air was brisk and sharp, the ice rink behind them adding an additional chill. And none of it was a match for the heat in Brody's eyes.

Brody walked her to her building door after treating her to a scrumptious Indian meal and this time she felt no awkwardness or hesitance before he kissed her. She fell into his arms, hungry for a sense that this could work, that they could share the passion she wanted with him without disaster. She savored his taste, the feel of his strong arms wrapped around her, the hard press of his big body against hers. Her stomach danced with needy anticipation and without meaning to, she ground herself against him, wanting to feel every inch of him.

The tell-tale twitch in his pants proved he was as affected by their kiss as she was, but it was a warning she forced herself to heed. Reluctantly, she eased back, not out of his arms, but far enough she could look up at him.

"Thanks for such a wonderful day," she murmured.

"It doesn't have to end."

He cupped her cheek in his big hand, his leather glove feeling deliciously erotic against her skin. She swallowed hard. Oh how she wanted to invite him in. But she just didn't dare yet.

"I… I need more time," she said.

She braced herself for his disappointment, or his arguments. She fully expected him to push the issue because most men had with her in the past. She was prepared with excuses, things she hoped would be reasonable enough he wouldn't dump her.

If he did, she knew they weren't meant to be. A man who couldn't wait on sex wasn't worth her time. But it would hurt with this man.

To her relief, he didn't do any of the things she dreaded. He just nodded, with that very slight, sexy smile tugging at his lips, and he kissed her again. Her pulse thumped hard at the seductive sweep of his tongue and delicious pressure of his lips against hers. She was panting by the time he straightened away, and afraid she'd throw caution to the wind and invite him up anyway.

Before she could, he brushed her cheek with one gloved finger then wished her a quiet goodnight.

She watched him walk away, standing just inside the lobby while she made sure he got a taxi, then she closed the door. Her relief was tempered by a surprising amount of disappointment—not at his respecting her wishes but at her own inability to do what she so desperately wanted to do with him.

Closing her eyes, she knocked her head gently against the wooden door, then turned up the stairs. She'd never wanted to be normal so badly in her entire life.

CHAPTER ELEVEN

Brody watched the swirling crowds of formally dressed party goers as he hunted for Ann and pretended to sip at his flute of Champaign. The exhibition game supporting the Special Olympics had gone really well that day, and despite his brutal hangover, he'd thoroughly enjoyed himself.

He really shouldn't have gotten involved in a drinking contest with his Nordic and Russian teammates. But they'd laid down a challenge, and some of the American and Canadian players had risen to the fight. He'd expected to do better—given his size he usually handled alcohol well—but the Russians brought out the vodka, and he'd been a goner. His only consolation was that he'd lasted longer than the Canadians.

But even with a dodgy stomach and a fuzzy head, he'd had a fantastic time during the exhibition. Now he was very much looking forward to seeing Ann all dressed up for the party. He was wearing the requisite tux—one Connor had helped him get when he'd first moved to New York—now all he needed was the beautiful woman on his arm. And only one woman would do.

When he finally spotted her, he felt his mouth drop open. Stunned was understating his reaction.

She was gorgeous in her dark blue dress, the cut modest, but the silk material skimmed her curves in a sinful seduction. She'd pulled her hair up into a loose bun on top of her head, making her neck look long and incredibly kissable. And her mouth, that gorgeous, sexy mouth of hers… She smiled when she saw him and the look went right to his cock. He had to swallow to wet his suddenly dry throat.

Had any woman ever looked so beautiful?

He handed off his mostly full glass to a passing waiter and went to join her, meeting her halfway because she was like a magnet he couldn't resist. For a long moment, he couldn't even find words to greet her he was so overwhelmed by her.

Finally, he blinked and made an effort to untie his tongue. "You look gorgeous," he said.

Her cheeks turned a charming shade of pink. "Thank you. You do too. You clean up well."

He straightened his lapels and made a show of preening at her compliment—only partly pretending at his pleasure.

"How did the exhibition game go?"

"It was great. Everyone enjoyed themselves. Thanks to my hangover, a kid half my size dropped me on my ass with a very clever check."

"Were you OK?" she asked through a grin.

"Only hurt my pride. But he was so pleased with himself, it was worth it. He'll be talking about that for years."

"You're a good man, Brody Evans."

He barked out a laugh that made a clump of his teammates frown at him. He ignored them because he was too thrilled with Ann.

"I wondered if you'd be hungover today," she said.

He winced as he led her across the room to get her a glass of wine. "Yeah. Sorry about that."

The challenge with his teammates had been a spontaneous thing and on a night when he and Ann hadn't had any plans to talk. Which apparently hadn't stopped him from drunk dialing her. Twice.

She chuckled as he handed her a glass. "Do you have any idea what you said to me?"

"No." He cringed. "Do I want to know?"

She laughed outright then. He loved the sound enough to face his own embarrassment.

"You were very cute. Kept telling me how much you like me and how pretty I am. There was a lot of ribbing from other men going on in the background, from what I could hear."

He closed his eyes. "Damn."

"I didn't mind. Even if you did wake me up at three in the morning with the second call."

"Ah, hell." He scrubbed a hand over his face.

"I would have preferred your teammates didn't hear how much you like my ass, though."

His groaned. "I didn't."

"You did."

"Fuck. That'll teach me to go drinking with the Russians."

She laughed again, which made all the humiliation worthwhile.

She rose on her toes, bracing one hand on his chest, and kissed his cheek. "It's OK. I like that you like my ass."

His heart rate tripled. The feel of her warm palm against his chest was like a brand. Her scent filled his head. She'd added a very faint perfume to her already delicious spicy scent and the combination was more intoxicating than the vodka had been last night. He wanted to bury his face against her skin and hunt out all the soft, warm spots where she'd applied that perfume.

He stared at her as she eased down and his hands twitched with the need to cup the aforementioned beautiful ass. Her expression turned serious. Her breathing increased, drawing his gaze to her breasts, so nicely framed in silk. His imagination filled with images of slipping that silk down, tasting all the pale skin he exposed, drawing her nipple into his mouth… He blinked and forced his gaze up to her face. In time to see her wet her lips with a quick flick of her tongue. His control almost broke.

"We should probably talk about something else," she said, her voice husky.

"Yes." He swallowed hard. "And we should walk."

She nodded and bit her bottom lip. He closed his eyes briefly and tried now to growl out loud.

They fell into step next to each other, not quite touching, as they circled the room, chatting with some of his teammates and a few of the VIPs. When music started, he talked her into a dance. Her silk dress shifted over her skin as he held her close, the sensation erotic as hell.

He wasn't really surprised he'd called her last night. His thoughts were full of her. He managed to focus on training, on the games, but off the ice, his world had become Ann.

Despite vowing to himself he'd give her all the time she needed, he was having a very hard time trying not to seduce her. He didn't just want sex with Ann, he wanted more. Much more. His feelings went a lot deeper than lust. So he wanted to do this right.

But his willpower was waning. He'd become too well acquainted with cold showers and his own hand over the last few weeks. Every nerve in his body lit up when she was near, like a constant spark of lightning. And it was all he could do not to drag her away to a dark closet so he could explore the glorious curves beneath her silk dress.

Even the thought of it left him edgy with need, and in danger of giving this posh crowd a show with his raging hard-on.

In an attempt to distract himself, again, from thoughts of fucking Ann, he brought up a topic he'd been avoiding. "So, we have a home game this weekend, and I have an extra ticket."

She narrowed her eyes.

He pressed on. "Would you like to come to the game? Watch me play live?"

Given her reaction to the first game she'd seen him in—and as far as he knew, the only hockey game she'd watched since—he hadn't invited her to a home game before this. She'd been eager to learn about hockey, but had shown no signs of actually wanting to watch the sport, or see him in action.

Her continued hesitance bothered him. Hockey was a huge part of his life. He wanted Ann to be a huge part of his life, too. But if she couldn't accept him for who he was on the ice as well as off…he wasn't sure what kind of future they had.

"You don't have to come if you don't want to," he found himself saying to fill the silence, then wanted to smack himself because he sounded like a child, pouty and insecure. Very sexy, Evans, he growled at himself.

She stroked her hand up his back as they swayed around the dance floor, and the gesture distracted him. He loved having her hands on him. She was always so damned warm. His imagination jumped immediately to how her warm hands might feel on his cock, and he had to force the thought down or risk embarrassing them both.

After what felt like a very long time, she said, "I think I'd like to see a live game. Will… Is it safe in the audience?"

He tried not to grin like a fool so he wouldn't scare her off. "You'll be safe. The home crowd is enthusiastic but not violent. All that stays on the ice."

"Will you be hitting someone again?"

"Probably." He wanted her to be prepared. "But remember, it's just part of the game. Remember I told you about checking?"

"Yes. But fighting is something else."

"It's actually part of the strategy. As much a part of hockey as a puck and stick."

"I know." She looked over his shoulder, her gaze turned inward for a moment, then she nodded. "OK, I can do this." She meet his gaze again. "I'd love to go."

He worked not to cheer, but he hugged her closer, hopeful and anxious all at the same time.

"Have I mentioned how beautiful you are tonight?" he asked, unable to resist.

"Yes. Thank you."

Her blushed charmed him.

She opened her mouth to say something else, then shook her head.

"What?" he asked.

"Nothing." She smiled. "Thanks for inviting me tonight. I'm enjoying this."

"Me, too."

He danced her off the floor and they wandered around the room some more, chatting with his teammates and their dates, some of the sponsors, he introduced her to the coach. All of it felt right. Having Ann with him, being with her felt right.

He just wished he knew if she felt the same.

CHAPTER TWELVE

Ann entered the Brooklyn Banking Center with the crowds of supporters, all dressed in the Empires' colors, sporting the teams' logo on hats and jerseys, some of them with their faces painted. The noise level was deafening, but all of it was enthusiastic, with several chants going up for the Empires even before she'd passed through the doors and into the stadium.

Her seat was an excellent one, just behind and a few rows back from one of the benches where the teams sat. Unfortunately, she was in the middle of a row, which meant she'd have to step over people to leave.

That didn't help her anxiety levels. She was already nervous about this game. She wasn't sure she could take the sheer emotion and not lose control. But she'd been working hard with Nathalie and Mr. Mendez. This was the test. If she could get through this game, be surrounded by and swept up in all this enthusiasm and energy, without losing control, then she might, just might, be able to finally take Brody to her bed.

She was getting a little more than desperate now. She wanted him so much she ached from it. But until very recently, every time she'd allowed herself to imagine him making love to her, her body got entirely too hot—in a bad way—and her hands flickered with flames.

Nathalie urged her to be patient, but given her feelings for Brody, patience was difficult.

She was much more comfortable with her control than she'd been two months ago. Over the last week, she'd been able to fantasize a little about Brody without actually lighting up. So she was hopeful.

She didn't want to consider what might happen if she failed tonight's test.

The players hit the ice for warm ups and the crowd erupted around her. She didn't stand until the anthem was played, despite the two men on her left spending the entire warm up on their feet and the group to her right jumping up and down.

Brody was easy to spot on the ice. He was huge, even compared to the other players. He glanced up once into the stands and raised a hand to her. She grinned and waved back, trying to be discreet, but the gestures still drew the attention of the men and women surrounding her. She ducked her head under their stares and concentrated on her breathing.

She could do this. She could.

Brody didn't look up at her again, at least not that she could tell. As the game started, he was all focus and attention to the rink.

The game was fast and rougher than the first one she'd watched. There was a lot of bumping and swinging and knocking other players hard enough against the glass to sound very painful. She tried to keep up with the play, but despite all Brody's lessons, things still moved too fast for her to follow. The line changes in particular made no sense to her. Even without understanding everything going on, she still enjoyed the first period a lot.

By the second period, she was cheering with the crowd every time the Empires got close to the goal. She forgot about her breathing exercises and her fire for the entire period, and when the break came, she realized she was excited, having fun, and wasn't heating up.

The thrill of that made her stomach dance with another kind of excitement—the kind that had everything to do with seeing Brody after the game. As the players hit the ice for the third period, she grinned, anticipation thrumming through her blood even as her hands stayed comfortably cool.

Things started out well for the Empires, but within moments of Brody's line hitting the ice, everything changed. One of the Empires got hit—taken out completely by someone from the other team. The poor man hadn't even seen the hit coming. For a heartbeat, the crowd was almost quiet in anticipation of him standing. But he didn't.

The game stopped. Everyone on the ice crowded around the downed player. The referees ensured the opposing teams stayed separated. The medical staff was called out.

The people around her talked about the penalty that would have to be given, arguing between a major penalty or a match penalty. She didn't know the difference, but from what she'd seen, there was no question there *would* be some kind of penalty.

By the time the medical staff carried the still unconscious man off the ice, the two men next to her were outlining strategies for the upcoming power play.

And then—no penalty. Nothing. The referee just resumed the game.

Chaos erupted in the stands. Shouts and screams, roars of outrage. Everyone was on their feet, fists waving, howling at the refs, screaming obscenities.

The emotional impact battered Ann because she was just as outraged as the crowd. How could they do *nothing*?

She hunted for Brody and found he was still on the ice. He wasn't watching the play at all, though. His focus seemed to be entirely on the man who'd taken out his teammate. Her heart started thumping hard. Oh no. He was going to fight.

Panic tightened in her stomach. Not for the impending fisticuffs. She'd only had to see him fight once to know he could handle himself. But she could feel her body temperature rising. The emotions of the crowd, knowing Brody was about to do something vicious, all combined to throw off her control.

She concentrated on slowing her breathing, ignoring the crowd's continued catcalls. But she couldn't look away from Brody.

When he struck, it was as vicious and merciless as she'd feared—and hoped. He hammered the guilty player, dropping his mitts and pummeling the man's face like it was a punching bag. The other player attempted to hit back, but his swings were weak and ineffectual, bouncing off Brody like pillows.

The crowd erupted again, this time in cheers, urging Brody on to more violence. When blood sprayed out from the other man's nose, Ann grabbed the chair armrest with one hand.

The feel of the armrest giving way under her grip pulled her attention from the fight. The metal had melted in her hand. She released her hold like she'd been the one burnt. She could clearly see finger dents in the metal. Panic pulsed through her again. She stood and tried to edge past the line of standing, still shouting fans. Their words made no sense to her now. All she could hear was the blood pounding in her ears as fear swept through her.

But all the wild gesturing and excitement meant a man bumped into her as she attempted to ease past. Without thinking, she gripped his arm. He howled, looking down at her with narrowed eyes, and she realized she'd managed to burn him even through his thick winter coat. Almost too terrified now to speak, she breathed out an apology and nudged her way out to the aisle.

Without looking back at the ice to see what had happened, she fled the stadium, taking refuge in the cold winter air.

Brody fully expected the match penalty and took it without argument. It was worth it to make that bastard pay for what he'd done to St. Laurent. As he headed to the tunnel, he looked into the stands for Ann. She wasn't there.

Worry followed him to the locker room. That fight had been even more bloody and vicious than the one she'd seen on TV. And watching a beat down live was very different to seeing one on the small screen.

He changed out of his gear, let one of the trainers check his hands—he had swollen knuckles but no major damage—then showered. He'd have to meet with Coach and do a few interviews with the press before he'd be able to leave. He'd warned Ann it would take him some time after the game ended before he could meet her. But now, the usual delays made him edgy.

Watching the last of the game from the locker room, he forgot his anxiety long enough to cheer when the Empires won. Then he went back to tapping his foot, impatient to get to Ann so he could check on her.

The team filed in a few minutes later, and for the next half hour, Brody did what was required. He got a lot of congratulations and praise from the guys—which he waved off. He was only doing his part for the team. He went into the office to talk with Coach—where it was confirmed he'd have a five game suspension. Neither he nor Coach MacArthur were very bothered by it. Brody would be back in time for the Winter Classic, and the suspension was worth it given the egregious actions of the other player.

He answered all the reporters' questions, doing his best to put on his typical easygoing acceptance of what had happened. But during it all, he worried about Ann, and it was harder than usual to focus on this part of his job.

Finally, after a brief talk with Semenov about the suspension, Brody got his chance to escape. By that point, the events of the game were secondary to his growing apprehension about Ann.

After making his way through encouraging fans and a few more reporters, he reached the place on the opposite side of the stadium from the team exit where he was supposed to meet Ann. She wasn't there. He hunted the passing pedestrians as the scents of cooking nuts from a nearby food cart flavored the cold December air. The streetlights surrounding the stadium were bright, but the stadium's wall still harbored pockets of shadows. He searched those too, trying not to let his frustration and worry show.

Where the hell was she? Had she left?

He took out his cellphone and checked—again—for texts or voicemails. Nothing. He flicked through to her number and started to call, just as he saw her come around the corner of the building, heading toward him.

Relief made his shoulders slump. He stuffed his phone back in his coat pocket and went to her, so happy to see her he almost missed how pale she looked.

Her hands were jammed into her coat pockets and her skin was nearly translucent under the yellow streetlights. Her eyes were huge and glassy, and she breathed in rough, rapid gasps.

"Hey, are you OK?" When he tried to take her in his arms, she jerked away. "Ann? Was it the fight? I'm so sorry. That was worse than usual. Are you upset?"

She swallowed visibly and shook her head, then nodded, then bit her lip. "It's... Are you hurt?"

He flexed his hands, though she wouldn't be able to see the damage through his gloves. "Nothing serious. I'll be fine by tomorrow."

"What happened after?"

"You missed me getting thrown out?"

She blinked. "They threw you out of the game?"

"I expected it. Got a five game suspension." He shrugged. "I'm more worried about you right now. You don't look so good. I mean, you always look beautiful, but you're very pale. Maybe we should go get a drink, put some color back into your cheeks."

She shook her head in a fast, jerky denial. "No. I can't... I have to go. I need to get home."

"Wait, what? I thought we were going out? Ann, damn it, what's wrong?" He pulled her into his arms, ignoring her protest because he was too worried about her. "Jesus, you're burning up. You're sick."

She scrambled out of his arms, so fast and so full of panic, his own panic spiked.

"Ann, please. Let me get a taxi. I'll get you home."

"No!" She shook her head again in that fast, jerky movement. "I'm sorry. I have to go. I..."

Tears filled her eyes, and Brody's panic went into overdrive. But before he could do anything else, she turned and ran. For a split second he didn't react, then he took off after her. If she was that sick, she needed help.

He pushed through a clump of milling tourists, grunting at their protests, but it was too late. Ann had disappeared into the crowds.

He had a sharp déjà vu moment of their first date, when she'd also run away from him. And his panic turned into full blown fear.

CHAPTER THIRTEEN

Ann pushed into her apartment, her hands still warm enough to heat the wood when she pressed it. She dropped her coat and purse on the floor just inside the entryway without touching anything, toed out of her boots, then went to her bathroom. She didn't even take off her clothes, just climbed into the shower, turned on the cold water and dunked herself under the spray.

Steam rose from her skin, warming the air around her despite the cold water.

Since the blue flames that burst from her skin weren't typical fire, they didn't react to fire retardants the way normal flames would. But cold water helped. It wouldn't prevent the fire entirely, but it was enough of a shock to her system to give her time to regain her control.

One of the more valuable lessons from Nathalie and Mr. Mendez.

She closed her eyes, with her head under the spray, and focused on slowing her heartbeat.

"Pi to the fifth decimal," she murmured. "Divide by twelve." She did that in her head. "Now add that." She focused on the numbers, the sound of her own voice echoing in the shower stall, the abstraction of the equations. Still with her eyes closed, she talked herself through a series of large number calculations, until finally she felt steady and calm.

Another trick Nathalie had taught her—if she focused on multiplying and dividing large numbers in her head, she automatically calmed because she wasn't thinking about her feelings or panic.

She eased out from under the water, taking a long, deep breath. The air wasn't steamy anymore, and the cold water was giving her goose bumps. Shutting off the spray, she stripped out of her clothes, leaving them hanging in the shower to dry, and pulled on her robe. Then she went to clean up her coat and purse in the entryway.

Her cellphone was ringing from the depths of her bag. She pulled it out, saw Brody's number, and pressed ignore, letting it go to voicemail. She couldn't talk to him yet. Her control felt tenuous at best, and it was all she could do not to revert to shutting down her emotions entirely.

But she was trying not to actually notice those emotions at the moment. If she spoke with Brody, everything would come rushing back.

Unfortunately, she couldn't ignore the sense of disappointment and failure that tightened her throat and brought tears to her eyes. She blinked them away and stumbled to her bed, curling onto her side and hugging her knees to her chest.

This wasn't going to work. She was still too dangerous, still such a mess. He deserved better, someone who didn't melt metal and nearly burn a stranger. Someone who could revel in her own emotions.

Someone normal.

She ignored the knocking on her door at first, knowing it was likely Brody. What could she tell him?

It took a few minutes before she realized the voice coming from the door wasn't a man's. Frowning, she went to look out her peephole. Nathalie stood in the hallway, hands on hips, shouting for her to open up.

"What are you doing here?" she asked as she let Nathalie in.

"Brody is having a heart attack worrying about you. He says you're sick with a severe fever and won't answer your phone. He's afraid you're passed out in a gutter somewhere. He's searching the streets for you and sent me here to see if you made it home."

Ann closed her eyes, guilt poking at her control but not enough to damage it. "I didn't realize... I'm sorry." She opened her eyes and faced her half sister. "I'm not sick. I don't have a fever."

Nathalie held her gaze for a long moment before nodding. "I see." She glanced around. "I think we'd better talk. Just let me text Brody to tell him you're here and safe."

When Nathalie was finished, Ann led her to the long, narrow living room and motioned her to the couch opposite the exposed brick wall. "Would you like something to drink?"

Nathalie waved that away. "Sit. Talk."

Ann told her everything, from the fight to nearly burning a man in the crowd in her panic to leave. When she was done, she felt both better and worse for having admitted everything out loud.

"It's hopeless, isn't it?" she asked. "I'll never have a normal life. I waited too long to get help."

"Stop. You've only been working on your control for two months and then only practicing with us a couple times a week because of your job. Just give it time."

"Time won't help me with Brody. He's not going to wait around forever."

"If he's worthy of you, he will."

Ann tried to smile at Nathalie's fierce tone, but she failed. "It's not that, it's… It could take me years before I'm able to control myself enough to have a normal relationship. I don't *want* him to wait that long. It's not fair to him. He's such a good man." She glanced away, swallowing hard. "I really like him, Nathalie. I could…I could love him. But what's the point when I can't even take him to bed without worrying about burning down the building?"

"If this wasn't such a serious conversation, that comment could be very funny."

Ann scowled. "When other people talk about burning up the sheets, they don't mean it literally."

Nathalie snorted a half-laugh. "I get it. I do." She patted Ann's knee, then quietly, said, "It might be a little late to break up with him, though."

"Why?"

"Men don't charge around town in a panic over their sick girlfriend if they're not…invested. Yours isn't going to be the only heart broken."

Ann tried to wave that way. "I'm sure he'll be fine. It's only been a couple of months."

"Sometimes that's all it takes."

"You and Alex have been together for a while now, right?"

"A bit over a year. But I knew I was in love with him a lot faster than that."

"What are you saying?"

"There are just as many emotions involved in a breakup as there are in staying with someone. Worse when two people are in love."

"We're not yet." But the declaration sounded hollow even to Ann.

"Deny all you like. That's your choice. Break up with him if you feel you have to. But just know it won't make things any easier. Not for either of you."

"What else can I do?"

"As I see it, you have two choices. One, give him up and move on, putting off relationships until you're confident of your control. Which, by the way, you might never be if you don't test it."

Ann hated the idea of giving up Brody. She didn't want to. But it felt like the only option. "What's my other choice?"

"You work harder at your control and take a chance with Brody. We can use the excuse of you supposedly being sick to disappear for two weeks. You can come stay with my dad and train full time. My grandma is back from her trip to Spain, so she can help, too. I'll come out when I can around my work schedule. We'll push you, hard, test you and train you. Like boot camp."

Ann stared at Nathalie as she considered the offer. "Will that work? Can I cram learning better control like that? This isn't a college exam."

"You're highly motivated. Anything is possible. But, if at the end of the two weeks, you still don't feel you can maintain enough mastery over the pyrokenesis to have a relationship, you'll have to have the hard talk with Brody."

Ann swallowed and stared at the rug covering her hardwood floor. It was a chance. Slim but real. If she didn't take it, she'd definitely lose Brody, and she'd always wonder if she'd sacrificed what could have been the best thing in her life because she was afraid to try.

She'd never even hoped for what she had with Brody before coming to New York. Now, could she really let the chance at happiness go without a fight?

He would fight.

So would she.

She straightened her shoulders. "I'll go pack a bag now. You're sure your father won't mind a house guest?"

"He'll be delighted. I'll call him while you're packing." As Ann headed back down the narrow hall to the bedroom, Nathalie shouted after her, "You'd better text Brody, too. He won't give you the space you need to train otherwise."

Ann took her time composing the text, wanting to ensure Brody would give her space but not worry too much. She hit send then pulled out a small suitcase. And as she packed, she allowed hope to settle into her heart.

She could do this. For him. For herself. She would do this.

CHAPTER FOURTEEN

B rody hated that he couldn't go see Ann, hated that she still wasn't taking his calls, though she did send him a few texts. He hated more that he didn't fully understand what was happening.

He flopped onto his huge couch and flicked restlessly through TV channels, gave up, dropped the remote on the coffee table, and resumed pacing his apartment—the same thing he'd been doing for two fucking weeks when he wasn't at the gym or out for a long run. He'd started and stopped at least twelve different books, unable to focus on his favorite, non-hockey pastime. He'd probably run the equivalent of five marathons. And he'd trained harder than he'd ever trained in his life. It hadn't done a thing to ease his frustration. Even grueling workouts at his boxing gym hadn't helped.

Both Ann and Nathalie assured him Ann just had a bad flu—contagious according to a doctor, Nathalie said. Too contagious for him to see Ann. But after two weeks, he was beyond worried. If she was still sick and contagious after this long, could it be *just* a flu? What if she was sick with something worse and they weren't tell him?

What if she wasn't sick at all?

He didn't even have his job to keep him distracted, damn it. He hadn't minded getting suspended so much because he'd assumed he'd be spending the extra time with Ann. Instead, when he wasn't working out like a madman, training to stay in shape but without the actual games to shed his restlessness, he paced his apartment, fretting like an old woman, irritable because he felt so damned helpless.

At least he was starting back to work tomorrow. He'd gotten the call just that morning that he was confirmed for the Empires' next game.

There'd been a media thing going on since St. Laurent's concussion and Brody's suspension, led by a reporter out of Montreal. A huge blowup, questioning why the player Brody had beat up hadn't gotten a suspension but Brody had. There'd been a lot of debate in the sports media, and all of it could have caused the Empires problems if not handled right.

He'd been ordered not to respond to the controversy, so he had politely refused to answer any questions reporters threw out him. He didn't actually have much to say about it anyway. He'd been too concerned about Ann to do more than notice the debate peripherally. At the moment, how the NHL handled penalties and suspensions was the least of his worries.

He paced into his kitchen, contemplated his empty fridge, and considered ordering takeout even though his appetite wasn't great. He needed to eat if he was getting back on the ice. Ignoring the phone and pile of takeaway menus next to it, he wandered back out to his living room.

He couldn't shake the feeling that Ann's illness wasn't just an ordinary flu. He wasn't even sure why that kept nagging at him. Probably because he had too much time to think.

She'd just gotten sick so fast, right after seeing his fight… And he couldn't ignore the sense that his fight had something to do with what was wrong with her. Which, for reasons he couldn't entirely explain, made him think of that first week when he couldn't see her. All of his worries got tangled together until he was sure his fight, this illness, that first week were all related. Unfortunately, without any actual information, worst case scenarios haunted him.

She'd had a violent ex-boyfriend, or her parents had been abusive, or she'd lived through some other violent encounter, and his fight had triggered a serious episode of PTSD.

She really was sick, maybe even dying, and she didn't want him to know.

She was married and her husband had caught her at the game.

Though, if the problem involved Ann being married, he was sure Nathalie would have told him by now, if only to get him to stop pestering her about Ann's health. Maybe. Nathalie was as notoriously private as Semenov and it was impossible to get anything out of either one of them if they didn't want to talk. But still, he doubted Nathalie would leave him like this if Ann really was married. She'd at least give him a warning hint.

So it probably wasn't a lurking husband. But some sort of violence in Ann's past seemed more and more likely. And he felt shittier and shittier for encouraging her to go to that game.

She should have just told him she wasn't ready yet, damn it.

He flopped onto his couch again, scowling at the silent TV. He'd already gone for a run that morning, but maybe another would help wear him out. They had the Winter Classic in two weeks. There probably wasn't such a thing as over training for that.

Christmas was coming, too. He'd hoped to spend that holiday with Ann. He'd already bought her a present.

Pounding the couch a few times, he stood, intent on going for another run, but stopped when his cellphone rang.

He pounced on it, answering before checking the caller id. "Hello?"

"Brody?"

"Ann. Jesus, are you OK?" It was such a relief to hear her voice, he actually had to sit again. "How are you? What's going on? Can I come over?"

He winced. He hadn't actually meant to ask that just yet, before he even knew what was wrong. But he was desperate to see her and make sure she was well.

"I'm sorry I've been out of touch. I'm feeling better now. I think." Quieter, she said, "I'd like to see you."

Thank God. "Where, when?"

"My place? Now?"

"I'll be there as soon as I can. Sooner if I can move traffic."

Her laugh was soft and a little strained, but still a laugh. He'd take it.

Because of a car accident on the Brooklyn Bridge, it took Brody ages to reach Ann's building. Thankfully, his taxi driver knew Brooklyn and, once they were over the bridge, had broken a few laws to get Brody to his destination quicker. He paid the man well, then hurried up to her building's front door.

By the time she buzzed him in, he was practically jumping out of his skin with desperation to see her. He didn't even bother with the elevator, just sprinted up the marble stairs to her third floor apartment. He paused long enough to steady his breathing before knocking.

She answered immediately, as if she'd been waiting. "Hi," she said with a small smile.

She was the most beautiful thing he'd ever seen in his entire life.

"Hi," he answered before sweeping her into his arms.

He hugged her close, not sure he could do anything else in that moment, even if he'd wanted to. To his relief, she hugged him back and some of the tension in his gut loosened.

When he could finally relax his grip a little, he leaned back to look her in the face. She wasn't as pale as the last time he'd seen her, but she did look tired.

He cupped her cheek with one hand, registering the healthy warmth of her skin. "How are you?"

"Better." She gripped his wrist and rubbed her cheek against his palm. "Come in."

She led him down a long hall decorated with framed pencil sketches, past two closed doors, and into a long but narrow living room with an open kitchen to the right. One wall was exposed brick, giving the place a very classic New York vibe. The hardwood floor was covered by a huge Persian rug. The furniture was leather and looked expensive. The entertainment center was bigger than anything he would expect her to have, so he assumed it belonged to the colleague she was subletting from. The kitchen was small but neat, with updated appliances. Everything smelled faintly of lemon and strongly of Ann. Being surrounded by her lovely scent made him a little dizzy.

"Nice place," he commented.

Until that moment, he hadn't really thought about the fact that he'd never been invited up in the two months they'd been dating. To his own irritation, he found himself wondering what her bedroom looked like and which door it was behind. He shook off the thought.

She glanced around the space and sighed. "I'll have to give it up in May when my colleague returns from his sabbatical." She motioned him toward the couch. "Would you like anything to drink?"

"Ann, what's been happening? I've been going out of my mind

worrying about you." He took her in his arms again because he couldn't seem to keep his hands off her. "Have you really been sick this whole time? Why weren't you in a hospital? Were you in a hospital?"

"It's complicated. Brody, please, let's sit."

He didn't want to sit. What he wanted more than anything else in the world was to pick her up, carry her to bed, and spend the next few hours making love to her. But he knew they had to talk.

When they settled onto the sofa, he pulled her close, keeping his arm around her. He felt wrong not having his hands on her, and since she wasn't pushing him away, he intended to hold her.

"I'm sorry about the night of the game," she said quietly, leaning into him. "More sorry that I couldn't really explain."

"Ann, are you in trouble? Did my fight trigger some sort of... issue?"

She puffed out a half-laugh that sounded more bitter than amused. "Issue? That's a good way to put it." She shifted a little to face him. "I can't explain everything, but I did have a reaction of sorts."

"Like an allergy?"

"No, not an allergy."

"Psychological? Did it trigger some PTSD?"

She frowned. "What? No. Nothing like that. It's just, I'm not good around that much emotion and violence. I thought I'd be OK. I wanted to be OK. Because if I could handle the game, I could..." She looked down at her lap as she trailed off, not meeting his gaze.

He lifted her chin. "Could what?"

"I could finally invite you here."

He glanced around the apartment with a little frown. "Am I missing something?"

When he faced her again, she was smiling, just a bit. "Apparently." Then she leaned into him and kissed him.

The gesture surprised him into stillness for a split second. She opened her lips and pressed closer, and he couldn't have resisted kissing her if the world was falling apart around them.

He wrapped his arms around her, savoring the much missed flavor of her mouth, the soft pressure of her lips against his, the playful dance of her tongue with his. She tasted so good, so perfect, and he'd missed this so much. He caressed his hands up her spine, and she shivered, pressing her body as tight to his as their position on the couch allowed.

Because he needed her weight on him, he lifted her to straddle his lap, then he ran his hands up into her hair, tunneling his fingers through the soft silk to hold her head as he deepened the kiss. She moaned, and the sound licked along his nerves, driving him a little closer to insanity.

She leaned into him until his head rested on the back of the couch, then wiggled forward, rubbing against his erection. It was his turn to moan. He could barely think anymore, but he knew they both had too much clothing on. And that he wanted a bed for this, not the couch.

He just couldn't drag his mouth away long enough to ask where the bed was. Dropping his hands to her hips, he squeezed and ground up against her, thrilled when she moved one of his hands to her breast. Oh, yes, he wanted that, too.

Still too much material in the way, though. "Off," he grunted, tugging at her buttons.

She didn't bother with the buttons, just pulled the long-sleeved shirt up over her head and dropped it behind her on the floor. Her bra was a pretty deep blue silk that perfectly cupped her extraordinary breasts. He leaned in and licked the valley between her breasts, cupping one and going for the fastener on the back with his other hand. She dropped her head back, holding his head to her chest. When the fastener gave way, he pushed the silk aside to get at her skin, taking her nipple into his mouth for a hard, desperate suck.

Her trembling only encouraged him to take more. He pinched her other nipple hard enough to make her gasp and writhe in his arms.

"You like that?" he murmured into her skin.

"Yes. Harder."

"Yes." He barely recognized his own voice, it was so deep and raspy. God, she felt good. He'd known they'd be good together from their first almost kiss, but this…this was perfect. He caressed and sucked, playing with her breasts until she was panting and grinding her hips against his cock. He needed to get their pants off soon or he'd come in his jeans. Not exactly the way he wanted their first time together to end.

"Bed?" he asked.

She wiggled off his lap, took his hand, and hauled him up off the sofa. "This way."

They stumbled back down the hall as he held her from behind, continuing to knead her breasts. It made getting to the bedroom awkward, but he couldn't keep his hands off her. She giggled as they tripped into her room, the sound as sexy as anything he'd ever heard.

He only looked around her room enough to locate the neatly made bed in the center. Then he spun her in his arms to face him and kissed her again, dropping one hand to grip her ass while he wrapped his other arm around her waist to hold her upright. She was a lot smaller than he was, but stronger and sturdier than she looked, taking everything he gave her. He loved it.

He backed her to the bed and dropped onto the mattress with her sprawled on top of him. "I love having your weight on me," he murmured against her mouth.

"I like being here. Finally." She slipped her hands up under his T-shirt and pushed. "You need to get rid of some clothes, though."

"Absolutely." He sat up long enough to strip off his shoes and all his clothes. Most of his concentration was on her, though, as she stood to slip out of her jeans.

For a beat, he forgot to breathe. She was stunning, all soft skin and curves, lush and sexy.

He was still trying to find his voice when she sauntered back to the bed and climbed onto his lap.

"I've wanted you like this for a long time, Brody. In my bed, naked and hard."

"I think my head just exploded."

She grinned. "So long as nothing else has exploded. Yet."

"Fuck."

She laughed, and the sound might as well have been a lap of her tongue up his cock. The thought of her mouth on him was a little too much to take. Especially when he had her heat and wetness pressed so close to his cock. He wasn't even inside her yet, and he was a stroke away from orgasm.

"You're killing me," he groaned and flipped her onto her back. "I need a distraction."

"A distraction?"

"Yes." He looked over her body, beautifully sprawled before him. "Ladies first. Just in case."

"What?"

She looked so adorably confused, he couldn't resist her. He settled between her legs, bringing his mouth to her core. He met her gaze for an instant, then licked into her. She half sat up, her hand in his hair like she might push him away, but as he found her clit and swirled his tongue around the sensitive bud, she dropped back to the mattress with a gasp.

"You like that?"

"Oh, yes. No one's ever…"

She trailed off on a moan, but he got the point. And it thrilled him to his bones to know no other man had done this for her. If he had any say in the matter, no other man ever would either. He licked and sucked, savoring her taste and flavor, better than any meal he'd ever eaten. He held her hips, keeping her close as he took her to the very edge. She trembled and writhed until he was sure she was close, so very close.

Then he felt her pulling back, resisting, trying to push him away.

He looked up. "Are you OK?"

"Yes. But I'm… This is too much. I'm going to come."

"Good." He grinned. "That's the point."

"But…"

He licked her again, giving no mercy, and she stopped resisting. He pushed her, taking her to the edge, letting her hang for a heartbeat, then he pushed her over, holding her as she cried out and bucked against him. He watched the orgasm take her even as he continued to suck and lick, knowing he'd never seen anything so exquisite in his life.

"Beautiful," he murmured against her damp curls.

She went limp, her eyes closed as she panted. He kissed his way back up her body, then nuzzled her neck as she wrapped her arms around him. Her skin was warm and flushed, and she smelled like vanilla and cinnamon and sex—a perfect combination as far as he was concerned.

"That was what you meant by 'ladies first'?" she asked, her eyes still closed.

"Of course. What else?"

"No one's ever said that to me before."

"You've known a lot of stupid men in your time, then?"

She grinned and opened her eyes to look at him. "Apparently."

He kissed her, holding her close, his own demanding need a nagging beat he held in check because he wanted to hold her more than fuck her in that moment.

That resolve lasted until she pulled a condom out of her side table. Then the need to fuck her overwhelmed his softer urges. He slid into her wet heat, grateful she'd had one orgasm already because he wasn't sure how long he'd last now. She felt so good, too good, and he couldn't think anymore.

He did try to make it last, setting a slow, steady, hard rhythm. But she was so tight, so wet, so hot, he just couldn't hold back. She wrapped her legs around his hips, her fingernails bit into his shoulders, and any attempt at control failed him. He pounded hard until his orgasm ripped from him in a long, breath-stealing moment of bliss, made even better when she cried out his name and her inner muscles pulsed around his cock.

When he could manage it, he sat up enough to cup her face in his hands and study her. Her hair was mussed, her lips swollen and red, her face flushed, her eyes sleepy and sexy. She looked thoroughly loved.

A vision he could spend the rest of his life savoring.

Chapter Fifteen

When Brody went to the bathroom to clean up, Ann took a moment to study her hands. There'd been a moment, when he'd been licking her, when she'd been sure her control would slip and everything she'd been working toward would be ruined.

But she hadn't been able to stop her own out of control desires and instead of fighting, she gave in, letting Brody take her into an orgasm unlike anything she'd ever felt before. Only as she was coming down from the brilliant shattering of her orgasm did she realize she hadn't lost control of the fire.

Her skin was warm and tingly, but not in that dangerous way. Her body pulsed in pleasant waves of satisfaction. And her hands were cool.

She'd done it!

In more ways than one, she thought with a little giggle.

Brody walked back in and caught her laughing. "What's funny?"

Nothing about him, that was for sure. He was magnificent naked, all hard, cut muscle and strength. She'd never been particularly enamored of men completely nude. Frankly, penises always looked a little weird and funny to her. But everything about Brody was beautiful to look at, and she enjoyed the sight thoroughly as he rejoined her on the bed.

"You're still smiling." He sounded very smug.

She couldn't really blame him. He'd earned that arrogant assurance. She cupped his cheek in one hand, because she could without hurting him, and kissed him.

"I'm very happy right now," she said against his mouth.

"Thank God, because so am I, and I want to keep this up for the foreseeable future."

She laughed. "We will have to leave bed eventually. Your suspension ended today, didn't it?"

"It did. Damn it. I would have preferred this for the last two weeks to all the running I've been doing."

She focused on his shoulder, afraid to meet his gaze when she said, "I'm sorry about that. It was necessary, though."

"I don't care now. I'm just glad to be here with you. The rest of that stuff doesn't matter."

She sighed, relieved he wouldn't push for more information. Nathalie had asked if she intended to tell Brody about the pyrokenesis. Ann still didn't have an answer to that question. She wanted to be open and honest with him, completely. But if he found out…

The thought of him looking at her the way her family would if they'd ever found out, of him calling her Devil's spawn and walking out of her life, after all she'd done to get to this point, was a future she just couldn't face.

Maybe they could be happy with just this one little secret between them? It wasn't absolutely necessary she tell him.

Even as they snuggled and talked about unimportant things, a knot formed in the pit of her stomach. She was certain now she was falling in love with Brody. Keeping a secret from the man she loved went against her every instinct, but admitting her curse to him seemed impossible.

When he kissed her, and the kiss turned into another delicious exploration, she decided to just savor being with him, able to make love to him without danger or worry. They had time. She had time now. She'd think about this later.

*****

His next training session went great. He was welcomed back by his teammates like a conquering hero, which was a little weird, but fun. And when he hit the ice for his first game, the crowd erupted in cheers. He took it all in good humor, just glad he'd been able to do something good for his team.

And like icing on the cake, the Empires won the game.

Between being back to playing the game he loved and spending every moment outside of hockey with Ann, Brody was pretty sure he'd discovered heaven.

The only irritating little blight to his happiness was the unexplained time Ann had disappeared.

He'd told her it didn't matter. He didn't want it to. But his brain kept circling back to those two weeks when he hadn't been able to see her, the week after they'd first met when he wasn't allowed to call. And he couldn't get past the fact that whatever was behind those things was important. Important enough to ruin his relationship with her.

He tried to ignore the suspicion and worry when he was with her, and he mostly succeeded. When he was training or in the middle of a game he could forget his concerns, too. But in those rare between times, commuting home, the taxi to her apartment, a solitary run, the nights he'd spent in a hotel room during the Empires' last away games, the suspicions raised their ugly heads and poked at him relentlessly.

In the days leading up to the Winter Classic, he knew he should be more focused on the game than anything else. And he tried. He really did.

Unfortunately, he was too curious and relentless. And he failed miserably at ignoring the nagging mystery.

He managed to get through and even enjoy Christmas, wiggling out of introducing his twin to Ann only because Connor went back to California and Brody used the approaching Classic as an excuse to stay in New York. Despite his brother's curiosity, he really really didn't want to introduce him to Ann until he was more sure of their relationship. Ann found all this very funny, which made his jealousy an acceptable sacrifice.

But two days before New Year's Eve, his curiosity and concern finally got the best of him.

"Tell me something I don't know about you," he said to her as they sat on her couch pretending to watch a zombie movie.

"Like?"

"I don't know. I don't know it."

She rolled her eyes. "Well, there's one thing…"

He tried hard not to show his anxiety and only display mild curiosity.

"My first name isn't really Ann."

"What?" He turned a little to face her.

"That's my middle name."

"OK. What's your first name and why don't you use it?"

Her cheeks turned a pretty shade of pink. "Chastity."

"Chastity?" He blinked, leaned back from her a little to look at her closer. "Your full name is Chasity Ann Bell?"

She made a face and nodded.

Well, it wasn't the secret he was digging for—while trying not to appear to be digging—but it was an adorable secret nonetheless. "Chastity."

She narrowed her eyes at him. "If you ever call me that, I will hurt you. I hate my first name."

"What's wrong with Chastity?" He pressed his lips together so he wouldn't laugh.

"Chastity Bell?"

"Very melodious."

"It's awful. Do you know how often I got called Chastity Belt in school? Besides, what scientist is called Chastity Bell?"

"Well, I think it's cute."

She scowled. "I'm serious about hurting you if you call me that."

"Fair enough." He brushed a strand of hair behind her ear. "I got my name from a movie."

"Really?"

"Connor and I both were named after movie characters. My mom's favorite movie was *Highlander* and my dad's was *Jaws*."

"Brody from *Jaws*, right? The character Martin Brody. Why didn't he name you Martin?"

"My dad liked Brody better." He shrugged. "Could have been worse. They could have named me Hooper or Quint."

"Quint Evans? Not as bad as Chastity Bell, but OK, I see your point." She snuggled back under his arm again and faced the TV. "I've never seen *Highlander*. What's that about?"

"Oh you have missed out." He went on to tell her about the beloved family movie.

In the back of his head, he continued to brood. His ploy had failed miserably. But what had he expected? If she hadn't explained already, she wasn't going to just drop the news at such a casual question.

He'd let the unspoken go too long and now he didn't know how to bring it up without upsetting her. He tried to convince himself he didn't need to know, that he didn't want to know. But he was a terrible liar—especially with himself.

The movie credits rolled, and he took the excuse to kiss her, loving the way her entire body softened against him. He buried his fingers in her hair, enjoying the silky texture, trying to lose himself in her feel and taste and ignore his own irritating curiosity.

She pulled back a little, breaking the kiss, and narrowed her eyes at him. "What's wrong?"

Damn. "What?"

"You seem distracted. Is it the Classic?"

He really wanted to lie and say yes and get back to the kissing. He didn't want to be distracted when he was with her.

He opened his mouth to say yes, but instead said, "Those two weeks when you were sick…" He winced even as the words tumbled out. "Sorry. I'm having trouble letting it go without knowing what was wrong."

"You think I'm going to make you sick?" she said through a forced smile, without looking him in the eyes.

"No. I know I said it didn't matter. I shouldn't have asked."

"But it's obviously bothering you."

"It is. I'm worried."

"About?"

"That what kept you away will come back to haunt us." Well, he was all in now. He might as well lay it all out. "I'm worried whatever went on during those two weeks is tied to that week after our first date, when I couldn't call you. I'm worried there's something serious you aren't telling me."

"It's nothing." She rose and went into the kitchen, making a show of putting dishes from their takeout dinner into the sink and tidying.

He really wanted to let it go because she was upset and he hated upsetting her. But he couldn't. He just couldn't let it go.

"Ann, I really like you. A lot."

She smiled at him over the counter. "I like you too, Brody. A lot."

"I want this thing between us to…go somewhere. To be important."

"But?"

He swallowed. "But I'm afraid whatever you're keeping from me will prevent that."

"What do you think I'm hiding, exactly?"

Her tone had bite but also a slight tremble, like she was covering anxiety with anger.

"I don't know. I can imagine all kinds of things…"

"Not this," she murmured, so low she probably didn't mean for him to hear.

"What the hell is 'this,' Ann? Please. I'm worried about you."

"Me? You don't have to worry about me."

"Of course I do." It was on the tip of his tongue to just say the words, to tell her he'd fallen in love with her. But with this hanging between them, he couldn't get the words out. "Are you in trouble? An ex? The IRS?"

"No. How many times do I have to tell you there is no ex, no husband, no boyfriend, or anything?"

"Your parents?"

"No. We rarely even speak these days."

"Family? A health issue?"

She winced, a barely perceptible tic, when he mentioned health issues.

"Is that it? Something is wrong with you?"

This time she flinched, almost like he'd slapped her, and looked away.

"Ann? What's wrong?"

"Stop pushing, Brody. It's none of your business."

"Like hell it's not. Are you dying?"

"No."

"Contagious? Is it cancer? Something worse?"

"No. No. No. Please. Stop. I'm not... I can't talk about it."

He ran his hands over his face and up through his hair. He shouldn't have started this conversation. "Are you going to disappear on me again?"

She stared at him, but didn't respond.

"I see." He stood. "I'd better get going. We have training tomorrow."

She closed her eyes, ducking her head, but not fast enough for him to miss her hurt. He wanted to take it all back. He wanted her to tell him this wasn't true.

But knowing she might disappear at any moment, that she wasn't even going to deny the possibility, was worse than any punch he'd ever taken.

He snatched his coat from the back of a chair at the kitchen counter, waiting for her to look up, to look at him, to tell him to stay. She didn't, and his heart broke a little more.

"Goodnight," he murmured.

He was at the door when she called his name. He paused with his back to her.

"I'm sorry," she said.

Nothing else. Just sorry. He wasn't even sure what she was apologizing for. He nodded and left without looking back. If he looked at her, he wasn't sure he'd ever recover.

Tears leaked down her cheeks as she curled into a ball on her lonely bed, missing Brody more than should have been possible. She should just tell him. Just get it over with. At least he'd know why he was leaving her.

She squeezed her eyes closed. Tonight had been bad enough. She'd never get over seeing him look at her like she was a freak.

Everything she'd gone through, all the work so she could really be with him, and she'd still driven him away.

Now what was she going to do?

CHAPTER SIXTEEN

"What's wrong with you?" Semonov asked as they came off the ice.

"Nothing." Brody focused on pulling off his mitts.

"You have a fight with Ann?"

"None of your business."

"You want Nathalie to talk to her?"

"Stay the fuck out of my business," Brody said evenly, without looking at his goalie.

"Whatever the fuck is wrong, get over it then. You're no use to us tomorrow like this."

"Fuck you." Again said evenly as he walked away. He didn't need his teammate pointing out he'd been a disaster during practice, so distracted his energy was low and his reactions pathetic.

He already knew it.

Stomping through the locker room, he disposed of gear, showered, and dressed, ignoring the other guys. He wasn't in the mood for light conversation or trash talk. When Reiner Jahr accidentally bumped into him, despite the friendly apology, Brody got in his face. He wanted to beat on someone badly and the big Norwegian was the only guy on the team Brody figured could stand up in a fight with him. They faced off for several long, tense seconds as the locker room fell quiet around them.

Then Brody blinked and backed off. What the fuck was wrong with him?

"Sorry," he said to Jahr. He ignored the looks he got as he left.

He'd taken the train to practice instead of his car, because he didn't trust himself behind the wheel at the moment. The ride back into Manhattan from Tarrytown didn't help with his anger, but it gave him time to feel even more like an asshole after the way he'd acted with Jahr. He never fought off the ice, except when he took time to train at a boxing gym so he'd be a better fighter on the ice. He didn't get into bust ups with his teammates. Ever. He usually broke up the fights.

Ann had knocked him so far off balance, he barely recognized himself. And he had only himself to blame. He'd pushed her for answers she wasn't ready to give. Worse, he'd gotten answers he wasn't prepared to hear.

He needed to call her, find a way to fix things. Problem was, he couldn't punch his way out of this. He had no idea what would fix things between them.

He switched to the subway at Grand Central. A few brave souls tried to talk to him, cheering the team on tomorrow, still congratulating him on that last fight before his suspension. He couldn't enjoy the conversations like he usually did, though he made an effort to be friendly. Something must have shown in his expression, because none of the fans took up much of his time, mostly leaving him to his brooding.

He got off the subway two stops early so he could walk a little.

The city was already crowded with people preparing to celebrate New Year's Eve, even this far away from Times Square. He kept his head down and ignored the bump and push of people, letting the sharp, cold air cool his anger as much as was possible. The wind coming in off the river wrapped around him like an icy hug. The familiar scents of his neighborhood, the pizza restaurant, the hot air and chemical soap from the local dry cleaners, the falafel food cart on the corner soothed him a little more. He almost hated to go inside.

At the door to his building, he glanced back up the street, considering extending his walk for a while longer. There was a party at Chris Emmerson's house tonight, just friends and family since the players had to keep an early night. He'd decided not to go, but maybe he should. Nathalie would be there. Even though he'd told Semenov to stay out of his business, Brody really could use Nathalie's help.

He glanced at his phone to check the time. He could walk another hour and still be back in time to get ready.

He'd just started to turn away from the lobby when a soft voice broke over him, freezing him in place.

Very slowly he faced Ann. She was just outside the building, like she'd been waiting in the lobby and had walked out when he turned away.

"Can we talk?" she asked. "Please."

She had her hands jammed into her coat pockets and her head tilted down, looking at him but not quiet meeting his gaze. Her hair was tucked under a wooly hat with the Empires' logo on it, a few blond strands escaping to wisp around her cheeks in the wind. Her skin was flushed from the cold, but beneath that red, she looked pale.

"Come on up," he said, turning back to the lobby, and holding the door for her.

He waved absently at the doorman as they walked to the elevator.

It took an act of will not to pull Ann into his arms once they were inside. Instead, they stood awkwardly on the ride to his twelfth floor apartment.

He let her in ahead of him, then took his time taking off his coat, gloves, and scarf at the door, needing a few moments to steady himself. Taking her coat to hang might have been a mistake because the material carried her scent and that scent filled his head, making him want to ignore the needed conversation and just take her to bed.

That made him feel pathetic, so when he offered her a seat on the couch he was sharper than he meant to be. She flinched, and he cursed silently.

He sat in the big recliner chair next to the couch and waited in silence. He didn't trust himself to start the conversation, even though he knew he should at least apologize for pushing things the other night.

She stared around the living room for a bit, looking at everything but him. She'd been here a few times, but they mostly went to her apartment. It was closer to the Brooklyn Banking Center, the Empires' home rink, and he liked how cozy her place was. As he waited for her to start, he wondered what she saw, what she was thinking. And it was on the tip of his tongue to ask, because the silence was stretching his nerves to breaking.

Finally, she faced him fully. "I'm sorry about our fight. You deserve an explanation."

"I shouldn't have pushed." He tried not to sound grudging, but he was too wound up to make it a proper apology.

"No, you're right. I've disappeared on you twice. I never have explained. If...if we're going to have more than sex, I should have been honest. But I don't know how to be."

He frowned. "What's that mean?"

"This is something I never talk about."

"Does Nathalie know?"

"She's my sister."

"That's not an answer."

"Yes, she knows. She's been helping me."

"With what?"

She swallowed visibly and looked away again. "I don't know if I can tell you, Brody. My parents…" She trailed off and shook her head. "Never mind."

"When I asked if you'd disappear again, you couldn't say no. Why and where would you go?"

"I don't know."

"Why are you here if you aren't going to be honest with me, Ann?"

She raised her hands, a gesture of surrender, and pressed her lips together. He saw the dampness in her eyes and had to grip the armrests to keep from going to her.

"Do you want more with me than sex?" he asked. A question he should probably have asked the other night.

"Yes."

"We can't have that without honesty."

"Have you been honest with me?"

"About everything." Except one little thing. He hadn't told her he was in love with her yet. But that wasn't a lie, just an omission.

She flinched. "Brody…" She closed her eyes, and a tear leaked out.

That little drop of moisture almost broke him. He leaned forward, not sure what he intended to do, but knowing he couldn't just sit here while she cried.

When she opened her eyes, when she looked at him with her jaw set and her gaze fierce, he froze in mid-motion, then slowly sat back.

"Fine." She nodded. "Fine. I'm going to be honest. Please, please don't…"

"Don't what?"

"Just…" She shook her head hard and said, "Watch my hand." She held it up, palm facing the ceiling.

He scowled. What the hell was she doing?

Ann concentrated harder than she'd ever done before, focusing all her attention on controlling the fire. She'd managed to start the fire on her hands once or twice without her entire arm erupting into flames, but only in the safety of Mr. Mendez's basement. Part of her was terrified if she tried this, she'd burn down his apartment. But she had to at least try. He deserved that much.

Nothing happened for a long moment, and then the tingling in her palms got more intense, and the heat built. She narrowed her eyes, a physical attempt to get the fire to do the same, stay in a narrow little ball on her palm. When the blue flames burst to life, she gasped, surprising even herself with the show.

She kept her attention on the fire ball, afraid to look away and break her concentration. Now came the tricky part, putting it out and calming the heat. *You can do this*, she chanted to herself. *You've done it before. Just close your hand and breathe away the heat.*

For a heart-stopping moment, the flames engulfed her fist, getting bigger rather than going out. She breathed a little deeper and envisioned pulling the flames back into her skin where they belonged. When they vanished, she opened her hand and wiggled her fingers, smiling just a bit. She'd done it. Her heart was thumping hard from the short burst of adrenaline, but she'd still done it. And not destroyed anything.

That thought reminded her that Brody was watching, and she might still have destroyed something. She hesitated and then forced herself to face him.

He was pale, his eyes huge, his jaw slack. He blinked at her, looked back at her hand as horror spread through his expression. Then he crossed himself.

Her shoulders slumped. She couldn't wait around to hear the epithets, the curses and accusations. She stood and fled, pausing at the door long enough to grab her coat before she slammed out of the apartment.

He didn't follow. He didn't even call her name.

Brody found Nathalie standing at one side of the party with Semenov, quietly talking and drinking a glass of Scotch. She blinked a few times when he stormed up to her.

Brody ignored the way Semenov moved to stand between him and Nathalie. "Has she called you?" he asked.

"Ann? No, why?"

"Here." He handed her a ticket to the Classic. "Make sure she comes to the game tomorrow."

"Why?"

"I need to talk to her."

"You want to explain what's happened?"

"In private."

Semenov growled. "You're not going anywhere with her without me."

"Does he know?" Brody asked Nathalie without looking at his goalie.

Her eyes narrowed again, and she pursed her lips. "Let's find a more private spot."

He trailed her and Semenov to a quiet nook off the main living room area.

"Tell me what you know," Nathalie said when they were safely out of earshot of anyone else at the party.

"Pyrokenesis? That's what she's been hiding."

Her brows rose. "You know the real word for it? That's a good start. Tell me what happened."

He told her everything, because he needed her help. Because Ann turned to her for help.

"Why do you want her at the game?"

"I need to talk to her."

"If you call her out as Devil's spawn I will kick your ass, Brody Evans."

"What the hell are you talking about?"

"Her mother. Her parents. Didn't she tell you about them?"

"A little. Only that they were religious nuts. What do they have to do with anything?"

"That's the reaction she was expecting from you."

"Why would I react that way? I'm not a religious nut." Then he remembered. He'd crossed himself. A knee-jerk reaction he'd barely thought about, something from his youth. He only ever went to mass on Christmas these day, and didn't really consider himself religious anymore. But he'd been raised Catholic, and some things had just been ingrained.

"Fuck." He ran a hand through his hair. "She got the wrong idea from my reaction." But she should have known better. She should have known *him* better. She should have trusted him. He pushed aside the hurt. That wasn't important now. "I really need to talk to her, Nathalie. Tomorrow. I can't wait until after the game."

"You sure you can play like this?" Semenov asked.

"Not all three periods."

"Why not see her tonight? Or before the game?" Nathalie asked.

"She won't answer my calls and she's not at her apartment tonight. She'll answer your call. And I won't have time before the game

120

because of all the media stuff. We need a minute of privacy. We can squeeze that in during the first period break. If you two will help."

She exchanged a look with Semenov, unspoken understanding moving between them.

Finally, she said, "I'll try. For her sake. And for the game."

He smiled a little at her last jab. "Can I ask you something?"

She nodded.

"Why did Ann come to you? Why did she think you could help her with the pyrokenesis?"

Semenov drew himself up, as if ready to put an end to the conversation.

Nathalie waved him away. "My mother called me Devil's spawn before leaving me and my father. She told Ann that my father and I were minions of the Devil. Who better to go to when you have a fire 'curse'?"

"You don't believe in that devil," he commented.

He hadn't wanted to intrude on her privacy, so he'd never come out and asked her about her religion. But his curiosity hoped she'd discuss it with him one day because he was fascinated by it and the differences between being a green witch and a Wiccan.

"No," she said, "but Ann didn't know that before we met."

"You *were* able to help her, though. You understood what was happening?"

"She's got a lot better control now. She'll need more training, but she's going to be fine."

He didn't miss how she'd sidestepped actually answering his question. "You'd make a good politician," he said.

She snorted a laugh.

"You'll make sure Ann is there tomorrow?" He didn't even try to hide his desperation.

"Are you breaking up with her or fixing things?"

"I'm hoping to fix things. I love her."

"Even with this talent of hers?"

"Of course."

"Then I'll make sure she's there."

Ignoring Semenov, he snatched Nathalie up in a big hug. "Thank you." He set her on her feet and grinned at Semenov's scowl. "Don't stay up too late," he told his goalie, just to irritate him more, then he left the party.

He had some planning to do.

CHAPTER SEVENTEEN

New York City hosted the Winter Classic at the Queens Bank Stadium. The place was a huge, open-air baseball stadium with lots of room to walk on the field level and a friendly, eager vibe as the hockey fans flowed in through the gates.

Ann hadn't been here before, since she'd never gone to any sporting events before meeting Brody. She wasn't entirely sure why she was here now, except that Nathalie had insisted. She owed her sister too much to refuse. Still, being around the crowds of enthusiastic fans reminded her too sharply of the last hockey game she'd attended and the chair armrest she'd melted.

Nathalie took her arm as they went up the escalator to the field level from the main rotunda. "Stop fretting. I'm here with you this time. You'll be fine."

Ann forced a smile. As they pushed through the crowds to their seats—a section near the ice reserved for the teams' family and special guests—she gripped Nathalie's arm tighter.

"Why does he want to see me?" Ann asked. Again.

"To talk. I'm not saying any more than that because it's between you guys to settle this."

"You should have seen his face. I can't take him looking at me like my parents would."

"He won't. I already told him I'll kick his ass if he tries."

"He's almost a foot taller than you and regularly gets into fist fights on the ice," Ann pointed out.

"Ha. I'd still kick his ass. He knows it, too."

Ann grinned.

They settled in their seats just as the two teams hit the ice to warm up. She couldn't help looking out for Brody, both dreading and hoping for the moment he'd look up into the stands and see her. But he didn't look their direction. He was all focus and attention, stretching, practicing shots, and running through drills.

She tried to convince herself the fact that he wanted to talk to her was a good thing, that he hadn't brought her all this way just to tell her they couldn't see each other anymore. Why bother? Hope and fear thrummed through her blood, making her pulse pound a little too hard. She focused on calming her nerves, keeping her control. Having Nathalie next to her helped.

When the first period began, despite herself, her stomach tightened with dread and expectation. She could barely watch the game, her every nerve anticipating her meeting with Brody.

As the clock ticked down and the buzzer sounded, Nathalie stood. "Come on. You two won't have much time."

She let Nathalie lead the way, as they took the stairs down to the ground level, flashed their passes at a guard, and were let in through a locked door to the sub-level where the locker rooms and media rooms were located. Ann stared at the milling crowds in horror. How would she and Brody talk with reporters everywhere?

"Why here and now?" she hissed at Nathalie.

"Because he insisted. Come on, Alex said there's a place around the corner here…"

They made their way to what looked like an equipment storage room, stacked neatly with baseball bats, bases and other things Ann couldn't identify but which she presumed had something to do with the stadium's usual purpose as a baseball field.

Nathalie waved her in, said, "Good luck." Then walked out, closing the door behind her.

Ann blinked, alone in the room full of sports equipment, not sure what to do now. She wasn't even sure how to get back to her seat if Nathalie didn't return.

A little bubble of panic swelled in her stomach. She practiced her breathing, working at calming her nerves, and tried hard not to think about her reasons for being here.

The door opened a minute later, and Brody, in full gear, stepped inside, closing the metal door behind him with a quiet clang.

"I can't stay long," he said, not coming any farther into the room. "The break goes faster than you'd expect."

"That's fine."

"I needed to see you."

"Isn't that uncomfortable?" She gestured to his skates. They had blade covers on them but still weren't designed for walking on concrete.

"It's fine. Takes too long to lace up again if I take them off."

They fell silent for a moment, Ann not sure what to say.

"So," Brody said into the tension. "You're a firestarter. That's why all the running away?"

She bit the inside of her cheek but nodded.

"Were you ever going to tell me? If I hadn't pushed, would you have admitted the truth to me eventually?"

"Maybe. I'm not sure. I wanted to, but…"

"Your family."

"Nathalie explained?"

"A little."

She shrugged. "It's a curse I've lived with my whole life," she said, finding a kind of relief in admitting this to him out loud. "I shut down my emotions so I wouldn't lose control of it. But that wasn't working anymore. Nathalie has helped me gain real control, though. I…probably won't burn things down now."

"Probably?"

"I'm still learning."

"Is that why that game, my fight upset you so much?"

"A lot of emotion can still be difficult for me."

"That's why you put off sex for so long?"

Her cheeks heated. "I was afraid I'd hurt you," she murmured.

"Have you ever hurt anyone with the fire?"

"No. Well, almost a few times. But no. I've damaged things, though."

"That first date, when you ran from the restaurant…?"

"I was losing control. I made my water boil."

"Why were you losing control?"

"Because you made me feel. You made me forget not to."

He took one step closer, then stilled, balanced expertly on his blades. "Now?"

"Now what?"

"You can deal with emotions now?"

"Mostly. My hands are a little warm right now."

"I'm not sure whether to consider that a good thing or not."

"As long as I don't set a baseball bat on fire, you could consider it good. I'm in control right now, Brody, but I'm also…emotional."

"How emotional?"

"I'm not sure how to answer that."

He stared at her, his gorgeous face still and impossible for her to read. He'd kept his tone neutral, though his voice was deeper than usual. She had no idea what he was thinking or how he felt, and it left her edgy. She didn't fidget, she didn't dare touch anything at the moment, but she did have to concentrate on breathing normally and keeping her pulse as even as possible.

"You don't trust me," he said quietly.

"What?"

"You weren't going to tell me about the pyrokenesis because you don't trust me to be different from your parents."

"No, that's not it." But it was, and they both knew it.

"You thought I'd react the way they would. You didn't trust me to handle it. Thought I'd just throw away what we have because of this."

She glanced away. "You did cross yourself."

"A knee-jerk Catholic reaction that had nothing to do with how I felt about your talent."

"Curse."

"Talent," he hissed, emotion finally working its way into his voice. Emotion that sounded and felt a lot like anger. "After everything, I can't believe you'd think that of me. I can't believe you wouldn't trust me."

"That's what you're upset about? I can turn my hand into a ball of flames, and you're worried about whether I trust you or not?"

"Of course. I love you, and you think I'm some sort of ignorant fanatic. How the hell else am I supposed to feel?"

Hearing him say he loved her took her breath for a moment, and she had to blink a few times before she could ask, "The fire doesn't…doesn't scare you?"

"Damn it, Ann. I thought you knew me better than that. I told you I read everything."

"About pyronkenesis?"

"And psychics and ghosts and ESP and *everything*."

"But you don't believe in all that stuff, do you?"

"I maintain an open mind to all possibilities. And I resent that you'd clump me in with close-minded numskulls like your parents."

She swallowed hard and let out a slow breath. She hadn't even considered that. She did trust Brody. But she'd been too afraid to look past her own knee-jerk reactions.

"I'm sorry, Brody," she said. "I'm sorry I didn't tell you *before* you forced it out of me. I'm sorry I didn't trust you to understand. But understanding of something like this isn't really part of my experience—outside of Nathalie and her family."

He raised his brows a little and nodded, but he wouldn't meet her gaze.

"Can you forgive me? Can you give me a chance?" She took a step closer. "Can you trust me?"

"I don't know."

"I love you, too. If that helps."

He scowled. "That's playing dirty."

She smiled. "Please, Brody. I'd like the chance to earn your trust." She closed the space between them. Because of his protective gear, she couldn't get as close as she wanted, and his skates made him even taller. She laid her hands on his chest and eased as near as she could. "Please, Brody."

His scowl was fierce. "Damn it. I haven't been able to resist you since the moment we bumped into each other at the physical therapy center."

The tension in her stomach finally started to ease as he wrapped his arms around her. The position felt clunky and a little uncomfortable against all the hard protective gear, but she didn't care. Just having his arms around her was glorious. The only place she wanted to be.

"I had Nathalie bring you here," he said, "because I wanted to make things right between us. I don't want to lose you. And I don't want you to be afraid of telling me anything."

She sighed. "I'd like that, too."

"I want you to trust me."

She nodded.

"You really can, you know."

"I'm figuring that out."

"About damned time." He shook his head. "You drive me insane. And I love you."

She chuckled. "I love you."

He tugged her upward a little and she took the hint, climbing up onto the top of his skates so she'd be closer to him. She wrapped her arms around his neck, her stomach dancing with pleasure now. Then he kissed her soundly. She sighed into him, relieved and grateful to be here.

"Will you show me how it works?" he asked, lifting his head and brushing a strand of hair that had escaped her hat back behind her ear. "How you do that thing with the fire on your hands?"

"If you really want to see. I'm still learning how to start the fire on purpose and put it out again. But when we're someplace without a lot volatile substances around, I'll show you more."

He grinned, that familiar easygoing grin she loved so much, the expression that showed off his dimple and made her heart thump hard.

"Can't wait," he said.

He leaned down for another kiss just as someone pounded on the metal door. "Damn. That's my signal. Gotta get back." He still kissed her, quick and hard, before releasing her. "Can I meet you at your place tonight? We have some making up to do."

Her nerves danced, giddy with anticipation and desire. The look in his eyes promised she'd enjoy making up with him.

"See you when you can get there," she said, waving him off as he hurried back to do his job.

Just as she started to leave, though, he popped back into the room. "By the way," he said, "I love you."

He didn't give her a chance to say it back before hurrying away, but the parting declaration left her grinning like a fool all the way back to her seat.

The Empires won the Classic. And all of New York City celebrated with them. Ann enjoyed the festivities, knowing it would be ages before Brody could get away and meet her back at her place. The train ride from Queens to Brooklyn took a while, because she had to go all the way through Manhattan to get home, but the subway was packed with people celebrating the Classic win so she didn't mind the ride.

Brody knocked on her door later that night, back in street clothes, looking more handsome than ever, his eyes glowing with heat and fun.

"Congratulations on the win," she said, letting him in.

She'd barely closed the door before he pulled her into his arms, kissing her hard and with such passion it took her breath away.

She pulled back just enough to say, "By the way. I love you."

He grinned then kissed her again, walking her backward to her bedroom without breaking contact.

They tumbled onto her bed, and Ann felt so right having him here. The hours of fear and heartache fell away, leaving such a profound relief, it left her dizzy.

She rolled him onto his back and strip him out of his clothes slowly, savoring each inch of him, kissing and licking and enjoying every taste. He groaned when she took his cock into her mouth and she smiled, loving the sounds he made, the way he felt. She loved him. More than she'd ever hoped to love anyone. More than she thought she was capable of loving someone. And that filled her with joy.

He was trembling when he pulled her back up his body for a kiss. With his hands in her hair, she held her close, all his own emotions right there in the press of his lips and the dance of his tongue. When he stripped her, when he explored her body with his mouth, she felt an acceptance she'd never experienced before. There was freedom in his touch, and so much emotion.

"Mine," he said when he slid into her, rocking his hips gently against hers. "You're mine."

"You're mine, too." She cupped his face with her hands, holding his gaze as long as she could even as her body wound tighter. Then she finally had to closer her eyes, as her orgasm took her, but she carried the deep, harsh sound of his own orgasm over the edge with her.

For long moments, they lay tangled together, breathing deeply, no words necessary. She savored the sensation. Finally, with no more secrets between them, she could love him without hesitance or reservations.

"I love you," she murmured into his hair, because she just had to say it again.

"This is the best first day of the year ever," he said.

She laughed.

"And that is my favorite sound in the entire world."

"You're the only person who's ever made me feel this way, Brody."

"Good. I intend for things to stay that way."

"Does this mean I'll finally be allowed to meet your brother without you worrying?"

"No. I'll still worry. But before you meet him, I'll make sure he knows I'll beat him to pulp if he hits on you, so we should be good."

She laughed hard and kissed him. "Thank you."

"For what?"

"For accepting me. For giving me..." She waved her hand in a small circle. "Giving me all this."

"You accept me for who I am. How could I do any less?" He sat up a little and narrowed his eyes. "You said you have to move out of here in May?"

She nodded, glancing around with a little sigh. She'd really grown to love this apartment.

"Move in with me."

The comment brought her gaze back to him. "What?"

"Move in with me. My place is big enough. Or we'll get another apartment. Or a house. I'll make my brother buy us one."

She laughed at that. "We will not make your brother buy us a house. We can take care of that on our own. Eventually."

He frowned. "Is that a no to moving in with me?"

"We've only be dating for a few months. We've only just made up again."

"I don't care."

She sat up and looked at him, at every inch of his beloved face. "Are you serious about this?"

"I'm always serious."

"You are rarely serious. Except maybe about hockey."

"And you. I'm very very serious about you."

"Brody."

"Don't say no. We have until May for you to consider it. Don't say no."

"I don't need until May to consider moving in with you." She

132

leaned down and kissed him. "If, in a few months, you still think you can live with someone who can boil water with a touch, I'll move in with you."

He grinned, then he pounced, rolling her onto her back and kissing her, his enthusiasm making her giggle even as she kissed him back. The sheer joy of that moment left Ann breathless and lighter than air, brimming with more emotions than she could name.

For the first time in her life, she saw a bright future ahead for her, full of love and companionship, the only flames those in a cozy fireplace on a winter's night while she snuggled in the arms of the man she loved.

CROSSING THE LINE

(Emersons #2)

Stacey Agdern

CHAPTER ONE

Kayleigh

Usually, the first thing Kayleigh Emerson noticed when she walked into The Poutinerie was the smell. The sudden blast of the distinct gravy, cheese, and potato mixture usually welcomed her better than any sign on the door.

This time, vision took priority over smell. A guy—young but not too young, judging by the stubble on his jaw and the six pack she could see under his shirt—grabbed her focus. He was the perfect sort of eye candy.

She shook her head at her own idiocy, but also to force herself to stop staring. Still, she smiled his way as she walked further into the shop and sat down at a corner table. Even from her changed vantage point, she still couldn't help herself. Instead, she went with the flow and let her eyes follow the hottie as he continued to sweep up the area in front of the counter. His hair was dark and ended just above his shoulders. His ass was tight, his arms were...perfect. Muscled but not the muscles of a bodybuilder. They were lean, and his shoulders? Illegal. Especially from the back.

Then he turned and the world stopped. Clear blue eyes zeroed right in on her, the corner of his mouth kicking up in a dangerous half smile. She was caught and should have been embarrassed. But she wasn't. Sadly, she was in no mood to do anything other than look at this adorable specimen of humanity. And she drank him in.

"*Mon neveu*," the owner explained with a grin as he came over to greet Kayleigh. The grandson of my father's best friend. "So he is, as you anglos would say, mon nephew. He will play with your brother starting...*lundi*?" Alain scratched his head. "*Néanmoins*, I get him to sweep while I have him, before his head blows up like a *ballon*."

The words in the Quebec French that reminded her of orchestral winter camps in Montreal (as opposed to her very strict Parisian childhood violin teacher) went through her head, and she understood some of it. Alain's very hot nephew would be playing on her brother's team starting Monday. He was adorable but untouchable.

Damn it.

"Max, *s'il te plaît, mettre la brosse sur le mur et bring la dame*, some of my best."

"*Ouais, mon chef.*"

She watched as the hottie, Max, put the broom down and turn toward the counter. Her eyes were locked, focused as he picked up a bowl of steaming hot poutine and brought it over to her.

He didn't move like any hockey player she'd ever seen, and she'd seen a bunch of them. She couldn't stop watching him as he came closer. It was a problem.

Except it wasn't. 'Cause it didn't feel like he was showing off for her, didn't make her feel like he had turned into a prancing peacock. It was just...him.

"*Ton poutine*," he said, his smile even more radiant.

"Thanks," she answered, allowing his voice to break into her thoughts. "I'm Kayleigh."

"Max," he replied, his eyes twinkling.

"You can talk," the owner said, "but you need to sweep."

Max

"You can talk," Alain said, "but you need to sweep."

Max St. Laurent looked at Kayleigh, first with his eyes, and then with his *percée*, the genetic inheritance that was both a blessing and at times a curse. That intangible extra sense told him she wanted to continue their conversation, that her curiosity was overwhelming, and her interest high.

And so he smiled and let himself be lead into conversation with her. She told him she was a violin player, that she wasn't from New York, and that she enjoyed this part of the city.

Sometimes he did have to tend to his chores, but she didn't mind; she had a large bowl of poutine and once she'd finished, he brought it to Alain for a refill.

"You...you don't have to do this," she said, gesturing to her full bowl. "I..."

He shook his head. "I'm not," he said with a grin, sitting back down on the bench. "But I am...grateful for the violin players of the world. My mother is French, and I think she would perish without the violin in this world."

She laughed, and her smile was warm and friendly and everything he probably shouldn't be investigating further. "I don't think my brothers and I would have survived childhood without poutine."

"*Franchment?*" he managed before he realized he'd spoken in

139

French. Again. "Sorry. Really?"

The serious expression on her face made him smile. "Yep. Winter in Saskatchewan would have been horrible without poutine, so I think we're even."

He couldn't help his laugh, and as Alain pointed to the corner of the restaurant floor, he realized he didn't want to leave her so quickly. But out of the corner of his eye, he saw her sudden surprise. The shock plain on her face, the nerves suddenly exploding.

"I'm sorry to cut this short," she began when he came back to the table, "but I have practice tomorrow morning and a binder of music to memorize. I'll see you?"

He nodded. "Yes," he managed. "Of course?"

She smiled, even though Alain was suddenly, vehemently trying to keep her from paying the bill.

"*Absolument pas*," Alain said, shaking his head. "Because of your brother, you are family, *non*? So no, you cannot pay. And please do not try, OK?"

He watched her sigh and nod, defeated. "OK," she said. "One day."

She left the shop, waving in his direction. She would be trouble, he realized. Her brother was on his team, and she fascinated him.

"That," Alain explained as soon as she was out of earshot, "was Chris Emerson's younger sister. She is...family, OK?"

He nodded. He understood. This would be difficult. Dangerous. *Merde.*

CHAPTER TWO

Monday

Max

Morning and the pounding of his alarm came faster than he wanted, visions of a woman with gravy on her nose haunting his brain. But he'd been summoned to the Empires' Tarrytown practice facility by his coach, and being late was not an option. So he showered, ate a quick breakfast, and headed to the closest subway.

Luckily, the subway followed his agenda; he could buy his train ticket in French; and the large marble Grand Central Station was easy enough to navigate. After a short, picturesque train ride, he got off at Tarrytown.

The train station itself was quaint, with a great view of the river. There were benches alongside the station house, and he sat down on the nearest empty one and waited. After a while, he wondered if he was doing the right thing.

Finally, Max reached into his pocket and grabbed his phone. Fumbling with the device, hoping it wouldn't let him down, he searched for the all-important email from his coach. It said he was supposed to take a particular train which would arrive at the station at a certain time, and he'd done that. Nothing else. Did he have to get a taxi? Should he have taken Alain up on his offer to drive?

Deciding he'd be better off acting than waiting, he stood and began to walk, following the sidewalk south toward the long line of taxis. He saw marble and brick, tons of cars, and the large village hall. The bustle and hustle of a small town, he decided with a grin. And it was nice.

"St. Laurent?"

He turned, seeing recognition and a bit of confusion in the eyes of the Empires' head coach. "Yes," he said, knowing it was important to speak in English.

"Jim MacArthur," he said holding out a hand.

Max took it. He wasn't an idiot.

"Had to drop my wife off at the train, so here I am. Welcome to the big show."

"Thank you, sir."

"You have your gear, or did they tell you not to bring it?"

"I put a...package together."

The coach nodded again as they headed toward a nondescript sedan. "Fine. It works. We'll speak, you'll see the facility. And then we'll talk some more."

He could only nod in response as he got into the car and settled in.

"Good," the coach said as he pulled away from the station. "You're a two-way player. Those're what we need this year. We've been stuck with injuries. Tons of them. And we need to be ready for anything. Which means you may need to play both offense and defense."

Max had played both offense and defense as long as he'd been playing hockey. "Not a problem, coach," he answered, not having to think about the words.

"Good. How much time do you need to switch?"

Max shrugged and tried to quantify the time in the best way he knew. The coach deserved an honest answer; the man would be, if necessary, altering his in game strategy for this particular purpose. "I prefer to have a full game in each, so at most I can switch each game. But if you need me to switch in between periods, I need an intermission at most."

"You have a routine, I take it? Mental or physical?"

"Both," Max said. Coach was drilling him, and so he would, once again, give the best answer he could. "When I am preparing to play offense I spend more time during warm ups on forward momentum, the backward for defense. But also I use a different stick, a different set of pads, different hand position…"

MacArthur nodded. "And if we need you at center?"

Max had expected this. Centers had been injury prone this year; he had asked one of the Stratford assistants to teach him the basics during practices. The man had done so as the Stratford head coach looked on with a smile on his face. "I could try," he said. "It would be a different preparation but…"

"Good. Goldman told me you'd be working on drills for centers. Very smart of you. You're already a two way, so adding another position won't be too difficult. Just let us know if you get to the point you feel like you're taking on too many roles.

He nodded. "I will, Coach."

"Good." As they continued to drive through the small town, Max found himself looking at the scenery.

"And by the way, we're sending you to do a commercial."

He paused, held his breath. "Yes?"

"It's a New York advertisement. Each team needs to send one foreign-born player. You'll be around internationals who play for all the other teams who've lived in this city for a while. They might be able to help you adjust." The coach smiled. "Think it'll be good for you despite your history . You up for it?"

Max knew, unfortunately, what the coach was talking about. His linguistic flubs had been legendary down in Stratford. "Yes sir."

"Very good."

Kayleigh

After a long day's rehearsal, Kayleigh found herself glad that Chris and Melanie had decided to hold the party welcoming Bryson 'Bryce' Emerson, her and Chris's older brother, to Brooklyn in an ice cream shop. Not just any ice cream shop; it was the shop that made the best ice cream in Brooklyn, and had a gorgeous party space filled with glass windows and comfortable tables. And its convenient lack of alcohol on premises made it a perfect space to celebrate a guy who'd just gone through rehab.

By the time she arrived, she could see in the small crowd of friends and acquaintances Chris and Melanie, Melanie's sister Emily (who was also the PR person for the Empires), and Emily's boyfriend Mark Smythe, a hockey player for the New Jersey Palisades.

"Hi, Kay," Bryce said as he saw her. Her brother the artist looked healthy, and she loved that. His eyes were bright, he was clean-shaven...even his hair looked healthy. But there was sadness in his eyes. "Save me."

She raised an eyebrow. "And why would you need saving?"

"Chris is hovering."

She laughed and threw an arm around him. "Chris always hovers.

He hovers, he herds, he…supervises because he loves. He's always done that."

Bryce nodded, and she saw the guilt there. "Yeah."

Both she and Bryce knew that Bryce's own trouble with drugs and alcohol had forced Chris to become the de facto oldest sibling; the last thing she wanted to do was push the dagger in further.

"Anyway," she said in an effort to change the subject. "Have you tried the ice cream?" Chris and Mel had assured her there was going to be an ice cream buffet, and she was looking forward to finding her new favorite flavor.

"It's amazing," Bryce said. "I blew through one bowl already, so I'm pacing myself. I figure I'm going to be living near here for a while, so I have time, you know." He shrugged. "I'm going to make a go of it, you know? Take it seriously. Take advantage of the fact that I'm near you guys and the art scene and…well not in the wilds of Saskatchewan."

"Good," she said. "I'm glad."

"Why are you glad, Kay?"

Speak of the devil. She shook her head and gave her brother the hockey player a look. "Hello, Chris," she said as she gave him a hug. "How are you?"

"Party is in full swing, good ice cream, good siblings, can't complain. Speaking of which, since I have you both here with me, aside from the fact that I'm thrilled to say this…"

"Here we go again."

"I love you, Bryce," Chris answered, his eyes brightening. "Anyway, I wanted to remind you both that there are a bunch of different family-related events that I expect you both to be at during the Classic."

"As long as Kayleigh isn't appearing with the Philharmonia…"

She turned around and grinned at her conductor. Arun Singh was talented as heck, able to maneuver his way through the many different ensembles the New York Philharmonia included, and a really good guy to boot.

"Hey, dude, glad you could make it," Chris said, a grin on his face. "I wondered if you were coming when Kay came in by herself.

"No problem. I had to wait for Jonathan, who's settlement conference went awry for some reason he refuses to tell me."

"So," Chris continued, focusing on Arun, "what's the deal with the Philharmonia?"

Kayleigh sighed. As per usual, Chris wasted no time, and she was glad that Arun was there to answer his questions.

"Right. So the mayor and a few of the borough presidents got together and decided that, starting next month, over the two and a half month period until the Winter Classic in Queens, there will be a series of events that will take place in Manhattan, the Bronx, Brooklyn, and Queens."

"Yeah," Chris nodded. "Yep. Family skates in the Bronx and in Queens, skating with the team in Brooklyn and Manhattan, and winter fairs where we're supposed to sign or something..." He shrugged. "But what does that have to do with the Philharmonia?"

"Well." Arun grinned as his husband Jonathan, who'd joined the group, rolled his eyes. "Who wants to be shown up by Columbus, who had a partnership with the symphony around their all-star game, or Boston who had an orchestra at their Winter Classic?"

Chris nodded, understanding. "Okay? So what did they do?"

"Or really," Kayleigh interjected shaking her head at everybody, "What am I going to do?"

After stealing the cherry from Jonathan's bowl of ice cream, Arun cleared his throat. "So all the winter fairs are going to have evening concerts attached to them. The music's going to be a bunch of different things…haven't figured the total specifics out yet. But closest I can think of is a fusion, a traditional-modern hybrid."

Kayleigh nodded. "So who's going to play?"

"Aside from you?"

The ensemble that's going to play the fairs, and the Classic itself, is going to be a combination of the plugged ensemble, which is more classical fusion, and the main ensemble for filler."

"By Classic you mean…"

"National Anthems, walk in music for both teams, then back up the groups that are playing during the intermission."

All three Emerson siblings nodded.

"Sounds like you're going to be a busy beaver," Bryce said, breaking the silence.

Kayleigh shook her head. "If I can survive it.

CHAPTER THREE
Manhattan
Event: Skating with the Empires at Bryant Park

Kayleigh

Kayleigh hadn't realized the time until the antique miniature grandfather clock on the wall in her living room started to chime. She cursed, angry she'd promised her hockey-playing brother that she would attend this crazy weekday event, then carefully put her violin in its case on the dining room table and raced into her bedroom. Skillfully avoiding the piles of books and clothing on the floor, she skidded to a stop in front of her closet door, threw it open, and began to rummage through the mess.

"Please," she whispered, "please let me find this." Two seconds later, her battered and bruised skate bag was in her hands. She let out a huge sigh.

After the skate bag was in her possession, finding her purse, jacket, shoes, and a fresh ponytail holder was easy. Even finding a taxi going the right way down 5th Avenue was a piece of cake. She had promised her brothers that she'd attend the Skating with the Empires event at Bryant Park, and it was a good thing she wasn't going to be late. Especially considering, first, her brothers would kill her if she was late, and second, she had to leave early to prepare for the evening's concert.

Unfortunately, the odds she was going to strangle someone were getting exponentially larger as the taxi approached the public park and the large crowd forming in front of it. "Dear god," she muttered.

"I have never seen it this bad," the taxi driver replied, shaking his head. "I can drop you here?"

"Here" referred to a spot in front of the mid-Manhattan library. The sidewalks in front of the smaller library were practically empty. "I'll take it," she said. Grateful, she swiped her card, gave the cab driver a huge tip for his trouble, and got out to examine her surroundings. There was still a teeming mass of people.

She was screwed.

She crossed the street as soon as it was possible, ignored the craziness of 5th Avenue and headed toward an entrance of the park.

"Trying to get in?" asked a man.

She nodded, fishing through her purse for the ID and letter she thought she'd put inside. Finally, triumphant and relieved all at the same time, she stuck the letter in her coat pocket and looked up. Dancing bright blue eyes met hers. "Yeah," she said as her heart pounded against her chest. She knew him from somewhere but couldn't place him. "Wait."

He paused, waited, and then smiled.

"You're Max. From the poutine shop?"

He nodded. "*Ouais*. And you're Kayleigh?"

"Yeah. That's me," she replied.

"Heading to the...*patinoire*?"

She loved the sound of his voice and his accent. "Yep. Heading to the rink. Trying to deal with this." She gestured to the crowd. "It's going to be interesting." She shook her head at the slight smile on his face, then wondered if he'd understood her. "As I said, this whole day is going to be interesting."

Max nodded. "They were trying to tell me there's a separate entrance, but I…" He waved his hands, brandishing long calloused fingers in the air, as if he were expecting to grab words out of the ether. "Their accents. So…" He shrugged. But it was the sort of elegant shrug-made-art Parisians were gifted with at birth. Not what she'd expected to see from someone who spoke English like he'd come from a small town in Quebec. But she nodded all the same, and realized if his English was as horrible as it seemed, he was going to have trouble understanding most people who carried the native accents of any of the five boroughs.

"Yeah." She put her hand in her pocket and pulled out the letter. "It says something about the back end…by the carousel and the shops?" She shrugged her shoulders. "Makes no sense to me."

"Can I?"

He'd shoved his fingers into his gloves, but the movements of his hands were still graceful under the bulk.

"Of course." She passed him the paper, touched his gloves with hers, and waited.

Then he smiled, and she thought her heart would stop. "Do you want to…try and find the…way in?"

"Yes." Despite the cold, she felt warm.

Max

Max walked down the street with Kayleigh until it felt like he was skiing uphill. Too many people, too many directions. "Wait," he

150

managed, not caring what language he'd spoken in but hoping she'd understand him.

She nodded, thank god, and stopped just off the sidewalk. He caught up to her, making his way through the crowd to arrive alongside her.

"You OK?" she asked.

He nodded. "*Trop*…so many people," he said, forcing himself to at least speak some English despite the fact he knew she'd understood his French. "I don't want to be…rude, but, well…" he shrugged. "It's difficult to…be careful, you know?"

Once again, she nodded. *Tabernac* it felt good not to have to explain. He was used to pushing hard, used to being aggressive, but not in a place where people did not know how to push back. Or push back like they did on the ice.

"You ready?" She asked like he'd needed to take a breath.

He smiled back at her, having composed himself. "May I?" he asked, raising his left hand and placing it at the small of her back. He waited, focusing completely on her. No nerves, anger, or upset. Just…a happy surprise. Like he was a knight or unicorn. But he focused still, waiting for her to *show* something. "I…it's not," he began, as if the words would make her speak.

"It's fine," she said, her smile burning his heart. "It's OK, you don't want to lose me, and you're too nice, and too strong, to push people."

He shook his head. "*Non*." Then paused. "No. Not…in this group of…"

"St. Laurent!"

The English words flew through his mind like autumn leaves, piling off to the side at the sound of his name. "*Ouais*?" Then he remembered the person who'd called him by name probably didn't speak French. "Yeah?"

The guard's response was loud and came with a grin. "You want the players entrance. It's around da corner and…"

He blinked. "Eh…"

"Thanks," Kayleigh said, as if she hadn't missed a beat. "I appreciate it."

"You are?"

She put her hand back into her pocket to take out her invitation. "Here," she said, giving the paper to the security guard.

The guard looked up, his face confused, the paper still folded in his hands. "Can read dis"

"Family member," she said, probably clarifying the words on the messy paper. "One of two. Not his though," she said, laughing.

The security guard nodded and gave her back the paper, which she put back in her bag, then directed them toward the exit, nodding at them both. "Thank you," he managed as he let her lead him out.

The guard waved in understanding. "Yer welcome."

As they walked away from the entrance, he leaned in to whisper in her ear. "Saved me."

She grinned back at him before she took his hand and let him lead her past the carousel and the shops, toward the entrance security had suggested. "Saved you, huh?"

He nodded as they turned the corner. "*Ouais. Vraiment.* You saved me from, eh…death by accent."

She laughed louder. "That's hilarious," she said, her voice lost through her laughter. "Death by accent. Unbelievable."

He grinned back at her. "You did, you know, hear the evidence."

"Oh, dear lord," she said, her laughter holding her words back. "Oh, my gosh, yes. You were so right."

But even more right, was the way she felt in his arms. And he could tell, *percée* or no, she felt the same way.

Kayleigh

Max made Kayleigh feel comfortable, which was something she'd learned to treasure. Her high-maintenance ex had made her feel as if she had to change who she was to make him understand her, and she'd had enough of that, whether with friends or a boyfriend.

Unfortunately, talking to him for about five minutes confirmed that his English was atrocious, even though he had an adorable accent.

Now, as they approached the player's entrance, she wished they'd had more time. "This way," she said, trying not to let the disappointment show in her voice.

And then out of nowhere, she felt his hand on her back again, then his arm around her shoulders. She relaxed into his touch. It wasn't just comfortable, it was practical. Yes. Practical. There were too many people milling around the Bryant Park shops to just walk together without some kind of connection. It was just…smart.

"This is nice," she said. "I'm glad I saved you."

"I was lucky," he replied. "Very lucky. Maybe…"

He'd let the phrase drop, and she wasn't happy about it. But she understood; she was his teammate's sister. Not to mention, her hockey player brother was, to put it mildly, an ass.

"Maybe next time I could save you?"

She didn't answer, mostly because they'd arrived at the player's entrance.

"St. Laurent's fine, and you." The guard looked at her. "Letter?"

She pulled the paper out of her pocket, and handed it over. "Here you are, sir."

The guard took it in his hand, and she watched as he inspected it, the expression on his face getting more puzzled as the minutes passed. "Goddamn it. I can barely see what's on this. This fuckin' looks like

153

you pulled it out of your ass. Who the fuck are you? ID please."

She grinned at Max, who was looking confused himself as they stood there. "Kayleigh Emerson," she replied as she reached into her skate bag to grab her wallet. "I'm Chris Emerson's sister." She passed her ID over to the guard and held her breath.

"Fuckin' A right she's Emo's baby sister," said a second guard as he came over to join his colleague. "My old lady? She's obsessed with classical ; tickets to the Philharmonia for Christmas, and she's a happy woman . Anyway…this girl? My old lady's favorite. She's like a muse come to Manhattan." The second guard then smiled at her and rolled his eyes. "Sonofabitch, and you're Lucky Seven, hm?"

Max, predictably, and adorably, blushed. "Yes…"

"Good. You." The guard pointed widely at a cordoned off area. "St. Laurent, you go there. And you, Emerson." He pointed at a door on the opposite end. "Need to go this way. You got people in there, family and stuff."

Instead of following the guard, much to her surprise, Max paused and smiled at her. "This was nice," he said, his grin as bright as his eyes.

She grinned back at him; apparently his expression was capable of stealing her words. "See you inside?"

He nodded, then paused. "Save a skate for me, maybe?"

She didn't answer him because she was dumbstruck. And despite everything else that would be waiting for her, she wondered what it would be like to skate around the rink with him.

CHAPTER FOUR

Max

It was a horrible idea to have *thoughts* about a teammate's sister, yet there she was when he closed his eyes. Improper thoughts shoved aside, Max headed into the part of the dressing room area set aside for the players. Like the other locker rooms he had been in on this level, each of his teammates had a locker containing the things they would need for the event. Thank god he found his locker without trouble.

The solid wooden bench in front of the temporary space welcomed his weight. He sat down and closed his eyes, attempting to block out the flutter of emotion from all areas of the room. *Sérénité*, he thought.

Once grounded, he reached for his skates, lacing them up in a way that allowed his ankles to breathe a little bit.

"All right," the assistant coach for defense shouted. "Eyes here!"

Immediately, he began to clap, following the team protocol; it was how they showed the coach they were ready and listening.

"So," the head coach began with a grin as he paced back and forth along the length of the locker room. "I see everybody's made it? Including Mr. St. Laurent, hm?"

He blushed; but there was a genuine smile on the coach's face.

"In all seriousness, I'm glad we're all here, because god knows we need days like this." The coached stopped and gazed at the group. "This, today? A little bit of fun. We're going to have a good time, we're going to skate, and we're going to mingle with everybody. But we're on a tight game schedule, so don't overdo it. And please, for the love of anything holy, I beg of you. Don't do anything *dumb*."

The coach looked at a few players, and Max saw him focus on Emerson.

"Me?" Emerson said, grinning. "Why would you think I would do something dumb...?"

"Cause you're the one out of everybody who has the most family here," the coach replied. "This is one of the earliest events surrounding the Classic, and you have two family members already in attendance."

Emerson laughed. "My two siblings live in the New York area. Oh!" He smiled at the coach. "Before I forget, I want everybody to pay attention."

Max could feel the sudden intensity focused on the man who wore the 'c'; it mirrored his own.

"So we're going to skate and have a good time this afternoon. And then we're going to go home, change and be on our best behavior because we're going to see *my sister* play. Not the New York Philharmonia. My sister. Which means you need to give *my baby sister*, and the rest of the ensemble she plays with, the proper respect."

Baby. Sister.

Merde.

"Lucky Seven? You got a problem?"

Max shook his head. "*Non capitane*," he replied, the French instinctively tripping off of his tongue as he sat up at attention. "No problem. Just thinking about how…amazing this is going to be."

"Better starstruck than lovestruck," his defense partner muttered.

Lovestruck?

Merde.

That would be horrible.

Kayleigh

By the time she'd finally made it out of the changing room and onto the Bryant Park ice rink, tons of people were already skating. She could see happy faces, and every facet of New York's population represented; it looked like a veritable United Nations, and made her delirious with excitement. And, she thought, it was only the first event in this city wide lead-up to the Winter Classic.

She began to skate, taking very easy laps around the edge of the ice, neither too close to the railing nor too close to the center, where some of the hockey players were making idiots of themselves in front of a few small children. Both her brothers were in a corner with Melanie and Emily. From what she could tell, the small group was either in an intense conversation or playing a stupid game.

And as she wanted to involve herself with neither, she continued to skate around the rink by herself. As she did, she caught random glimpses of other hockey players she recognized as they skated around with family members and other random people.

"Can I have this lap?"

"Of all the ice rinks in the world," she answered as she looked up to see Max standing beside her.

The clueless expression on his face made it clear he hadn't caught the reference. So she shrugged her shoulders, smiled, and reached out her hand. "Why not?" she said.

He nodded and took her hand in his. They began to skate side by side. And it was wonderful. He didn't force her to speed up or slow down. It felt comfortable.

"I love this," she confessed. "It's crazy but…"

Suddenly, he'd moved them both to the left, then the right.

"There was," he managed "someone who…would fall on the ice. I did not…want you to *sois blesse*."

"Hurt? Me?" She laughed, then stopped when she saw the serious expression on his face. "I appreciate it," she said. "But I'm fine. I've been doing this for a while."

Once again, she was forced to acknowledge how pretty his eyes were when he smiled. "But they have not," he answered, worry in his voice. "They…do not have control, and you would end up in their fall."

"Thanks," she answered, understanding what he meant despite how awkward his phrasing was. "I appreciate it. In fact. I liked it."

Max

She liked it.

The strange, happy warmth that came from spending time with her stayed with him as he went back to the apartment to change for the evening. He took a quick shower and changed into the blazer and dress pants he'd brought with him from Stratford. Maman would never have forgiven him if he hadn't brought proper dress clothing.

Finally he arrived at the concert hall, comfortable in his blazer and dress pants. Thankfully, it didn't take long for him to find his teammates.

"Glad you all made it," said the captain. "Quiet, and we sit together.

Enjoy the performance."

He sat down next to Evans and stared up at the stage. According to the program, there would be a few different selections. Different pieces, different composers. Some he'd heard before, and some he hadn't. He was looking forward to it all the same.

As the lights dimmed, he sat straighter in his seat and focused his attention on the orchestra. Not the muddle of feelings he was getting around him, but the lowering of the conductor's baton and the beginning of the concert. He let himself get lost in the motion and the music that followed.

Of course, he couldn't help the way his gaze followed Kayleigh as she stood for her solos, and how wonderfully she played. She was magical…

The snicker and the elbow from the other side forced him to remember he was in public. With his teammates. And that he needed to keep his guard up.

"He'll kick your ass," Evans said.

Max blinked, confused. "Eh?"

"Emerson. You're mentally undressing his sister. Take it down fifty notches in public, mm?"

He huffed out a breath and hoped he wasn't pink with the blush. "She's amazing with…*le violon*. She is…"

"Chris Emerson's baby sister."

The tone was quiet enough, and final enough, that Max forced himself to focus on the music, and hopefully not so obviously on the violin player.

Kayleigh

Kayleigh came out of the side entrance, ready to join the excited group of people who'd come to see her play. It had been a beautiful night.

"You were wonderful," Chris enthused, his bright eyes and proud-brother expression making her smile.

"Goddess," Chris's girlfriend gushed. Melanie always gushed after a performance.

"You're amazing," Bryce added. She liked when her oldest brother smiled. "So proud of you. I think you sparkle…"

"No sparkling!" she joked. "We're from an area too close to Washington state that people are already talking."

Bryce rolled his eyes. "It's not that bad." He patted her on the head as only he would. "Seriously, Kay. You can't be so pop-culture obsessed anyway. Aren't you a classical musician?"

Once again she sighed at the artist who was her brother. "It's hard to play classical music in the modern world without having one foot in it." She leaned in to her brother's ear. "And if you insult those books in front of Arun, he'll hurt you."

Her brother shook his head. "Kayleigh. I love you," he said as he walked away, exasperated in a way she didn't care. Yep. Bryce as she knew him was back. And she loved every annoying minute of him.

"This does not stop getting good, Kay," a familiar voice chimed.

"Ohmigosh," she gushed as Sousanna, her best friend from high school, caught her up in a huge hug. She must have left her boyfriend to watch the over the Elk, the bar they owned not far from the Poutinerie. "So glad you're here, Sousa."

"Course, girlie," Sousa replied. "You know I'll always come when I can." Then she paused, staring at the cluster of hockey players who stood about twenty feet away. "What's up with that?"

"Chris probably gave them the 'stay away, she's my sister' speech."

"Oh boo, that sucks."

"An understatement to be sure." Kayleigh sighed. "I don't even know why he's so protective. Damn it. I've been in New York long enough to warrant a reunion! At Julliard!"

"Because you're his baby sister," Sousa replied. "And hockey is so fucking tribal."

Team was team, and family was family, and hockey was both. But at least she wasn't the only sibling who had to deal with Chris's overprotectiveness. Bryce also got the Emerson sibling babysitting treatment. Of course in his case, she'd always thought it was warranted…

"Uh, oh. Upset hockey player at twelve o'clock…"

Once again, Sousanna's voice broke into her thoughts. Kayleigh turned in the direction her friend indicated, meeting Max's bright blue eyes. He grinned; she hoped he was grinning back at her.

"You think blue eyes is going to cross the border?"

She sighed and shook her head. "Rookie," she informed her friend. "Totally not going to happen."

"So why not send him a something?"

"What do you mean?"

The look on her friend's face was the 'you've lost your mind, and I need to fix it' look she'd known since they were kids. "Give me something *to give* him."

Understanding hit her, so she took the program, the pen Sousa gave her, and gave Max *something*.

Max

Both Emily from the PR office and Emerson had each cornered him during intermission and told him he needed to avoid the first chair viola player.

161

Emily had said some random collection of words, too quickly and too close together. He didn't really get it, only her insistence and her concern. So he nodded. Thankfully his captain had seen him coming back from the bathroom.

"Dude doesn't think it's possible that a hockey player can speak more than one language," Emerson had said. "Avoid him like the motherfucking plague." Max understood that. So when he got back to his seat, Max took another look through the program, made a note of the first chair viola player, and resolved to avoid him.

Except it was hard to avoid someone while they were heading toward him like a cannonball. And he couldn't get away.

Merde.

He needed help, a diversion, and he wasn't sure how to get one. And then he remembered he wasn't alone. He turned toward Evans.

"What's wrong?"

Putting this situation into English would be difficult, but he'd manage it. "This man...the viola player. I have been told to...avoid him. He is...not believing that an athlete that is...can speak two languages."

"Ah. He looks pretty intent on talking to you." Brody patted him on the shoulder, confirming he understood. "Leave it to me. Duck and hide. I'll take care of him."

Max nodded and headed off, grateful for the assist.

"Thank god you stepped away from him," said the tall woman who had moved next to him. "I did not want to deal with that guy."

"Any particular reason?"

"He's an asshole," she replied without a pause. "I genuinely find him as interesting as a piece of rubber. You, however, I find fascinating. As does one of my dearest friends."

He blinked. "I don't...I..."

She grinned back at him. "It's fine. You're adorable. She likes you." She took something from her pocket and passed it over to him. "She expects you to use it."

And without any other word, she left him alone to figure out what to do.

From: Max_SL7@empiremail.com
To: K_emerson@nyharm.com
Thank you for this. I enjoyed the concert. Wonderful choices of music, and the ensemble plays beautifully.
I hope to hear from you soon.
Max

From : K_emerson@nyharm.com
To Max_SL7@empiremail.com
Hey. It was great to see you at the concert. Yes, you had to be there, but still…
Chris is a dork. Ignore him if you have to.
K

From: Max_SL7@empiremail.com
To K_emerson@nyharm.com
Thanks. You play well. It's hard to get that sound out of a violin. My mother used to take me to the symphony. I tried to play when I was younger. It did not work. I admire you.
Max

From: K_emerson@nyharm.com
To: Max_SL7@empiremail.com
Like the dodge on the comment about my brother. But it's OK. I'm his sister. I'm allowed to call my brother names, even if you don't think you can. And thanks.
K

From: Max_SL7@empiremail.com
To: K_emerson@nyharm.com
Can you wear gloves? Even without fingers? Or does that make
playing difficult?

CHAPTER FIVE

Max

While the team was in the middle of a bizarre schedule which had them free during the week and playing back to back game on weekends, Max got an email from Emily Gould in the team's PR office. The email demanded his presence at the premiere party for the commercial he'd shot a few weeks earlier. Since he was looking for something to do that wouldn't get him into trouble, it was easy for him to comply.

"So this is the story," Emily began as they arrived at the venue, a hall on 36th and Broadway. "Mingle, talk with everybody, have a drink, make nice with everybody. But not too much because someone from the mayor's office will come and get you when it's your turn to run the press junket. I'll go find out who's there, and I'll take you through. Sound good?"

He nodded. "Thank you," he managed as he waded into the party itself. High ceilings, waiters in black tie, tons of mixed up emotions, to the point where he took refuge in a glass of seltzer, not wanting to risk anything further.

But within two minutes of leaving the bar, he'd began to talk to people. The most fascinating was Pedro Dominguez, the center fielder for the for the baseball team whose stadium was going to be used for the Winter Classic. With the help of two different sports reporters—a Spanish reporter whose name he couldn't understand, and Pierre LeBlanc, a reporter from one of the Quebec based sports networks—acting as translators, he and Pedro were having a really good conversation.

"It's your turn, Mr. St. Laurent," said a representative from the mayor's office.

After saying his good-byes to everybody, he followed Emily to where the press was set up. First were the reporters from print and online publications, some of which he kept up with; he got a kick out of telling them that he liked their sites

Next were the TV reporters: the hockey network, followed by the network devoted to covering the Empires. He also managed to tell them how much he appreciated their time. Then came the other networks that wanted what Anglos called "sound bites."

Those were easy, and even though it took a while to get through it all, he was proud of himself. No major mistakes under the bright lights of the cameras. He took his time, breathed, and listened. He also made sure that Emily Gould remained in his line of sight.

"Good job," she said as they headed into a small room just off the end of the long junket. She grabbed a bottle of water from the counter and passed it to him. He smiled in thanks, opened the bottle and drank down about half of it.

"Thanks," he managed once he'd drunk enough to soothe his throat. "I think…"

"You're doing fine, Max," she assured him, clapping him on the shoulder. Even though his *percée* told him she was terrified, he took the assurance as it was given. "One more to go."

He nodded. He knew. That was the interview he was really nervous about.

The major network covering hockey that season had sent their famous sideline reporter, Clint Beauchamp, to see the commercial and to interview the hockey players involved. Max's interview was going to be part of the features aired during the network's coverage of the Winter Classic.

"Now remember," Emily said. "Beauchamp is…dangerous."

Dangerous was an understatement. Max knew the rumors, and once he'd been called up to the Empires, he was told the rumors were true. Clint Beauchamp, a former coach turned beloved (by the fans) sideline reporter, had a reputation. He was known for deceptively calm interviews that lead into questions designed to trip up even the most prepared player.

"I know your history," Emily began.

He nodded. His history of linguistic screw-ups during all sorts of public situations was rather legendary around the AHL, especially in Stratford where he'd spent a year playing for the Empire's affiliate.

He watched Emily look around, making sure they were alone. "Beauchamp is going to exploit it," she said softly. "He's got a vendetta against…the league, the teams, who knows? He likes to prove that his players were the best prepared for interviews, and he is ruthless."

He swallowed, took a deep breath, and then reached up and ran his index finger and his thumb around the collar of his dress shirt, adjusting it without the benefit of a mirror. It was something he could focus on without showing Emily he was also scared out of his fucking mind.

"St. Laurent?"

"You're up," Emily whispered unnecessarily.

Max smiled back at her and made a quick gesture searching for approval.

Emily nodded.

"Last minute pointers?" he asked.

"Just watch yourself with this guy," she replied after a moment. "The infamous tricky question will come out of nowhere, and you have to be prepared for it."

Max nodded in return, though he wasn't quite sure how the word deceptive actually applied. But he felt Emily's sincerity and headed toward the podium set up for the national network.

"Nice to meet you," the bald-headed gentleman said in a bit of a raspy voice, taking his hand.

"Same," he replied, smiling.

And the conversation began. Beauchamp was from Montreal and knew about Max's years in Juniors. They spoke about the fact he played both offense and defense, how much he enjoyed being in New York, and how Brooklyn reminded him of Montreal—the city he'd spent most of his life outside of.

"So how did you get the nickname Lucky Seven?"

Thank god.

Max started to laugh as he remembered the incident and thought about the words he'd use to tell the story in the easiest way possible.

"I don't know; it was something that happened along with the jersey, you know? I wear...I am number seven, and I scored...the first time on the ice in Brooklyn, and they thought 'number seven... lucky.'"

The interviewer's genuine laugh made him feel relief. "Very lucky you're the only rookie in this group, barely got your peach fuzz off your skates."

Right. Rookie. Peach fuzz?

Tabernac.

"Well, you know…you get your moment when you can, and maybe take your chances and do…what you can to be part of the team and of the sport, and do your best."

"Already sounding like a pro at this."

If he thinks I'm a pro already…

"So what's this about?"

Simple. To the point. Quick. Easy.

"Well, this is a campaign of athletes who play for New York teams who are from other countries. We…were being sports ambassadors to New York. Showing the city has the flavor of so many countries. And my segment was me saying…welcome to New York in French, so you know, that's '*Bienvenue à New York.*'" He shrugged. Smiled. "It was a good thing for New York, a good thing for Les Empires and a good thing for hockey….to be made part of this."

"What's it like? Being around other New York athletes?"

Easy question. Easy answer. Simple. Simple. "It's great, of course. It's wonderful to see the love they have for the city and their sports, and how they make…parts of their countries live…in New York. It's like…"

"Halloween? Frankenstein?" Beauchamp laughed, but his smile wasn't friendly. And in the back of his mind, Max could feel Beauchamp's emotions start to gather.

He could work with gathering emotions and an out, courtesy of Alain. "Possibly," he answered, laughing himself. "My uncle, you know, he told me about how much this city loves to celebrate the holidays…Halloween…you know with the parade in Greenwich Village and the excitement. And the parades of Thanksgiving…"

"Yeah, New York knows how to celebrate. What do you think of…"

And suddenly Beauchamp's emotions exploded…like a thunderbolt or a volcano or…a bomb. All he could feel was the pounding headache produced by his *percée* in response to Beauchamp's anger and jealousy. There was so much of it…and focused right on him in a way that made him think it was deliberate.

He took a breath instead of grunting in pain, carefully brushed his eyes with his fingertips and blinked. "Erm…I what did you?"

Beauchamp laughed, anger and jealousy turning to satisfaction. Satisfaction he could handle. "So," Beauchamp said, "what do you think of New York weather?"

Max answered the question, but from the horrified expression on Emily's face, and the smile on Beauchamp's, he knew the damage had been done.

Merde.

Kayleigh

There were two huge folders of "Winter Classic and related events" music, and Kayleigh swore she'd played every piece of music in them twice. Including *three* different arrangements of Vivaldi's *Summer* that the Plugged ensemble was testing. Her fingers desperately needed a massage, but she was too tired to walk down the block to her favorite little massage place.

Instead, when she got back from practice, she collapsed on her couch and called it a day. She was contemplating ordering dinner when the phone rang. The caller ID said "Sousa," and she always picked up the phone when her best and oldest friend called.

"'Lo?"

"Turn on the TV."

There was an urgency in her friend's voice, and she wasn't sure why. "What?"

Sousa sighed on the other end of the phone. "It's about to get interesting. Turn on the TV."

"Good interesting or bad interesting?" she wondered aloud.

"You, my friend, need to judge that one for yourself."

Kayleigh nodded, even though she knew her friend couldn't see. "Sure then…"

Then she held the phone between her ear and her shoulder and carefully, sadly, got up from the most comfortable couch she'd ever owned. Then, following some instructions a friend of a friend once had given, she stretched her arms, then her legs. Sufficiently stretched, she crossed the living room and grabbed the remote.

Remote in hand, she walked to the couch, flopped back down and pressed the on button. The TV flared to life, lighting up the half-darkened room to the point where Kayleigh needed to cover her eyes. "Ouch," she said.

"Did I wake you?" Sousa asked.

"Nah. Long practice, came home, collapsed on the couch and forgot to turn on the light. So what channel am I watching?"

"Four."

She turned to one of the major networks and waited.

"In other news earlier this evening, athletes from all of New York City's major sports teams gathered together for the premier of an advertisement that showcases the international flavor this city has to offer."

She sat back and watched the Swedish goalie for one of the other New York hockey teams, the Dominican outfielder from the baseball team from Queens, and the Japanese right fielder from the Bronx baseball team all talk about their sports."

"Here we go," Sousa said. "This is it…"

"Defenseman Max St. Laurent from the New York Empires had this to say…"

As they switched to the footage of Max's interview, her heart started to race. His responses were slow and clear, which boded well for him. He was also adorable. And then…what?

As the silence extended, she wanted to smack the usually annoying journalist with her shoe. Finally, she watched as the adorable Frenchman realized he'd been asked a question, then managed gamely to answer it.

"Oh, boy," she said.

"Oh, boy is right," Sousa replied. "I take it you two have been emailing?"

"Yeah," she said. "There was some kind of emailing and he emailed me back but I hadn't…."

"So what are you going to do now? After you've seen your adorable Frenchman on TV?"

"Send him an email?"

"Do it now," Sousa ordered. "He needs it. Bye." And with that, her friend ended the call, leaving her to send a very important email.

From: K_emerson@nyharm.com
To: Max_SL7@empiremail.com
I saw you on TV. You're still awesome.
K

From: Max_SL7@empiremail.com
To: K_emerson@nyharm.com
Relieved to hear that, thanks. Not feeling so awesome (?) now.

From: K_emerson@nyharm.com
To: Max_SL7@empiremail.com
You are. You held your head high and you were wonderful. And making an effort.

From: Max_SL7@empiremail.com
To: K_emerson@nyharm.com
Merci

CHAPTER SIX

Max

Tabernac.

The entire team had heard the interview. He'd had enough of the snickers, the weather maps, the silly puzzle, and the stuffed squeaky sun.

Merde.

He smiled, despite his embarrassment. Especially since he could feel the genuine horror from his teammates. They were laughing with him, embarrassed for him. And in a few isolated cases, proud of him. "OK, thank you," he said, bowing. "Really. I am touched that all of you spent your off time watching me on television."

Even his defense partner grinned and presented him with a French-English meteorological dictionary. He shook his head, grinned back, and put the heavy tome away before settling down into the usual rhythm of practice. But practice itself was in no way usual. It was hard, fast, and it felt as if the world was doing its best to keep his brain in the game, and not on last night's moment of idiocy. He had to focus on the ice, the puck and the game. And work. Hard.

As per usual, the entire team worked, too; the forwards, the wings, the centers, and the defensemen. Puck handling and stick handling first, then passing drills. He even got a few moments on one of the power play practice groups, then his penalty kill unit got about five seconds. By the time he got in front of the net, Semenov didn't even break a sweat as he turned away his feeble attempt at a shot. Only a cretin would shoot with his hands in the defensive stick position.

Coach MacArthur was pleased with the team's efforts on the ice. Max didn't need *percée* to see it, but he felt it nonetheless. There was also something else; a worry behind the pride. And worry from his coach made his stomach turn.

"Great practice, guys," Coach Mac boomed. "Back here tomorrow for video. Also the two power play units need to come early. We need to drill this thing into submission." And then he turned to Max. "St. Laurent? I need to see you. In my office. Ten minutes."

The team broke up and headed toward the locker room. Of all people, Emerson clapped him on the shoulder. "Careful, buddy," he said, his tone joking, his fear just below the surface. "Just be careful."

Max nodded at the captain, taking the man's sage advice at face value. *Merde.* He was in for it. But all he could say was, "Yes. Absolutely. I will."

He headed into the locker room, grabbed his things, and took the quickest shower he'd ever taken. As he dried himself off and got dressed, he tried to figure out what he might be confronting, and did his darnedest to calm his raging mind.

He found himself focusing on the fact his coach was not angry. The man was frustrated. Proud and he felt a tinge of exasperation. That meant a couple things, he decided as he grabbed his bag and headed toward his coach's office. But in the end, the most important thing was to make sure his coach realized how serious he was. He was working hard, and would continue to do so. The opportunity he'd been given meant a great deal to him, and he'd do whatever it took to stick as a pro.

Resolved, settled, he knocked on the door.

"St. Laurent?"

"*Ouais, Chef,*" he began without thinking.

Merde.

English. "Yes, Coach MacArthur."

"C'mon in. It's open."

He nodded, took a deep breath and tried to see past his own fear. Frustration and worry and urgency from his coach. As he shut the door, he took another deep, cleansing breath before turning to his coach. *Keep it simple. Slowly. Slowly.* "I…"

But his coach shook his head, gesturing him to a seat in front of his desk instead. All he could feel was sadness. "I don't want to hear one word out of you. Not one."

He was silent as he sat down, focusing on Coach MacArthur's face.

Now it was his coach's turn to sigh, and he found himself overwhelmed by the disappointment rolling off of the other man.

"You did great during your segment of the commercial," Coach Mac began, a bit of pride in his voice. "Wonderful. You also represented your team well in most of the interviews you did during the press thing. That tells me you're making a genuine effort. You mean it. But these flub ups, these mess-ups of yours. They're…"

"But…"

"Not one word, St. Laurent. I mean it. You need to *listen.* I cannot tell you how important it is to me personally that you're making the effort to learn English. Whatever that effort is, it shows."

Max wondered how the coach would react if the man understood how little he was actually speaking English outside of practice and scattered emails...

"And nobody likes that reporter anyway. But he messed you up. And if he can, then any reporter worth their salt can. Which means you're not fluent enough. And here's the thing. The Classic. Obviously it matters in the standings, but it matters for the league's publicity. It matters for the team. If they mess you up there, again? It's not just you who's messed up, it's the team. Because it will be everywhere."

Max swallowed.

"And the thing is, the organization wants you to play up here. We think you're ready and we think you're going to be here for a while. So instead of sending you back down to Stratford to keep you out of that spotlight, this is what we propose. It's a simple proposition. If you're not fluent or whatever you want to call it by the time we play the Winter Classic , we're hiring you an interpreter. And the cost is coming out of your salary."

There were no words he could say. He was in trouble.

Merde.

Kayleigh

One of the new pieces was first on the agenda at the Philharmonia's full practice: an arrangement of an aria from Carmen. Kayleigh found herself having to focus. The arrangement was a bit interesting, but in a good way. It was fast, furious and forced her nimble fingers just beyond their limits.

Finally, the piece was the way Arun wanted it, and he gestured to the ensemble to put their instruments down. "Good job, everybody," he said, pride in his voice. "We'll take five in a minute and come back to the Vivaldi. But before that, I have an announcement.

Announcement? Another announcement?

She sighed, then realized she wasn't the only one. It was all she could do to keep from laughing.

"This isn't bad, guys," Arun qualified, his hands out in a motion of surrender. "So there's been a change to this year's schedule."

Another change?

She bit her tongue, holding back any possible comment she might have made. The rest of the orchestra wasn't as successful; she could hear the undercurrent of chatter around her. She just shrugged her shoulders and held her breath.

"Yes," he continued. "I know. This has been a tumultuous year already and we haven't even made it into December. But this year, we are getting a gala holiday party."

Gala? Holiday? What???

She sat up straighter in her chair, carefully holding on to her violin.

"Because this year presents more opportunities for subscribers to spend time with orchestra members, as well as increased opportunities to gain new subscribers and charitable contributions, the board decided it would be a better use of time and money to give the Philharmonia a reward. Thus, instead of the midwinter charity gala, this year, we will have a mid-winter orchestral gala. Orchestra members, some selected board members and invited guests will attend. Attendance is mandatory. Plus ones are allowed. Dress code is black tie. Now take five, and we'll go back to Vivaldi after the break."

Kayleigh sighed. The very last thing she wanted to do was to have to deal with some of the members of the orchestra on an off day when she wouldn't otherwise have to. It was one thing to see some of them when she wanted to but this?

"Aren't you excited about the gala?"

Speak of the devil. Joe. One of the very last people in the world she wished to see.

Instead of answering him the way she wanted, she bit her tongue and focused on putting her violin back into its case. She absolutely did not want to go to this gala. But she wouldn't tell Joe that. She had no desire to socialize with him. Especially since the man reminded her of an overexcited Chihuahua, and there was nothing she liked less. "Sure," she said, picking words that would get her out of the conversation as quickly as possible. "Black tie, right?"

"Yes. Formal setting for us requires black tie." He paused. "And it would be better for you to bring a date. It seems…awkward if you don't."

"Sure," she said, preparing to leave Joe before he had a chance to continue the conversation. Because he wasn't who she wanted to talk to. She needed to talk to Arun. Immediately.

And as soon as she put her violin case back on her chair, with a peripheral "Excuse me," to Joe, she headed toward Arun. Thankfully, her friend had stepped away from the podium, and smiled when he saw her standing in front of him.

"Kayleigh, how are you?"

"Do I have to?"

Arun laughed, and rolled his eyes. "Not willing to mince words, Kay?"

She shook her head. "Not so much. Come on," she pleaded. "Do you know what December is going to be like for me?"

Arun threw back his shoulders. "I do, or don't you remember discussing this a few weeks ago?" he replied. "I'm guessing your parents are coming in?"

"Yep. And most of my relatives and half the province of Saskatchewan. It's like my brother's never played in a hockey game before."

The sound of Arun's laugh was almost enough to make her smile. "And haven't you already noticed that 'the powers that be' were already making special arrangements for you? You know, your addenda to the schedule where you were told you didn't have to attend certain events?"

She nodded, remembering the papers she'd been handed three days after the original schedule went out. "Yes. And…"

"This is not on the list of events you can miss. No buts, no excuses if not something major."

Fuck.

Resigned to the inevitable, she prepared to head back to her seat.

"Oh, and Kayleigh?"

She turned toward Arun. "Hmm?"

"I'm going to bring Jonathan," he said, his voice barely above a whisper. "Could you…bring someone as well? He'll need someone to talk to."

She nodded; she couldn't say no to her conductor. Especially when he was a friend asking her for a favor.

"Someone to take his mind off of how nervous he is, maybe a hockey player?"

"Like they grow on trees," she said, laughing.

"Please?"

Once again she nodded. "Sure, Arun. I'll see what I can do." If she were being honest with herself, she knew exactly who she'd ask. Except it was a horrible idea. A very bad, horrible, no good idea. But that didn't stop her from thinking about it.

Max

Merde.

He was screwed. *Tabern…*

180

"*Hein, petit,*" his grand-père said, laughing. "*Arrêt* with the *tabernacs* or we're going to put you in that church two blocks north."

He laughed against the broom. He'd desperately hoped he'd be able to sweep out his frustrations on the floor of the poutine shop. Apparently, this was not going to happen. Especially when grand-père was in town, watching the shop so Alain could go fishing before the period he called 'peak poutine season' started. "*Désolée,*" he said, his voice full of regret. "I…"

"No," Grand-père said, halting the apology with a smile. The World Series was on the television, a French language broadcast courtesy of a Quebec sports station that took pity on the shop. "S'OK. So what's causing the trouble? Your schedule? You need a…"

"Another head is what I need," Max answered earnestly. "I have to…be better at English, or I'm going to be forced into a translator."

"So it is the language. *Merde.*" Grand-père swept at the counter with a towel. "Is there someone you can ask for assistance with English? *Un Anglo*? You know, what about a pretty girl…"

"*Arrêt!*" Max shouted, half laughing, half shaking his head. His grandfather meant well, but the idea…well… "I don't know." He paused and drummed his fingers on the countertop. "Maybe." But would she? Would Kayleigh help him? Not that he'd mind having the excuse to spend time with her, but *tabernac*…

"*Mon dieu,* it's like you have the world on your shoulders, *petit.* Be smart, *hein*? Not…like you search for the cure to cancer, you know?"

He nodded, smiled and sighed. An email wouldn't hurt. The worst she could say would be no. And he could live with that.

Kayleigh

There was only one place Kayleigh felt comfortable going when she was on the verge of making a bad decision: Sousa's bar. So immediately after rehearsal, she got on the subway, got off at the stop that took her to the right part of the Village and walked the few blocks to the Elk (not the poutine shop).

The Elk itself was a nondescript spot with a comfy atmosphere. Wooden bar with hand-carved bar stools and leather cushions. Small tables in the corner and a stone fireplace. She was there often enough nobody looked twice at her as she walked in with a violin case.

"Hey, Kay," Sousa said as Kayleigh walked in. Her friend was behind the bar, swabbing it down with a cloth. "What do you want?"

"The Good Ship Bad Decision," she replied, shaking her head as she sat down on a stool. "Dear god, Souze."

Sousa began to make her drink—a Shirley Temple with a shot of vodka. "So what brought this on?"

"So there's this gala," she began as she reached for a water glass. "The management turned it into a gala for orchestra members only, when before it was for subscribers. Kind of a way to get everybody together and…relax? I guess?"

Sousa nodded as she passed her the drink. "Go on."

"So anyway, I don't want to go to this thing. Really don't. For reasons."

"Which don't involve the viola player that deserves his bow shoved up his ass?"

"Yes. And definitely do involve the fact I am tired, what with the fifty million things I need to do…"

"Yes. Yes. Yes. Go on."

"And I especially don't want to invite someone."

"Come again?"

Kayleigh sighed as she took a swallow of her drink, letting the fizzy soda dance around her tongue. "See, Arun freaked out because he's bringing his husband, of course. Problem is, Jonathan's a total sports guy. So Arun asked me to bring someone, preferably a hockey player, to talk to Jonathan so he's not bored." She took another drink and sighed. "Basically."

"And you're thinking of asking the guy you had me give your email to?"

"In a nutshell. Hence the Bad Idea Express."

"It's not a bad idea," Sousanna replied matter-of-factly. "He's hot. You're asking him if he wants to go with you to a gala."

"He's on my brother's team. He's barely comfortable talking to me when my brother's around."

"You and he have been emailing, right? And is your brother going to be attending this gala?"

"Yes," she replied. "We've been emailing, so it's not going to be a random email out of nowhere. And no. My brother is not invited. He is not my guest."

"Not your date, thankfully. So, again, what's the problem?"

Kayleigh sighed, reaching for anything she could think of. "His English is not the best. What if he can't keep up a conversation with Jonathan? What's the point of bringing someone who can't have a conversation with Jonathan, when the express purpose of bringing someone is to keep Jonathan occupied?"

"Does he have a cute accent? I mean what's the point of an accent if it isn't…"

"You're not even listening."

Sousanna glared at her, then swiped the bar with a towel. "Just because I think you're being completely idiotic doesn't mean I'm not listening to you. I hear every single word, Kay, even if I don't want to. Yes. He's on your brother's team. But you knew that. And he *still* emailed you after I gave him your email address. So he has trouble speaking English. I'm sure Jonathan will ignore that particular fact because he will be talking to a hockey player. And maybe forcing him to speak English will help him learn."

"But..."

"So what's the harm, Kay? What's the problem?"

"What if he makes a fool of himself in front of Jonathan and feels worse about himself? I mean, yeah, he could be better, but he could be worse, too..."

"Which him? The conductor? His husband or the Frenchman?" Sousanna poured another drink for a patiently waiting customer before turning back to Kayleigh. "I'm confused. You need to be specific with your pronouns, especially when telling this story."

Kayleigh put her head against the bar, defeat and exhaustion weighing her down. "What the hell should I do?"

Sousa, like the best friend she was, rolled her eyes before patting Kayleigh on the head. "Ask him. And then tell me how it goes."

Kayleigh sighed. "Fine. I'll do it."

From: K_emerson@nyharm.com
To: Max_SL7@empiremail.com
Got a question for you but I can't ask it over email. When can you meet?

From: Max_SL7@empiremail.com
To: K_emerson@nyharm.com
I have a question for you too. Are you free Thursday evening?

From: K_emerson@nyharm.com
To: Max_Sl7@empiremail.com
Yes. Where should we meet?

From: Max_Sl7@empiremail.com
To: K_emerson@nyharm.com
630 at Westside, between centre Javits and Penn Station?

CHAPTER SEVEN

Kayleigh

Kayleigh examined her surroundings when she got out of the brand new subway station. She rarely took the subway this far west, so she'd never taken the time to notice what the area was like.

Now, she took the time to investigate as she walked down the street toward Max's meeting place of choice. And she liked the combination of business and industrial, of new office buildings and old, crowded restaurants.

The place that Max had chosen stood out, and yet was firmly a part of the area. The doors opened to reveal a space that looked much bigger than the brick building made it seem. The wooden floors spread from wall to wall, the bar space to the left, the tables to the right. It was huge and cozy all at the same time. She looked around and took a breath.

He was sitting there in a corner table, waiting for her. She watched his shoulders, the way he breathed in and out with each passing minute.

It seemed as if he'd been there awhile, the way he seemed to try and focus on everything but the chair in front of him.

"*Ouais?*"

She blushed. She'd been caught. "Sorry."

He shook his head as he stood. And she couldn't help but watch him. Damn, he was graceful. Like he only seemed to use half of his muscles with twice…

"Are you here?"

She laughed. He'd caught her. Again. "I'm so sorry…"

"*Arrêt.*" His voice was wonderful, and she laughed. "*Franchement,* if you think you have to apologize for paying attention to me, or anything else, I…well," he shrugged. "It's OK. It's fine. Join me?"

She nodded, not trusting her traitorous tongue, and sat down across from him. "Why here?"

He laughed again as he brushed his fingers across the menu. "Good food, not…" He paused. "Not owned by people I know."

"An epidemic of that in this city," she answered before realizing he might not get it. "There's a lot of it."

He nodded. "Thank you," he said graciously before he seemed to realize he still hadn't answered her. "Yes…there is, for a city I don't… didn't really live in, you know? And not because I…"

She smiled. "Yeah. Do something special."

Max

He sat back and relaxed for the first time since she'd arrived. He'd been sitting there, concerned she wouldn't show, despite the fact she'd told him she would. They'd ordered food, a glass of wine for her, a Fin du Monde for him. It was nice, calming, relaxing.

"To problems," she said as her glass chimed against his.

"To problems," he repeated, the words swimming around his tongue. "May we both find the solutions easy."

She grinned and took a sip of her wine. "I'll drink to that."

He watched as she carefully sipped from her glass, focused on her expression as she swirled the wine around in her mouth.

"Just like I remember it. You?"

He reached out and took a sip of his beer, clasping his fingers around the cool glass, bringing the bottle to his lips. The taste reminded him of home, of winter nights with his father in front of the fireplace. "*Ouais*," he replied, because it would be difficult to explain exactly what the taste of the beer on his tongue made him feel in English.

She nodded, taking another sip of wine. "Problems, hm?"

He nodded. Sitting with her didn't feel like a problem; rather it made him feel like everything else was a problem, and she was… right.

"So what's your problem, exactly?"

"English," he replied, making an effort to actually speak in the language, no matter how much he wished to lapse into French.

She folded her arms and reached for the plate of nachos. "Clearly. I've never met a guy who was less willing to speak a language he was famous for attempting on a regular basis."

He wanted to laugh, and so he did. She had him pegged, of course. "I can…understand…faster than I can…reply. If I go too fast, I make… mistakes." His cheeks burned but he forged ahead anyway, ignoring her piercing emotions. "I cannot…*continu* like this. It bothers me."

"More than bothers," she said, "judging by the expression on your face. Pisses you off, more like."

He tested the expression on his tongue. It felt right. "Yes. It pisses me off."

"I see," she said.

And it did not take much for him to tell she actually did.

Kayleigh

"So," Kayleigh finally said. "My problem."

"Yes?"

They'd gotten that far. Of course it had taken dinner and two glasses of wine to keep her from losing her shit. She took a breath and a fortifying sip from glass number three. "I have to go to this…party. For the ensemble. Everybody has to be there."

He nodded, and he was focused. Though whether he was focused on her, her words, or something else entirely was another matter. It didn't make her any less nervous.

"And," she managed, forcing the rest of the words out of her mouth, "I need to bring someone."

He blinked, the bright blue of his eyes disappearing for an instant before returning. "You want…me to come with you?"

She nodded. And held her breath. His confusion was adorable but not helpful. She curled her fingers around the wineglass, allowing the chill to seep into her skin.

He shrugged, of course. "I figure you can help me with my English, I will go with you to the gala. We…" he paused and she could see him searching for the words, "we get along. And I think…it would help for me to speak English with someone who…does not mind I make mistakes."

She took a deep breath, and relaxed as his hand settled atop hers, the one that wasn't curled around the wineglass in a death grip.

"It's OK," he said, the sound of his voice more comforting than the wine. And then he grinned and said words that meant more to her than anything else possibly could have. "Let's order dessert."

And with that, she decided, they'd begun what was going to be a beautiful friendship.

CHAPTER EIGHT
Event: Brooklyn Winterfaire

Kayleigh

Soon after she made her bargain with Max, Kayleigh rediscovered that the only person busier than a hockey player was…well, someone with her schedule. But they'd managed to send emails back and forth and have a quick drink and a conversation at the poutine shop. Conversation was fun, and he seemed to genuinely want to try and learn the language.

Except life had just gotten crazier. She'd just found out her family was coming early to celebrate not only Christmas, but American Thanksgiving and Chanukah. Because, her father, the professor, informed her matter-of-factly, if they were going to have a Jewish daughter-in-law, they needed to learn about Chanukah firsthand.

As if that wasn't enough, the folder had gotten bigger and Arun had finally admitted that one of the Vivaldi arrangements would be the music that would herald the entrance of the two teams into the stadium. Which would be fine, except her brother was already asking for previews so he'd "know the time signature with which to swagger."

Thankfully, Max hadn't asked her stupid questions like that.

Strangely enough, Max hadn't asked her very much at all. Which surprised her, but she shrugged her shoulders and moved along. The team had just gotten back from a road trip (she was a horrible sister not to have paid attention to how the team was doing) only to plunge into the day's events.

Luckily, the first item on the agenda was an outdoor market. She was able to spend some time with Chris, Melanie, Bryce, Mel's sister, and her boyfriend, Mark Smythe, the Empires latest acquisition. Each of the players, except Smythe, had to spend time at the signing table, and she had to put some face time in at the orchestra table. Otherwise? It was going pretty well. Very laid back and…nice.

The concert afterward went well; the Bizet suite seemed to get the crowd clapping, which was always a plus. But the previews, one of the Vivaldi and a piece composed by one of the members of the band reuniting for the Winter Classic got a bigger round of applause than expected. She, however, was not surprised that the Corrs were pretty well known in Brooklyn.

But after the concert, she said goodbye to the relatives and headed toward the exit.

"*Attends*…wait…"

She looked up, waved, and waited for Max. She watched as he walked toward her, stunned as usual by the lazy-hipped movement beneath the coat. His hair was wet, his eyes were bright and damn it, he looked…perfect. Like those Montreal guys she remembered from orchestral summer programs, the ones who looked as if winter wouldn't dare make them cold. "Hey," she said. Except it was awkward. What else should she do? Hug him? Take his hand? Smile?

Argh. Damn it.

She did none of those things, opting to deal with the fact she'd forgotten her winter-warm gloves by shoving her hands in her pockets.

He broke through her thoughts with a smile that nearly knocked her over "*Allô*…hello," he replied, making an adorable effort to pronounce the h.

She grinned, 'cause how could she not, then shrugged. "How are you doing? You must be exhausted."

"I should be asking about you," he replied, concern in his eyes. He reached out to take one of the bags she was carrying.

"Nah," she said, putting her hand on top of his. "It's okay."

"Are you sure?"

Seriously?

Apparently he was, but the two bags she carried were light. "It's fine," she said. "Besides." She pointed toward the bag that contained her violin. "Precious."

He nodded, and there was the smile again. "I see."

"So where are you headed?"

"I have a few errands before tonight," he answered.

Tonight. The party her brother was throwing for the team, his friends, and invited guests. At his townhouse in Brooklyn. She and Max were clearly both going. She nodded, then pointed toward the subway. "Which way you headed?"

"Uptown," he replied.

There was a slightly confused tone in his voice, like he knew generally he was going, but not more than that. She had to ask. It was her duty as someone who'd lived in New York longer to make sure he was going to be able to get where he needed to go. It wasn't like it mattered or anything. He could always tell her no. "Where uptown?"

"It's this…pâtisserie. It's not a bakery…not the same thing. It's… French and famous. I think it's on…Sixty-Eighth?"

There was only one famous French bakery on Sixty-Eighth Street.

It was one of two New York outposts of a Parisian staple. It was all she could do not to grin back at him. "My place isn't far from there, actually."

"Have you been there? Do you know what I'm talking about?"

"You mean that place that's famous for its macarons? "

He blinked, confusion in his eyes. "Eh…that and a few other things, but yes."

"I've heard about it," she answered, "but I haven't been there yet."

It wasn't like she was angling for an invitation; he'd asked her a question and she'd answered.

"Would you like to?" he asked, uncertainty in his voice. "That is to say…would you like to come with me?"

Yes. Of course. Absolutely.

And yet she wondered if he'd asked out of obligation or because he wanted her there. "Sure," she finally said, still chewing over the matter in her head.

But all of a sudden, he looked confused, almost hurt, and she couldn't help but wonder why.

"I mean it," he said. "I would like you to come with me."

And if that wasn't the perfect invitation…

"OK," she said. "Just remember you need to speak English."

She loved the sound of his laugh.

"You drive a hard bargain," he informed her. "But OK."

Then he took her hand, and led her toward the subway.

Max

Subway rides usually took Max's focus. He couldn't just stand or sit like every other person on the train. He had to shield himself from their emotions, focus, but not too hard so he wouldn't miss his stop.

He'd done *that* a few times already.

But today was different. Riding with Kayleigh helped him relax. She was comfort, ease, and a very welcome surprise. And to have run into her without actually planning? Even more special.

Luckily, there were seats on the subway. He stood in front of her, doing his best to guard the violin she had on her lap.

"Thanks," she said, smiling. "It's not necessary though."

He shook his head. "You were...worried about the," he gestured toward the case. "It's *nécessaire*...you know?"

Thankfully she did understand. And grinned up at him until the subway came to a stop.

"We're here," she said.

He nodded, glad at least one of them was paying attention. "*Bon.*" He tried to use his body to make a path for her, but the subway riders made their own way.

"It's fine," she said, grinning, taking his hand in her own and practically dragging him off the subway and toward the stairs. "I think it's this one."

She sounded sure, but his *percée* said she wasn't. "Hmm."

"It's not far from my place," she answered, "but it's not the same exit."

He nodded, then relaxed as he followed her up the stairs and out into the sunlight.

"So why this place, out of all the French...pâtisseries in New York?"

He had to focus in order to force himself to speak English. It was as if she'd deliberately opened the door to the possibility of switching languages, but he needed to slam it shut, then lock it, otherwise he'd never learn. He'd promised her he'd speak English and, damn it, that was what he was going to do. Even if he couldn't remember the words he wanted to use.

"*Ma mère*…my mother, she's…Parisian. And she asked me one thing, you know, when I came up to the Empires? She knew I would focus on my hockey, and she knew Alain would make sure I didn't get into trouble in the Village, but she wanted me to…explore the city and find this place for her. So, my…taste for this place is her fault."

She nodded, and he could feel the concern as the silence stretched out. "So what do you think of this place? I mean…people talk about it all the time, and I want to know your opinion."

"It's…they…they're *agréable*?"

"They're nice, hm?"

He nodded, tested the word on his tongue. "Nice. Right."

She smiled at him, and he'd been around her enough that he could tell an explanation was coming.

"So the relationship between *agréable* and agreeable? They're called…a…false friend," she began not letting him down. "At least…" She paused, looking up at the sky for a few minutes as presumably she thought about something.

He watched her but tried not to focus too closely on her, because otherwise he'd miss her words.

"At least that's what I learned it as when I was younger. There might be a more sophisticated term for it. It means words that sound the same but mean different things in different languages"

Ah.

"OK," he confirmed, smiling. "So…let's go in and have some good French pastry?"

Her smile was the best he'd ever seen. "I'd like that."

Kayleigh

Max opened the door, and suddenly Kayleigh found herself in the middle of a huge crowd. A metric crapton of people were stuck close together, barely able to move.

"My god, apparently half the City of New York is here," she muttered.

He laughed. "More than nice, hm?"

She nodded, but Max was clearly focused on something or someone else. She watched as he looked behind the counter and inspected the people waiting in front of it, as if he were looking for someone. "Wow..."

He nodded. "Once I'd found it, I discovered people...who are not related but..." He paused, and she could see him search for words, this time as if he were looking into a little mental dictionary. "People who know the family know, well..." He blushed, and, god, it was cute.

"*Sept de chance!*"

Suddenly, a pathway to the counter of the brightly colored shop opened as if by magic, and Max made his way through while having a very easy and familiar conversation in pure Parisian French with someone who looked like he was in charge.

Kayleigh understood enough to figure out what was being said, basically eavesdropping as the two discussed how many macarons to get for...how many well fed people? And for how much money? Apparently not much as the guy in charge didn't even let Max pay half of it.

"*Quand tu gagnes un médaille d'Or pour Les Bleus, mon ami,*" the well-dressed older gentleman said, "*ou un championnat avec les autres, tu vas l'amène ici,* OK?"

They wanted him to win a gold medal, hm?

Max thanked the gentleman, taking the bags he was offered, but also not commenting on the gold medal requests. Which was interesting. But not as interesting as the force of his grin, or how quickly he returned to her side, and the way he ushered her out of the store.

She didn't say anything about what she'd seen until they'd gone outside, where the wind was still blowing and the chill sucking her dry. "So what was that?"

Max turned toward, her, leaned in and whispered. "A one man recruiting *comité* for the French Olympic team. He thinks I should... not try for Canada and go to play for France instead."

She blinked and stared at him before leaning in. "France has a men's ice hockey team? And you had that conversation in the middle of that huge crowd of people?"

He nodded. "Nobody...not so big deal about ice hockey in France, so...there...nobody expects, you know?"

She did, which didn't phase her. To most people, France was many things; the Eiffel tower, the museums, the shopping, the food, the wine. Maybe soccer. Not ice hockey. "Yeah." She smiled at him. "Does that happen often?"

He laughed. "The *comité* thinks they have a chance in...getting me to play. You know, the...grass is easier competition."

The look on his face was so adorably confused that she didn't correct him. "I think I get it," she said. And then she took a deep breath. "Thanks for letting me come with you."

This time, his smile was slow. "So can I walk you...home?"

"Yes," she replied. "You can."

They walked out of the pastry shop, her carrying her tote and her violin, him carrying the pastry box and a small bag that bore the name of the shop. It was a short distance between the shop and her apartment, and for once she wanted it to be longer. She was enjoying herself.

So much so that she decided to be a little bold. "So," she said, "what do you have to do before the party?"

"My…uncle needs me to help out."

The disappointment was probably clear in her face, because he leaned in toward her.

"I think he was lying about having a college kid to assist," he whispered, "and was doing it himself for some reason. So I do it, you know? Keeps me…busy? Humble. So many stories of people who play…they lose their shot because they end up partying. I sweep instead."

A small facet of his nature slowly revealed itself. He was a professional hockey player. By all rights, he should be spending the time he wasn't playing or practicing doing other things. She admired him more because used those open moments in his schedule to help his uncle. "Aaaah. I see…"

And yet the more she understood him, the more she understood why he was doing what he did, the less she wanted to leave him. Which meant she asked a question that made her sound desperate. "So no audience required?"

He shook his head, and she could see the disappointment in his eyes. "It's…I…" He sighed. "It will be…a mess," he assured her. "So…no."

"So I'll see you there?"

"Are we…here?"

She nodded. "Yeah."

"Oh."

He was obviously upset; she could see it in his eyes. "Yeah," she confirmed, gesturing toward the small building she lived in. "This is me."

"So…"

"You could come up?"

He shook his head. "I have to go…downtown to the shop."

"To sweep."

He nodded. And maybe the disappointment in his expression echoed her own? Why? What the hell…

This had happened to her too many times; there had been too many situations where feelings weren't expressed, and one person's friendship was another's heartbreak. But she had to ask. She had to know what was going on between them. Because then she'd know how to act around him. Maybe.

"So what is this?"

The words came out of her mouth before she could even begin to think about what she said.

He sighed, squeezed her hand and looked up at her. "I don't know," he answered. *"En vrai*…it really seems like…we are more than just getting along. But I…"

She sighed. Again. "Fine. Yeah. Whatever."

He shook his head as she let his hand go, then stepped toward her and pulled her close. "I was not clear."

She felt his breath on her cheek. She waited, saw the intensity in his eyes, like he was trying to decide what to do.

Kiss me or let me go already, will you?

And suddenly he did. She couldn't think. Hell, she didn't want to; she just wanted to feel. And, oh wow, did she feel. His hands, his lips, his tongue it…just was and…wow.

And when she pulled back, she felt a little better about herself, about life in general, and maybe love.

CHAPTER NINE

Max

Thankfully Alain had understood enough about the forgotten mandatory team gathering, with a little help from the email, to let him leave the shop after a 'cursory' sweep of the shop floor. Alain was also understanding enough that he let him put together a huge takeout container of poutine to bring to the party. He cradled it and the bag with the macarons as he got on the subway, headed downtown toward Brooklyn.

Finding his teammate's townhouse wasn't a problem. Dealing with the large amount of emotion that assaulted him when he walked inside was. He almost physically recoiled, something he hadn't done in a long time. But he didn't.

"You didn't have to do that," Chris told him as he took the bags. "They're going to be amazing, but you didn't have to."

He shrugged. "I couldn't see myself coming to visit, you know, without anything.

"It's a pleasure, rook. Really. Especially if the need to bring

201

something made you do what I think it did."

He blinked, confused. "Hm?"

His teammate sighed, pointed to the bag he'd picked up with Kayleigh. "My girlfriend will swallow those down in two seconds flat. From Paris. Damn, Lucky Seven."

Relief. "Then," he managed, "I leave these in your competent hands, *chef*."

"Excellent." Emerson nodded, then clapped him on the shoulder. "Beer is here, soda, everything. I think there's a good Quebec beer in the fridge. Upstairs there's both a dance floor and a video game tournament, chill rooms all over the house. Have fun, hm?"

Max popped into the living room, chatted with some people, then headed upstairs. He couldn't deny he was looking for Kayleigh, but he wasn't admitting it either. But he headed upstairs anyway, passing the room where he'd heard sounds from a video game, only to hear the driving beat of a recent pop song by a female singer about a clandestine rendezvous between two people who were hiding their relationship. He followed the music down the hall, where he saw a closed door.

As he opened the door, he could see that he'd found the room where they'd set up the dance floor. There were tons of people there, but he could see Kayleigh in the thick of it. She was gorgeous, bright, dancing to the beat with Melanie, his captain's girlfriend. He wanted to join them, but if he were being honest with himself, he'd admit that he wanted to dance with Kayleigh; watching her from the sidelines wasn't enough.

But dancing with her, on the dance floor her brother had set up in what was obviously Melanie's office, was a horrible idea, slightly worse than the bottle of beer he held in his hands. Mixing too much alcohol with his *percée* was something he never wanted to experience again, having done it once. And yet.

He couldn't stop watching her. He'd blame it on the song, but he knew that would be a lie. They weren't the couple in the song; his hair wasn't slicked back, he hadn't been dumb enough to wear a white tee shirt to a crazy party; she wasn't wearing red lipstick or a skirt. But she was Kayleigh, and that mattered.

He sighed, feeling the confused vibes from the people on the dance floor, knowing full well it *was* scary and weird he was just standing there, watching. So he took one sip from his beer bottle, making sure he labeled it, and put it down before making his way onto the dance floor. He followed the music, dancing along toward her.

"C'mon, rookie," said one of the other people on the floor, a woman he remotely recognized from some music video. "Dance with me."

But there was Kayleigh's hand. "If he's dancing with someone," she said grinning, "it's my responsibility as the sister of the host to make sure he's enjoying himself. And I take my responsibilities seriously."

He laughed, but let her pull him close. "Responsibility, mm?"

"Yep. I have a thing for sixties glam and confused francophones."

"Confused?"

"You are, aren't you?"

He shook his head, and danced with her, falling into the music, letting her sing into his ear. This was perfect.

Kayleigh

Kayleigh was dancing with Max, off to the side of the improvised dance floor. She hadn't believed the set up would work, but her opinion of had changed dramatically once she'd started to take advantage of it.

She was still dancing when the song changed; the driving beat of the fun pop song had ended and given way to something else. Slow, fun, with a very laid back singer. She squealed when she recognized what it was.

"*Hein?*"

She reached up to put her arm on Max's black T-shirt-covered shoulder. "I love this song," she told him. It was a country song, bright, fun, about a late-night drive the singer wanted to take with the object of his affections. "Dance with me?"

"Thought I was," he said, confused. "I mean."

"Yeah. You are," she grinned. She shook her jean-clad hips to the song. "But still…"

He nodded. Understanding. This was dangerous.

"One more trip ar0und the moon?" she sang along with the song.

And he nodded. Because she knew as well as he did that they were playing with fire; if Chris had an inkling of what was going on between them, he'd be pissed, and that was the last thing she wanted. So she stole a few more moments, and let him go when the song ended.

"See you later?" she said.

He nodded, smiling. "Off to the video game…to see how crazy it goes."

She raised an eyebrow. "You don't play? Apparently it's good for reflexes."

"I sweep instead," he said, his eyes twinkling. "I'm a much better… cheerer at video games, you know?"

She did. And then he left the room before they could continue talking, before they could spend another minute together. And instead of thinking about that, and what it could mean, Kayleigh threw herself into the next song. Thankfully, it was a happy pop song about a breakup gone well. Then she decided that she didn't want to stay at the party any longer. She was exhausted and not in the mood to drink, dance, or be around anything that would keep her from falling asleep.

She glanced down the hall, drawn by the happy sounds coming from Chris's game room; the tournament, thankfully had been a great idea. People were smiling, and she was so glad her brother and his girlfriend had figured out a solution to the problem of a comfortable party. But Max was there, and unlike him, she wasn't in the mood to watch people playing video games. She wanted to go home, and having made her decision, she headed downstairs.

Her brother was standing by the coat closet. "I'm heading out," she told him, smiling.

Chris nodded. "Late night. You have to be up, right?"

Kay nodded back. Rehearsal wasn't till late the next day, but if her brother was giving her an out, she'd gladly take it with the minimum of fuss. "Yep. I have early practice, so I need to get to bed."

"You taking the subway?" Chris asked.

It was late, and when push came to shove, she wasn't in the mood to deal with trying to remember which subway line was working and which one had decided to stop. "Gonna try and get a cab," she said. Especially considering in this part of Brooklyn, one called taxis on the telephone. So much more convenient than standing for hours on a street corner. "You guys have a number you use, right?"

Chris looked at her like she'd lost her mind. "Tonight you're going to try and get a cab. Really?"

"Yes," she replied. "I'm serious. More sense than trying to take the subway."

He rolled his eyes for some inexplicable reason, as if he'd already decided to implement a solution that made sense to him and nobody else. Then he took a breath and looked around at the group that had gathered near the coat closet. "Rook," he called.

There was only one rookie she knew on the team, one rookie who might be standing near the coat closet. "*Ouais*," that one rookie said as he joined them. "What can I do, *chef?*"

Awkward. Nerve-wracking and awkward. She wondered whether Chris was blind or willfully ignoring the way the room had started to crackle. Or maybe it was just her.

"You live in Manhattan, right? Above La Poutinerie"

Max nodded, and she could see tension in him. Damn it. "*Ouais, chef.* I do."

"Good. You need to escort my sister home. Right home. No funny business."

"*Ouais, chef,*" he replied as he settled in beside her. She watched as his hands flexed and fisted beside her, then focused on his heavy exhale as he shoved those hands into the pockets of his jeans.

"Kay. Eyes here," Chris said.

She still didn't like the expression on her brother's face.

"I'm not going to ask if you're OK with this, because it's happening. Now." He stepped toward her and put his arms around her. "Love you, little sis," he said.

And then he was gone, back to the rest of the party. Leaving her with Max. And she was nervous.

CHAPTER TEN

Max

He'd come down from the video game tournament in search of a snack, something to soak up some of the beer he'd drunk. He'd seen the food set up in the kitchen so he grabbed a plate.

Except as he was making his way over to the table they'd filled with food, he overheard the beginning of the conversation between Kayleigh and Chris. He tried to stay quiet as he grabbed a napkin.

"Rook?"

He had no choice but to put the plate and the napkin down, and follow his captain's instructions. He needed to take Kayleigh home and hide how it affected him. So he gave a basic answer, without feeling...

Elle etait nerveuse.

It was obvious and clear as anything he'd ever felt. Not surprising; he was nervous, too. Her brother had asked him to play the knight in shining armor, so he had to be chivalrous. Careful.

She bit her lip.

Tabernac.

He took a breath. "So," he said once her brother had gone back to the party. "I…I'm taking you home."

She grinned, and his heart jumped. But he was a knight, not a horny teenager. "Yeah."

She looked down, and there was a calmness radiating from her. "So…"

He put his coat on, made sure he had his MetroCard, his wallet, and his keys, and walked through the door. She followed him, clutching her bag between her arm and the puffy jacket she wore.

A smile. He took a breath, and took her free hand.

"You sure?" she asked. "I mean…"

He nodded; he got to spend extra time with her, even though he was trying to keep her safe.

Her squeeze of his hand broke his concentration, but regardless, they headed out onto the streets of Brooklyn. It was a beautiful winter night, and he let the silence envelop them as he tried to figure out which subway to go to. They were between two stations, and he wondered which would work better.

It felt good, comfortable…

And then concern, ice, just before he felt her hand slipping away.

"It's fine," she said, shoving her hands into her pockets. "Anyway."

It was not fine. Not fine at all. She was upset. And he didn't need *percée* to understand that. Didn't need to feel the hurt radiating off her to miss the tightness of her shoulders, the sudden speed of her walk through the streets of Brooklyn.

And then he realized what it was.

Merde.

She'd misinterpreted his attempt to be a gentleman and careful about his feelings in front of her brother as a feeling of obligation.

Yes. His captain had asked him to take her home, but it wasn't the only reason he was doing so. Then his concern about direction and safety must have looked like he didn't care. And she didn't have his *percée*. Which meant he had to tell her.

Which meant he had to catch up with her first. So he went after her. He followed her, fast.

"*Non.* Can…it's not…fine," he said as he walked alongside her. "I…*j'espere ça*…hope that this is better." And then he put his arm around her. Waited a beat, felt her happy surprise, then drew her closer. Then he kissed her cheek. "This? Very much better."

Kayleigh

"Yeah."

That was what she said, the almost word that came out of her mouth as he kissed her cheek. The one that maybe possibly covered up the fact that her traitorous heart had started to slam against her chest. Damn it.

In the middle of a cold, November night, it was easier for her to remember the reasons why genuinely acting on whatever was happening between them was a bad idea. He was a hockey player, a twenty year-old rookie, and a guy she was supposed to be tutoring. Not an object for her lust. Or any other four-letter words that began with l. Despite the kiss they'd shared earlier that afternoon, and anything else that may have happened between them.

But as his fingers trailed down her cheekbones, a grin molded his lips. And her once strong resolve melted in the face of a fire that blazed all the way down to her toes.

"*Bon.*"

A sip of ice water in that simple word. "English," she teased, grinning back at him.

He blinked, as if he'd forgotten what language he was speaking, then shook his head. "Sorry, I forgot," he answered, a rasp in his voice, but no sign of repentance in his eyes. "Am I able to...get extra credit?"

She giggled. Couldn't help herself. Because suddenly, halfway to the subway, she was thirteen years old, awkward and giggling at a guy with cute dimples and an even cuter accent. "You need to," she said as she reached into her pocket. "A great deal."

He nodded as they reached the subway entrance, and then looked back at her. But not...at her.

She turned, confused, only to see the fluorescently green taxi that was parked only two steps away from where they stood.

"Would you like to?" he asked.

It took her only a second to connect the dots in her head. "You sure?" she asked.

He grinned back at her, and dear god, that grin was going to kill her. "Would you rather take me on the subway?"

Once again she giggled, but this time, there was confusion in his eyes.

"I...am not sure what is funny," he managed. He was hesitant, slow but questioning. "Is there a...level of that word I might miss?"

Idiot. Of course he's not going to figure this out. He barely understands English, much less North American slang.

"Take me," she replied after taking a breath. "It also means... well..."

She trailed off, and once again she felt like that...well not thirteen years old. She'd aged up to eighteen. And she was entirely unable to explain, much less think about, the sexual connotation of otherwise innocent words.

But in that instant, Max's expression went from confused to bright and gorgeous. "Your lack of words tells me all," he said. "I think we do need that taxi, yes?"

She shook her head. "No."

Then she took his hand, and began to jog through the streets, doing her best to lead him toward the station that gave her better access to the subway she wanted them to take. "This way?"

He stopped, laughing, throwing his head back. "This is…"

"Fun, Max," she replied, grinning. "This is fun."

Max

This subway ride was…easier and harder. The car was empty enough for them both to get seats, and this time he sat next to her, bumping up against her hip and thigh with his own. He focused on her, on this express train that stopped near where he needed to go. The train sped through the night, and he couldn't breathe.

Expectation, nerves, and heat in her eyes. She looked back at him, then sighed. And kissed him.

Tabernac.

There was nobody else but her. The way she felt, the way her hands held his face, her hair in his hands, the way she felt against him, the…

She pulled back, surprise in her eyes. "Holy shit."

He didn't need his *percée* to understand what she'd said, even though she was speaking too fast for him to understand.

Fear. Surprise.

He reached an arm around her shoulder, pulled her close, and let her rest her head on his shoulder. "*Ouais,*" he said, forgetting what language he was speaking and not caring. "But…it doesn't have to be a mess."

She lifted her head from his shoulder, staring up at him. "What?"

"I'm...not going anywhere," he answered. "You don't have to worry about that. Whatever we do, we'll do, I promise you, I'm not walking away...unless that is what you would like."

She shook her head. "No." And then she blushed. "This is your stop."

"Would you like to come up?"

"I'm exhausted."

He let her hands go for a moment, held up his own, palms facing her. "No strings. You are tired. I...have a couch."

"I..."

"Would you like me to take you home? Make sure you get home safely?"

She paused, stared at him again. Confusion, exhaustion, and... surrender.

"Yes. I'll take your couch."

As the train pulled into the station, he smiled, took her hands again, helped her up from her seat, and let her lean on him as they got off the subway.

"*Viens, bébé*," he whispered. "Come on."

She leaned against him, let him lead her up the stairs and along the streets. She didn't ask how far to go, just...went.

"*Pas loin*," he whispered. "Not far from here, OK?"

"OK."

And quietly, as if he held the world in his hands, he took her to his apartment. Lord knew how he got her upstairs and onto the couch. A cup of tea later, he'd covered her with a blanket and left her to sleep. He wasn't sure if he was going to sleep. But he was tired enough that he had to try.

Kayleigh

It was the swearing that woke her up. Word after word in perfect Parisian French, followed by a list of phrases that would burn the ears off of any speaker of Quebec French worth their salt. Or *sel* as the case may be. She rubbed her eyes and looked around. She didn't recognize where she was, but the barrage of French was a dead giveaway that the couch she'd passed out was Max's.

She reached out and rubbed her eyes, careful not to roll over...and off the couch. It was comfortable; she'd give him that. And so much else. Because she started to smell coffee.

"Is that coffee I smell?"

"One of my mother's favorite phrases is '*Rien d'importance avant le café,*'" he said, his voice emanating from around the corner.

She got off the couch and headed toward the sound of his voice to find him in a baggy T-shirt and sweat pants, standing in the middle of a small, efficient galley style kitchen. "Oh, *merci a dieu,*" she said, grinning back at him. "Thank you to the coffee gods of the world."

He laughed. "I'm not like my mother, but I like the day better after I have coffee, or espresso or...something, you know?"

She did, and she nodded as she watched him work the espresso maker, her focus briefly shifting to the two tiny cups sitting to the left.

"Are you...do you need something special for breakfast?" he asked.

She shook her head. "No. Lucky for me, I'm not allergic to things I eat. Which is a very good thing. I try to eat healthy most of the time, but you know, I'm not perfect." At which point she stared at the box on the table. "What...what is that?"

He shrugged, and she could see the blush in his cheeks. "Once a week, a day I don't have a heavy schedule, I...well," he stared helplessly at the bag of pastry she remembered him carrying along with the macarons.

And the guilt was written all over his face. Was he expecting her to judge him for his pastry habit? Of anybody, she was probably the least likely. So she grinned back at him and shook her head. "It's fine, I'm not judging. In fact, I'm going to partake in your Sunday breakfast indulgence." She walked toward the table, and opened the bag. She could barely think on confronting the marvels of French chocolate and pastry that sat in front of her. "Oh, my god."

He put down the two cups of espresso before shrugging again and gesturing broadly toward the table and the box. "*Viens*," he said.

"Coffee and chocolate for breakfast?" she quipped. "I am not going to ask twice." She sat down at the table, and took a swallow of her espresso. "Oh my god this is beautiful."

"Sometimes you need it, no?"

She laughed. "Always, I think. I don't think I've ever said no to a cup of caffeinated something."

"*En vrai*?" he asked as he put napkins in front of them. "I mean… really?"

She nodded. "Caffeine's always been a…mental thing for me. Like, it works when I want it to. So I drink a lot of it. But I like it the best in the morning."

"Not me," he confessed. "I like it…but it…works when I do not want it to." He shook his head. "And chocolate? What are you feelings on that?"

"I'm not eating enough?" she ventured. "The fact that I haven't started eating one of the gorgeous things in the bag right there is a huge testament of my strength of will."

"Which," he said, "is entirely not necessary. So…go ahead and take something."

She grinned back at him. "If that's the case, than I will." And without waiting, she reached into the bag and pulled out the most gorgeous pastry she'd ever seen. Chocolate dust came off on her fingertips, and the flaky pastry crunched under her touch, it was so soft. If the rest of the pastries in that bag were like this one? She was going to die a happy woman.

Max

She was adorable. Covering her face with chocolate at his breakfast table. Drinking the espresso that he'd managed to make despite the machine's best intentions. And, *mon dieu*, she was comfortable. She was relaxed.

"Do you have…plans?"

She sighed, sat back in her chair, and he watched her pull back. Just a little. "I have to go soon, actually." A small sigh as she stared at the clock. "Laundry and a few other things before rehearsal tonight. You?"

"It's an off day, so I'm helping at the shop before heading to skate a little."

She nodded, sighed. "So…"

But she made no move to leave, which pleased him greatly. Except he knew this idyll with her wouldn't last. Because within five minutes, his grandfather, or some other member of his family, would call. Or Alain would be knocking on his door, wondering why he hadn't come down to help him with the shop.

"So," he added, his contribution to the conversation as intelligent as he'd expect.

But she didn't seem to have words either, which didn't make him feel better. Instead, they sat in silence fueled by the understanding that their time would be over soon.

Kayleigh

It took her longer than usual to get herself together and leave despite the fact that she didn't have very much to organize. Just herself, her coat, her purse, and the door. That was it. Yet it was damn difficult.

She could see he knew it too. It wasn't so much that he wasn't trying to make her stay; he knew she needed to go. He needed to go too. And yet...

"This is hard," she said, surrendering once again to the pull of that hard kitchen chair. "I mean, leaving."

He stared at her, and those eyes of his seared through her. Dear god, he was killing her.

"Would this help?"

And out of nowhere he stood. She followed, and watched as he walked toward her. Left, right, moving his hips, lazy and gorgeous. Purposeful.

Because she knew what he was going to do. He kissed her. Hard, seriously, full of everything he had. Walked back, still kissing her, not letting her go, and she sank into it, to him.

Still walking toward that door, still kissing her. He put his hands through her hair and pushed her back against the door. Metal, wood, she couldn't tell through the heavy coat she'd managed to put on. But his lips, soft, hard, punishing and just...

When she pulled back, she knew she had to go. Because otherwise, she'd never leave. And that would be trouble.

From : Max_SL7@empiremail.com
To: K_emerson@nyharm.com
Silly question...

From: K_emerson@nyharm.com
To: Max_SL7@empiremail.com
Very few questions are silly, but I'll answer whatever you're asking me.

From: Max_SL7@empiremail.com
To: K_emerson@nyharm.com
What's your address?

CHAPTER ELEVEN
The Bronx
Event: Family Skate at Yankee Stadium

Max

It was much easier to send Kayleigh an email than talk to her on the phone. He just liked that the emails forced him to use his English in a way he would otherwise avoid, and think about what he had to write before he did so.

Those emails became almost a diary; even when he was only separated from Kayleigh by a busy schedule, he'd email her. He told her about the crazy party he attended, where he had to steal his defense partner's phone and help make coffee for most of the rest of his single (drunken) teammates. He told her about how much fun he'd had with the kids from the special Olympics, how great it was to see the smiles on their faces, and how much he wished she'd been there that evening when the entire team was wearing tuxedos.

What he didn't talk about was the impending arrival of his grandfather, as well as both of his parents, who had been divorced for more than half of his life. At the same time.

It had started as a special gathering for new years and the Winter

Classic the next day before it extended. His father arrived first, scaring him by wanting to spend time together, maybe Christmas as well as New Years? Then his mother, who decided that he had no business spending Christmas alone with his father, said she would arrive earlier to prepare his tiny shoebox apartment when he had practice. And then, because that's how he worked, his grandfather decided that he would join them all so that none of them were alone for any reason.

He didn't want to talk about it, didn't want to think about it, especially since they all would be in town in time to see this evening's game. His grandfather and Alain would get both of Max's parents to the game. He would see them after.

But now? Now was the family skate in the Bronx, and if he was smart enough, he would be able to spend some time with Kayleigh and not just email her.

Kayleigh

After delays and planes and university hang-ups, her parents were supposed to arrive late that night, if not early the next day. They'd be just in time to light the last two Chanukah candles with Melanie and her family and experience a Christmas in New York. Unfortunately, that meant that she came to the family skate in the Bronx with the same family she'd gone to the family skate in Manhattan with: her brothers. And they were driving her crazy.

Not to say that she didn't love them. And as if that weren't enough, over the weeks and months they'd been spending together, Kay was glad to watch a bond develop between the reunited siblings that hadn't really been there before. Possibly because of distance, but more likely because Brooklyn, and Bryce's new resolve to stick to the treatment plan he'd been given, agreed with the eldest Emerson sibling.

"Come *on*, Kay!" Bryce bellowed, his long fingers beckoning her toward them as if she were breaking some cardinal rule by taking in the famous ballpark by herself. "Skate with your dear brothers."

"And risk being knocked on my arse?" She laughed. "No chance!"

"Come on, Kay," Mel shouted. "They'll drive you mad if you don't!"

Which, she admitted to herself, was absolutely, one hundred percent, true. Even if it was only Mel they were going to drive crazy. Being a good sister, she pushed off from the wall, skating toward where they stood at where center field would be. But in true Emerson fashion, her brothers lifted her up…

And began to spin her around. Her view got faster and faster, the famous ballpark passing quickly. "Damn it!" she shouted as she smacked one of the two culprits, probably both of them…most of them.

"Put me *down*, you buffoons! I was bloody freakin' right not to let you two…"

But when they did put her down, she was so dizzy that she could barely see straight. "Whoa…"

"Don't move…*arrêt* hmm?"

Max's voice hit her ear, as smooth as the French chocolate he'd sent her from a store he'd found when he was playing the Typhoons down in North Carolina.

"If I said you saved me again," she managed, "it would be…"

"Routine," he replied, grinning. "Now you tell me when, OK?"

And without him having to explain, she understood that he'd let her go when she felt she could stand on her own two feet.

"Breathe, OK?"

Which somehow she had managed not to do until he'd reminded her. OK, then. In. Out. Breathe.

And yeah, she realized as she found herself getting less reliant and more comfortable against his shoulder, this would be interesting. But she couldn't resist him. Especially when he was being sweet. Lord help her.

But there wasn't any help in sight. In fact, it was getting harder and harder to let him go, to leave the safety of his arms, and move away from the bright beacon of his lips. Even though somewhere in the back of her mind, she knew her brother would be pissed, not only because he was protective but also because Max was a teammate. But whether it was because he and Bryce were acting like assholes, or she was inspired by the winter breeze or the happy families skating across the ice on Yankee Stadium, she gave into the moment and kissed him. It was gorgeous, strong and beautiful.

But when she felt him pulling away, she let him. And the regret in his eyes was palpable. "Later," he whispered in her ear.

Then and only then, she smiled.

Event: Evening Game vs the Apples at
Brooklyn Banking Center

Max

Max knew there would be repercussions for that kiss. He'd managed to keep his relationship with Kayleigh quiet up until that point, though how, he'd had no idea.

There hadn't been a reaction from Chris after practice, not even during the quick bus ride back to Brooklyn from the Bronx. So even as he sat down in front of his locker, he shoved thoughts of brotherly vengeance aside in favor of visualizing his defense-based warm-up as he laced his skates.

"I saw what happened at the family skate."

Captain. Emerson. The voice sounded angry. And close. Max finished lacing his right skate, looked up at his Captain's expression and saw granite.

"You need to stay away from my sister. I don't give two shits that you're helping her or she's helping you. This helping shit needs to stop. I told you to stay away from her. You're too young and too fucking immature to give her what she deserves."

His *percée* was useful for once in his life. Emerson talked about his sister, but at the core of his captain's anger was betrayal. To Emerson, Max had betrayed some confidence. That was easier to deal with because he could understand where that came from. And for the first time, it didn't bother him. So he stood. But that was it.

"You're not saying anything. Open your fucking mouth and goddamn promise me you're not going to touch her again."

The captain waited a half second before continuing toward him. As if the captain had become an arrow, heading toward its target. And still, Max said nothing. There was nothing he could say that would stop this. Not then at least.

Faster, closer. He stood his ground, and then he ducked, pivoted and lightly grabbed Emerson's arms midpunch. "You don't need this," he whispered. Clear, soft and sure. "Not now. Not *avant…*"

Except of course it didn't matter because there was an elbow. It was hard, slamming into the center of his chest. He lost his breath, but caught himself right before he hit the ground.

The look on Emerson's face was beyond angry. *Merde.*

He didn't want to punch the captain. He had no desire to punch Chris in the face or anywhere else. Didn't want to punch Kayleigh's brother in the face.

But as the rest of the team came into the locker room, Jahr and

Karpov grabbed the captain to hold him back, while Smythe and a few others grabbed Max. Evans, for his part, came in and shook his head at them all.

"Can't we all just get along?" Evans wondered aloud, even as his hands were ready to push people further apart.

That made Max laugh. Then the rest of the team, now that the tension was finally broken, followed suit.

Kayleigh

Kayleigh found herself at the evening's game instead of the rehearsal. She felt horribly guilty, but the Philharmonia and the team had decided that her presence was more important at the game. So there she was, sitting in the stands at the BBC. As the third period started, she sipped on her soda and settled in to watch the action. The game itself was going pretty well; the team was leading after two periods, and nobody had made any stupid mistakes that resulted in unwarranted penalties.

She was sitting next to Mel on one side and some random person on the other. Mel made nervous noises every five minutes, and the woman on the other side had freaked out when Kayleigh had celebrated the Empires' last goal.

"Hockey's in my blood," she'd said unapologetically. "My brother's out there."

"As is your boyfriend."

Mel's whispered comment didn't require an answer; she wasn't going to let her brother's girlfriend and her interest in romantic relationships mess up her hockey watching mojo. Max was important, yes; she spent time with him, but he wasn't her boyfriend. And yes, he also kissed well.

"I've been watching my brother play in various places and guises for years when I could," she continued, ignoring Mel. "School, Uni," she shrugged. "It's always been fun."

But there was something in the air. And she wasn't sure what it was; were things too perfect? No injuries, no horrible penalties, nothing out of the ordinary.

"You okay?" she asked Mel.

"Fine. Enjoying the game when they're not acting like idiots…"

She'd ask Bryce, but Bryce was waiting at his apartment for their parents. And the last thing she wanted to do was to stress Bryce out with a phone call that asked about "things in the air." So instead, she sat back, settled in, and focused on the game.

Max

Third periods were always exciting, especially when the team was doing well. The ice felt good under his skates, and the home team was playing dumb, five minutes in. They'd just forced their top line to send the puck clear out of their offensive zone. Intent on nullifying an icing call, he skated after it, catching it on his stick before it went over the line. He skated it around the back of the net before making an outlet pass toward Smythe. It landed on his stick. He felt Smythe's relief and went back to position, watching the play as it developed. Smythe handed the puck over to Karpov before heading off to the bench for a change.

Max focused, tight, closely.

All of a sudden, he felt the shoulder, the elbow, and then the shove to the wall. He elbowed back but the push was too strong coming on the other way. There was a loud noise, and then there was nothing.

CHAPTER TWELVE

Kayleigh

Her breath stopped suddenly and completely as Max hit the ice. He didn't move. He wasn't moving. "Oh, god."

She didn't even know she'd stood, but she was standing and now she had to go…somewhere. Somewhere she could get to someone who would let her see where he was going. She had to. She absolutely had to.

Melanie, who was sitting next to her, took her hand. "It's fine…. really."

She shook her head, took a deep breath and headed out of the closest exit, toward the elevator, her heart in her throat. One of the guards downstairs took pity on her, leading her toward the player's entrance.

"You're family," the guard said. "We know who you are."

She could barely speak as she saw the stretcher, followed by three people who were speaking in rapid French. She could hear Paris in the woman's voice; she had to be his mother, and the man in Timberlands and a coat had to be his father. The grandfather stood to the right of the woman, half separating her from the father who constantly tried to stand by her.

She found herself trying to breathe, to force herself to do something that was slightly productive. Except all she could manage was one word. "Max…"

"We don't speak French," the paramedic said. "Who the hell can speak French here?"

Kayleigh raised her hand. "I do."

"Good." He pointed at Max's mother. "You tell her she and you can come with us. And put," he pointed to Max's father and grandfather, "these two in the taxi. Tell them we're going to Maimonides and we're off."

After following the instructions the paramedic gave her, she got into the ambulance and held her breath.

Somehow, after the harrowing ride in the ambulance, pulling up to the hospital only to discover that there were no French translators on staff was not surprising. A very helpful nurse explained they had a phone system, but the concept didn't erase the look of panic that remained on Max's father's face.

Also unsurprising was the fact that Max's mother didn't panic; the Frenchwoman seemed almost impenetrable. Ice and calm except for her hands. They shook despite the fact that his grandfather didn't stop massaging her shoulders.

Damn it.

Kayleigh wanted to snarl, but she didn't. And so she put up a nonthreatening finger. "I'll be back," she said in French.

Fast feet took her to the waiting room just outside. Past the bathroom that smelled like the cleanser they used, the tile floor that clicked against her shoes. Finally she fell against the simple chair near a window that had a view of the east river and pulled out her phone. She had three messages, the impudent device proclaimed. One of them had to be from her brother's girlfriend. She called her immediately.

"Kayleigh omigod…"

"Melanie? I need Emily's number. I'm at the hospital, and they don't have a direct human translator. I can speak French but not well enough. She has to have the name of the person they were going to get for Max."

There was a pause, and she heard the kind of rustling that usually meant the phone was being moved from one hand to another.

"Kayleigh? It's Emily. How can I help?"

"Do you have the name of or access to that translator? The one that they were going to get for Max?"

"Yes. I can call the one they'd had in mind for him. What did you tell my sister?"

"I told her that the hospital didn't have a direct French translator available and we need one. Now."

"Why the hell don't they have…"

"Because they have a telephone system, and the only live actual translators that will come into the rooms for patients are Spanish-speaking ones. And Max's parents and his grandfather are freaking out. And I can speak French well, just not the kind of French they're going to need to be calm."

"All right," Emily said. "I'll call her and tell her it's an emergency."

"Thanks Emily. Really."

Kayleigh hung up the phone and took a deep breath.

After finishing the conversation, Kayleigh headed downstairs to the main entrance to wait for the translator.

And leaving the floor, that room, for that long, hurt. She had no idea what was going on in Max's room, no clue what his parents were doing. More importantly, no clue what this person looked like. Every time she heard the sound of clicking heels against the tile floor, she looked up, hoping to see someone, but whoever had made those footsteps usually walked right past her, purpose or concern in their expression.

She took a deep breath and began to pace, trying to focus on something…anything other than the fact she was terrified of losing Max.

"I'm looking for Kayleigh Emerson?"

She nodded "Here," she said. "That's me."

"You need a translator?"

She swallowed. She had to say it. "My boyfriend's family is upstairs. They do not speak a word of English, barely at least, and the doctors have a phone system which doesn't work well enough, and the only hospital translators translate…"

The translator sighed. "Yep. Happens all the time. What language?"

"If you can, you need to switch between Parisian French and Quebec French…or some kind of something that fits them both in some way…"

"You know they're not the same, right?"

Kayleigh sighed. She wasn't an idiot, but she didn't have time for shenanigans. "Yes. I know. But his mother is Parisian and his father is a Quebecker. So you need to figure out what you can do to communicate to them both so that they both understand."

The translator nodded. "Take me to them."

She had to wait out in the hallway as the woman spoke to Max, his parents and his grandfather. She didn't have any official family status, and so this…well…

She paced the hallway outside of the room, holding her breath, trying not to lose her mind. He wasn't her boyfriend. Not really. He kissed well, and he had a nice smile…

And she was going to lose her mind.

Breathe. In. Out, as the clock ticked, the minutes passing by. People coming in and out of the room. Finally, the door opened. "He's going to be OK," said the translator, smiling.

"When can I see him?"

"That depends on his family."

"*Tu peux venir*," said an older gentleman with a smile that was achingly familiar.

"*Merci*," she answered, her voice tenuous but as pleasant as she could make it.

Without a thought, it seemed, his grandfather put his arm around her. "*Tiens, petit*," he said, his Parisian accent clear. "It will be OK."

And at that moment, she believed him.

CHAPTER THIRTEEN

Max

The light was harsh when he opened his eyes. The beds were soft. People were holding his hands. He blinked again. And nothing. Just people.

His heart pounded against his chest. No feelings, no nothing, no nerves. Clarity.

The realization was almost enough to make him pass out again.

But he held on tight and remained conscious. He was aware of the beeping monitors and everything that followed. Of the people in the room. He focused and felt his grand-père's worries, focused on his mother and felt her sudden calm, on his father and felt him, too.

Could he now *control* his *percée*? Had the knock on his head managed to make his life easier?

But there was no time to consider that, no time to even discuss it because there were footsteps. And Kayleigh.

He started to try and sit up, but all that got him were angry looks, beeping monitors and not very far off the pillow. And so he lay back down, taking Kayleigh's hand in the process. "*Tu es venu?*"

"Yeah," she whispered as she squeezed his hand. "I came. I'm here. Not for long though…"

He saw his father and the doctor nod.

"You'll be back?"

"I'll visit wherever you are."

And that was good enough for him.

Kayleigh

Kayleigh tried to visit Max. Many times. Nobody would let her see him. Not in the morning, not in the evening, not in the afternoon nor in the wee hours between any of those. Not at his apartment, not in his hospital room. It was as if he'd fallen off the face of the earth. At first she thought it was because he needed space to recover. But as time went on, so did her concern, and she began to try and get information from anybody she could talk to. Nobody. Not her family, not the team. Nobody.

On girls' night, three days before the gala, after way too many shots of tequila, she spilled the beans. "I miss him," she said.

"Oh my god," Sousa murmured pouring a glass of water and shoving it toward her as Melanie walked through the door. "You didn't see it?"

Kayleigh shook her head before taking a long drink of water. "Don't know what you're talking about," she managed, now that she was starting to feel her tongue again. "I haven't seen *Max*. I can't get near him."

Sousa shook her head, pity in her eyes. "Yep, it figures. There's this Quebec TV reporter…LeBlanc or whatever his name is? Anyway, he's been going on a whole bunch of different sports shows. He's been talking about how the fact that the New York dude didn't get penalized for Max's injury, but Brody Evans got suspended."

Apparently she hadn't been paying attention. "Evans got suspended?"

"Yeah."

"And why did my family not tell me this?"

"Because here's the thing. LeBlanc is basically saying, Why did Evans get suspended when the New York dude that hit Max didn't get a penalty? That Evans wouldn't have acted if the dude that hit Max got the kind of…disciplinary action he deserved for playing in such an unsafe manner."

"Which is amazing that he's doing this, but…"

"Anyway," Melanie said as she sat down and poured herself a glass of moscato, "apparently Max himself is locked up tight. Nobody's seeing him. Nobody even knows where he is right now. At least the ones who do aren't saying anything."

Emily nodded as she hung up her coat on the rack. "Yep. We don't even know where he is, either officially or unofficially. So no visitors, no nothing. Because of course, if anybody sees him, they're going to want to talk to him, and if we want to make it clear that he's injured, seeing him in public isn't a good idea unless and until he's cleared. You remember what happened with the Norwegian dude on the New York team last year? Nobody saw him, nobody talked to him. Turned out the injury was, in fact, as bad as they said, but you know, when we're pushing an injury inconsistency, it's always better to be safe than sorry and control the situation."

"I have to say," Kassie, the Floridian flautist who came to join them, said, "that it's kinda cool someone who the league needs to listen to is standing up for this. League's had a problem with enforcement consistency for a while, and seeing this officially neutral party say something in a way the league can't ignore? I love it."

Emily smiled for a moment then rolled her eyes. "Yeah, but LeBlanc is going a little apeshit."

"Better apeshit than letting this stand," Melanie informed her sister. "The officiating and the suspensions have been inconsistent and awful. And even you need to admit that."

"Which means," Sousa said meaningfully, "if you want to give Max something…send him something."

Kayleigh nodded, took long drink from her glass of water, and thought about her email.

From K_emerson@nyharm.com
To: Max_SL7@empiremail.com
I miss you.

From: Max_SL7@empiremail.com
To: K_emerson@nyharm.com
I miss you too. When is the gala of yours?

To: Max_SL7@empiremail.com
From: K_emerson@nyharm.com
It's fine. Seriously. Totally fine. It's in less than two days and you're not going to make it. I almost forgot about it myself except they reminded us in practice. Don't worry.

To: K_emerson@nyharm.com
From: Max_SL7@empiremail.com
Send me the details ;) you never know what will happen.

CHAPTER FOURTEEN

Kayleigh

Kayleigh had been primped and powdered to within an inch of her life, and her dress was killer. She knew she looked gorgeous, but she didn't have the heart for glamour. Not tonight.

Nevertheless, she shook hands and smiled with board members, charming them as best as she could, sharing stories of her childhood, explaining how the design of the rink had been altered to allow the Empires to watch the orchestra play during the intermission, and genuinely doing her best to keep her game face on.

And it worked, at least until she ran into Joe. "Thought you were bringing someone," he said.

The board members hadn't mentioned it, nobody else had. Not even Arun or Jonathan when she'd seen them in the coat room. "And that matters because?"

"It just makes you look bad, is all. You know. Most of us are settled in good sturdy relationships, and you...well are not," Joe replied.

She barely managed to get away from him, choosing to make a

beeline to the bar instead of telling the stupid viola player to fuck off. She leaned her elbows against the marble bar, took a deep breath and ordered a drink. Something strong enough to stop her brain from whirling.

"Come sit!"

She turned toward the voice; it was Jonathan. He sat, somewhat at ease, at a table no more than two steps away. She grinned, took the drink, tipped the bartender and headed over to accept the invitation.

"Thanks," she said as she sat in one of the empty chairs and smiled. "How are you doing?"

Jonathan smiled back at her and patted her hand. "He's going to be fine," he said, ignoring her question.

She was glad she'd swallowed the sip of her drink she'd taken before she started talking. "What?"

He rolled his eyes. "You told A that you'd bring a hockey player. You're as pale as a sheet. You went to the game where Evans got suspended and St. Laurent got injured, and you've been a mess since then. Doesn't take a brain surgeon to figure out you're worried about the guy you were supposed to bring. And you were bringing St. Laurent."

She blinked.

"Kayleigh, I'm a litigator, not an idiot. Though some confuse the two, the truth is that I spend way too much time making sense out of the crazy. And he's going to be fine, otherwise they would have had a press conference like they did with the other team and their goalie. The only reason he's under lock and key is because of LeBlanc." He looked down at his watch. "Give it about…say five more minutes, and then blow this overdressed popsicle stand and go check on Lucky Seven."

She nodded and smiled. "Thank you."

Suddenly she found herself genuinely relaxing. It was as if she'd been given permission to breathe again. Jonathan and Kassie were chatty and awesome enough to make her forget the people she didn't want to see...or talk to. Finally, there were footsteps, and Jonathan's face lit up in a way that made her realize Arun had joined them.

"You should go," he said as he came over to join them. "You've done your time, Kayleigh. Seriously. It's OK."

She raised an eyebrow and took another sip of her mystery drink. "You sure?"

Arun nodded, patting her on the shoulder. "Now."

She needed no more suggestion, no more prodding. "OK."

Max

Max'd had enough of waiting. He'd been hidden away at the very luxurious house of the team owner, so he had to fake symptoms he was not having until it felt...safe. Then he had to go see the doctor, who had a horrible accent. Apparently, it was because the team's doctor was from Boston...

But he did ask if he could dance. The doctor, as well as the other people in the room, laughed.

He was glad the only part of the response he caught was "yes."

As he and the team owner left the doctor's office, Monsieur "call me Arnie" Dawes wondered aloud, "So why do you want to dance?"

He smiled. Dawes's interest was genuine. So he spilled the beans. "I was...invited to an event by a girl...and it was formal so..."

"So you need to dance, of course." Then Dawes looked up at him, focused. "Event's formal. You have a tux?"

Merde.

He'd forgotten the tuxedo he'd purchased (and worn, and dry-cleaned) after the Special Olympics Gala. His family was with Alain doing something, and he was …

Merde.

Dawes smiled, clapped him on the shoulder. "I'll take care of it."

"I…"

"I can't let one of my boys go to a gala without a tux, Lucky Seven."

He nodded. The offer was genuine; his *percée* was never wrong. So he accepted.

Unfortunately, the fitting took a long time. He was lucky; the tailor was nice, even though he turned out to be another member of the unofficial recruiting committee for the French national team. Aside from that, it was good and put him into a tux, a sufficiently warm topcoat, and a car, with enough time to get to the gala.

And then there was horrible traffic.

But finally, he arrived.

"*Merci*," he said to the driver as he got out of the car.

There was a huge staircase to his left, and he started to climb it, two stairs at a time.

Except he looked up only to see a solitary figure in a long black coat heading right toward him. As the figure came closer, he was transfixed.

Kayleigh.

He focused his *percée*, and she was upset, worried, and concerned. She wasn't looking at him, so he went up another stair. The sound of his dress shoes hitting the stone steps echoed through the silent night, producing the desired effect. She looked up.

She was gorgeous, bundled up in that coat, her eyes wide; his *percée* told him she was curious, questioning, which meant she was trying to find the source of the sound. His heart pounded against the chest and his breath made clouds in the cold as he waited.

When her eyes stopped searching and met his, there was a split second before her heels started to pound against the steps as he opened his arms. He held his breath until she reached him, and he held her.

"I made it."

"You're here."

He shrugged. "I am."

Relief, joy, guilt, and something else came pouring out of her as she leaned toward him. Her lips met his in an explosion that almost knocked him over. He let himself get lost in her, his hands in her hair, the way she responded to his lips on hers, the sweet taste of her mouth…

She pulled away, breaking the kiss so suddenly it made his head spin. But instead of pulling away completely, she and put her head on his shoulder. "You're here," she whispered. "I…I didn't expect you to come. Wanted you to. But I just…"

"I wanted to…surprise you," he managed, the letters mixing on his tongue and ending up in a weird place between the English and the French. "I got the OK from the doctor today and I…"

Her responding smile was the most beautiful thing he'd ever seen. She put her arms around him, and he couldn't help himself; his lips brushed her cheek, matching hers as she turned just at the right moment. His fingers explored the strands of her hair that escaped from her hat.

"Cold?"

He smiled at her, the concern in her eyes melting his heart. "No." He turned toward the door. "In?"

She shook her head, and he could see she was filled with determination. "Home."

CHAPTER FIFTEEN

Kayleigh

S he barely remembered the cab ride.

All she remembered was Max, the feel of him next to her, how she couldn't wait to get him out of the tuxedo that peaked out from under his long winter coat, to break the unspoken rules they'd been following. She remembered the furtive kisses she'd stolen, the way his carefully tied bow tie came apart at the slightest movement of his fingers.

"You wore a tux," she murmured against his cheek. "You would have killed in a tux."

She saw the confusion in his eyes, then remembered who she was talking to. So she leaned over and kissed as close to his lips as she could get from her position. "You're probably gorgeous in that tux."

"Probably?" he said as he leaned toward her that little bit more, his lips landing on hers.

"Definitely," she murmured against his mouth. "Definitely."

"Do you want to go back?" he asked, his words hesitant and mostly lost in his accent.

She shook her head and breathed him in. "I want to get you out of that tux as fast as possible. Which means my place."

He laughed, and she loved the sound of his laugh. "OK, *bébé*. I… it's OK…"

For the millionth time, she was glad she lived in a walkup, a small building, right next to a coffee shop. She took his hand as the car pulled over, and they got out. But she didn't remember much about how she got them up to her apartment, only how fast their heavy coats, his jackets, her dress, and bra had found their way to the floor. The clothing littered the path, obscuring the hard wood floor from her frozen feet.

She expected him to say something, but he didn't. She turned on the light near her bedroom and let him lead her inside. Because he was amazing.

He had exquisite control over the way he moved those fingers along her skin. He kissed like his mouth was on fire and, dear god, his hands. Forward and backward around her breasts. She'd wanted him to touch her, had yearned to feel those skilled fingers against her skin. And now that she finally was, she wanted to roar in triumph.

Not exactly roar, but…luxuriate in the feel of him. His hands, now his mouth on her breasts. He was hungry and she would let him feast. All over her, as much and as often as he wanted. This would be amazing, special, and…dangerous.

Although his shirt had to come off. Yet as she leaned closer to it, he moved back. "*Non, petit, non bébé*," he managed, his accent deeper, "*non* yet. OK? We take it slow, hm?"

She sighed and nodded. The full force of Max's answering smile could have been classified as a lethal weapon. And in the remains of his tuxedo? Holy shit.

Max

There came a point where he wondered why he held off her questing fingers. Urged on by the desire he saw in her eyes, he gave up the fight. "*Viens,*" he whispered. "Come on…"

She did. Her hands made short work of the buttons on his shirt, and he found himself forgetting to breathe as she kissed him, His pants came down faster, her fingers easily exposing his body to the cold of his bedroom. He didn't resist her; he couldn't. He wasn't strong enough, and that was OK.

He let her push him back, straddle him. Her smile was dangerous as she pulled his boxers down, beautiful and everything he wanted. The feel of her hands on his shoulders put him in perilous danger of losing it all…

Merde

He flattened his hands on the mattress, pushing up to meet her mouth. "*Viens,*" he murmured. "*Viens, bébé.*"

"On my way," she replied against his mouth. Her chest against his, her legs suddenly around his waist. He moved slightly, and he entered her. She was wet, slick, and ready for him.

"What happened to taking it slow?" she murmured as he positioned his hips just so, moving inside her, trying to find the rhythm they both needed.

"We lost it," he managed, his ability to speak hampered by his breath and his movements. He hoped his words came out somewhat intelligently.

She came. God she came. So did he, thankfully. Tight around him, and oh. She fell onto his chest, put her head on his shoulder, and sighed, kissing his cheek. "I don't want to move," she informed him.

In response, he put his arms around her, hugging her close to him. "Don't."

And she didn't.

CHAPTER SIXTEEN

Max

It was a normal visit; any athlete had to visit the PT clinic before being cleared to come back from an injury, right?

He took a breath, stared up at the ceiling, and hoped he could find answers there. But there was nothing. Only busy, overwhelmed thoughts from the people buzzing around him. No nerves. No fear. Except for his.

Tabernac.

"Mr. St. Laurent?"

He looked up at the sound of his name. "*Oua…*yes?"

"Come this way."

He nodded, and stood up, trying to think of the best way to deal with the questions that ran around his head. *Merde.* He had to tell Kayleigh about his *percée*, his grandfather had reminded him. And it wasn't as if it was something he hadn't thought about. Just…

Merde.

"Mr. St. Laurent?"

The therapist, Nathalie—Semenov's Nathalie—had called him a second time, and he felt horrible. "Sorry," he managed, forcing the English words out of his mouth as he followed her into the exam room.

She patted the table, and he got on, closing his eyes and attempting to clear his mind. He failed. Completely. All he could think about was Kayleigh and how he couldn't lose her.

As Nathalie's hands began to do their magic, he felt something... different. She was suddenly separated from her emotions; she was witnessing something. He opened his eyes and saw her. She stood still; almost completely motionless, her eyes looking at almost nothing. He felt betrayal from her, but it wasn't hers. Felt observation and confusion, then resolution.

"Tell her," she said suddenly, conviction in her voice. "Whatever it is, tell her or you'll lose her." And then...was it...surprise, embarrassment? "Sorry," she said shaking her head. "Every once in a while, I read something and it gets me so angry I need to vent about it. Didn't realize I was talking out loud."

Max knew the excuse for what it was, understood it, and closed his eyes before responding. "*J'y*...I do the same, you know," he said, smiling in a way that he hoped was friendly.

Then he let the conversation go; forced himself to clear his mind. He let her work her magic, massaging out the kinks in his muscles, the places where his coach was most concerned about; on his shoulder, his back, his neck. When she was done, he got up from the table and looked up at her. "*Merci bien*," he managed. "And I will."

Because he had to tell Kayleigh about his *percée*.

Kayleigh

Kayleigh saw Max's number on her phone and grinned, waving to

Arun and Kassie in apology before leaving their lunch table stepping outside into the cold alleyway. "Well hello there," she said. "You got me during lunch break."

"So I have perfect timing for the first time in my life."

She giggled. "You do."

"Good." He swallowed. "I…I have…I need to talk to you."

"OK. Sure." She paused, sitting down on the ledge just outside the building. This didn't sound good. "What's up?"

"Can you come over?"

He was nervous. This was…bad. Serious. She wondered what the hell it could be. "Are you OK?"

"I'm fine…"

Fine. Emotionally messy not physically messy. "Can it wait? I'm in practice…"

She waited, waited to hear what he said.

"Yes," he said, his voice barely above a whisper. And then "It can wait until you get done with practice."

"So I'll meet you at 5:30?"

"Sure. Come to my place."

"I'll see you then."

Max

He'd been pacing since he'd put the phone down. A few minutes at the window, a huge bottle of Gatorade, then back at the window. Breathed in and out. Forced himself to sit down, make a cup of tea. He couldn't relax; he couldn't breathe.

He was going to lose her. And there was nothing to do about it except stare at the window, listening to the wind.

Finally, there was a knock on his door. "*Allô?*"

He opened it to see her standing there. He put his arms around her, held her tight, and breathed her in.

"Hi," she whispered. "Hi, there."

He kissed her. With her coat on, her bag still on her shoulder, he kissed her. Lost himself in the taste of her mouth.

But she pulled back. "I adore you," she said. "Just…adore you. But there's something on your mind."

He nodded; it was all he could manage.

Her hand brushed his cheek. "Is it the doctor? The PT session not go well?"

"It was fine," he said as she put her violin down. "A normal session."

"I'm glad." She smiled up at him, then fell onto his couch, folding her arms. "So what did you want to tell me?"

He couldn't get the words together; he was lost in her, savoring the moment as if it would be his last.

"Just say it," she said. "Come on."

Mon dieu.

Like it was nothing, and he could tell she meant it. But *merde*. "OK."

He took a breath and dropped his shields. Reached out, past the wall he now was able to build. And then he found her. Another breath. She reached for him, and he felt the sudden fear inside of her when he didn't take her hand.

"I…have…" He swallowed. *Merde*. "I am…" Yet another breath. As if oxygen would lift the English words out of his mouth so he didn't have to say them. "I can read…*les emotions*, how someone is feeling. I know…*en famille*, my family, we call it…*percée*."

She said nothing. She sat there, staring at him, like he'd lost his mind. And maybe he had.

Kayleigh

She stared at Max, trying not to focus on the flashbacks she was having to the first time she saw Bryce drunk, high and raving about something. This revelation was important to him, this secret of his, and focusing on her own frames weren't helping.

I can't do this.

But she nodded. "OK."

His shoulders didn't relax; he clearly wasn't convinced by her sudden calm. "I…am not your brother."

Holy shit.

She blinked, wondering when she'd had the conversation with him where she explained about Bryce's difficulties. Then she realized she hadn't.

She needed to sit down. She saw his fingers clenching, his body ready to spring, then reached for the kitchen chair herself. She closed her eyes, ran her hands through her hair then looked back up at him.

"I am not…the first person *en ma famille* to…be this way," he began. He moved toward the table and sat down across from her, his elbows on his knees. "*Mon grand-père*. He knew…what I had when I was small."

She nodded, tried to breathe. Followed the path of his fingers up his shirt, watching as he grabbed his collar, pulling out a necklace she'd once seen and never asked about.

"They…passed this down in my mother's family. Usually through the women, but I…" He shrugged. "Am special…?"

So he was serious. This was…something his family knew about. Either he had a mental illness, a delusion, or his entire family suffered from the same ideas.

"I can't…I have…"

He sighed and he stood, turned around toward the window. "This is the first time I have told anybody," he said softly. "I cannot…I do not know what I can do to help you understand."

She closed her eyes, knowing that if she left them open, she'd see him. And how painful this revelation was for him. But she'd never be anywhere if she focused on his pain and forgot about her. She wouldn't do him any good.

She couldn't stay.

"I…"

"It's OK," he said, his voice barely louder than a whisper. "You can…make it to the door?"

The memories of the last time she'd left his apartment overwhelmed her, how she'd almost never been able to leave on her own. And yet now, she got to her feet, focused on the door, and put one foot in front of the other toward the door.

"*À la prochaine*," she whispered as she closed the door behind her, not knowing whether it would be the last time.

She held her breath as she headed down the stairs that separated his apartment from the street, shoving her hands in her pockets and bracing herself for the cold just outside the door. It was nothing compared to the hole in her heart.

"Ah, *belle fille*."

A familiar voice in Parisian French. She looked up to see Max's grandfather's twinkling eyes.

"*Bonjour*," she said formally, her voice still scratchy from the tears she refused to cry. And then…in French, "He needs help. Please. I…"

He paused, then sighed. "Not all in the world is the same, you know? It is like…" he paused, scratched his chin. "They say in English that if it…what is that…if it quacks like a duck, it must be a duck?"

She nodded. "That's it."

"But, *petite belle fille*, it could be, you know the…trumpeting of a goose or something like that. You need to pay attention. Because it might sound like a duck, you know, but it's another something totally."

"*Non, monsieur*," she said, respectfully. "I've seen this duck before. I'm sure of it…my brother…my other brother. Bryson. He didn't get help for a long time, and…it hurt."

"Are you sure, *petite fille*, that you are seeing a duck? That *mon petit* grandson is a duck who needs to be treated like a duck? Or a goose who honks as well as he was meant to?" He reached out his hand, patting her shoulder. "You have to decide yourself, whether he is a duck to help or a goose to embrace…"

"Thank you," she said, as respectfully as she could manage. "I appreciate it. Thank you." She smiled.

And as she turned to leave, she could hear his voice.

"I too, *petite belle fille*, had to tell the difference between ducks and geese once upon a time."

When she finally set foot on the snowy cobblestoned streets, she was confused, her vision filled with ducks and geese.

CHAPTER SEVENTEEN

Max

His grandfather had told him not to worry about the "*petite belle fille*," but Kayleigh still remained on his mind.

Fortunately, her brother hadn't said a word when he'd seen the man at the first few practices after he'd been cleared. The team had left him alone under the watchful gaze of his parents (who were spending this visit looking quite cozy with each other, something he did not want to consider).

But, he mused as he continued to let the trainers put him through his paces, not even being alone on the ice was a good thing. He was grateful for the sound of the whistle.

He headed toward the boards, where the coach stood with a clipboard and a smile.

"Good," Coach MacArthur said, smiling. "You look amazing out there, but I don't want to shove you on the ice too quickly. Start preparing, Lucky Seven. There's a few more games, but I think you get two days in the press box and then back in the game before the

Classic. We're playing Toronto. Which means if we play like we're supposed to, we'll be back to par."

Max nodded.

"But the big kicker, Lucky, is that Dobrynin is back, playing defense in that slot with Evans. So we're going to need you on the offensive side. Emerson's line needs a winger, and it's not going all that great. I need to be able to move Driscoll down to the third line where he belongs, and you would fit that right wing spot with Smythe and Emerson. You good with that, Lucky Seven?"

Offense. He could do that. "OK." Words were hard, but *plus ça change...*

"Now get on the ice, we're all using that pond out there as tune-ups. We got an advantage in Tarrytown, so we're gonna use it. Get a couple laps in out there, get used to that kind of ice surface. Also maybe try the eye black...see if that'll work for you. Donnie'll have it in his box of tricks."

Once again, Max nodded. And started to organize himself.

Kayleigh

December.

A month that had been full of ducks, geese, and her family. There had been family celebrations, most of which allowed her to avoid the rest of Chris's hockey team. Chris himself, being smart, didn't ask; she didn't answer.

But it wasn't as if Max and the secrets he'd shared had been far from her mind; she'd had heartfelt conversations with her mother, her father and Bryce. About things she'd never wanted to understand. Until then.

She did miss Max. It was cold without him. But as she put her bow to the strings, she knew full well that until she figured out if he was, as his grandfather put it, a duck or a goose, she wouldn't go anywhere near him.

But this late in December also meant final rehearsals, and practice with the bands that would be playing during the first and second intermission at the Winter Classic. And so she closed her eyes, put her chin on the rest, and tried not to cry as the lead singer of the band playing during the first intermission sang about loss.

CHAPTER EIGHTEEN

Event: Family Skate Queens
Location: Queens Bank Park
Day before Winter Game

Kayleigh

She saw the reporter talking to Chris and Melanie, of course. Emily was trying to be official but Mark, her boyfriend and new member of the team, wasn't letting her. She leaned against the wall.

"You look bored, Kay," Bryce informed her. "You need to…smile."

She raised an eyebrow and stared at her brother. "You need to be quiet."

He laughed, and she put her head on his shoulder. "Love you, Bryce."

"Love you, too, Kay." He tousled her hair. "I see your boy out there."

She started to answer him, but she couldn't get the words out. "He…"

"Chris said something was wrong. 'Cause, I love you, Kay, but seriously, you've…" He paused, rubbed his head and sighed. "Does

253

he…is he…in need of a good doctor he could trust?"

This wasn't a time she could appreciate her brother's way too insightful nature. She also couldn't smack him. Instead, she settled for words. "I need to figure things out," she said, trying not to stare at Max. "I don't know where I stand."

"Where you stand?"

Her brother looked like he'd eaten a rotten egg. She almost burst out laughing at the sight, but was able to hold back the onslaught. "It's not him, it's me," she said, deciding that was the safest way to play it.

Now he looked wary. Wary was easier in the face of her parents' impending arrival.

"Come on, you two," her father said, the hat Chris had gotten him for Christmas covering most of his bald head. "Let's get a move on."

Her mother adjusted her scarf, then her perfectly coiffed hair, before shaking her head. "You'd better come along. There will be trouble later otherwise."

And knowing her family as well as she did, she followed her parents onto the ice, waving at the group as she did so.

Max

His parents were holding hands and laughing like two teenagers. This had not happened, not in a long while. He figured he'd be seeing the end of the world and not in a beer mug if things continued as they were. But he wasn't going to worry about it.

Until the music started playing.

It was a plaintive, song about loss.

Merde.

His grandfather chose that moment to skate over to him. "Ah, *petit fils*," he said, a smile on his face. "You realize that we…are skating on a baseball field."

He knew, of course. Especially considering Pedro had come to see this. His friend the outfielder was in a heavy jacket that proclaimed the name of the stadium's primary tenants. Signing autographs, waving to people. Staying as far from the ice as he could. *"Oui, grand-père,"* he answered formally, dodging out of the way of a skater so unstable he had to be related to Smythe, the team's Oklahoma contingent.

"You going to go to her?"

He shook his head. His grandfather's statement didn't need clarifying. There was only one "her." And that was Kayleigh, skating with the rest of her family, her parents and the brother that wasn't Chris. "She has to decide," he said. "I…need to wait."

His grandfather nodded. Thankfully, the man let the topic drop. But he couldn't help watching her. He didn't focus on her; he knew his heart wouldn't be able to take it.

New Years Eve
Location: Melanie and Chris's Townhouse
Brooklyn

Kayleigh

Family was everywhere. Which was a good thing. Chris had even managed to convince Alex and Nathalie to join the family gathering. Her parents, Melanie's, Melanie's sister, her boyfriend, his parents, her brother…a small gathering but a close one. Chris and Mel had set out hot cocoa, soup, tea, and hot toddies for those who weren't going to play hockey the next day. Like Max

Damn it.

She had to decide to fish or cut bait, to stay with him or run. And so she got up to get a glass of water.

The kitchen of her brother and Mel's townhouse was downstairs, she knew the way. And nobody decided to follow her, so she took a deep breath and ran the faucet. "Damn it," she said, "how do you believe something so impossible from someone so rational. How do you make that leap?"

"You either trust them or you don't," Alex said out of nowhere. "If you trust the person, even the impossible is possible."

"Thank you," she said. She took a deep breath and turned back toward where Alex was standing, glad for an answer. "Water?"

"Thank you."

And as she gave him the glass of water, she wondered what she'd do with his advice.

CHAPTER NINETEEN

Event: The Winter Classic
Location: Queens Bank Park

Max

S t. Laurent?"

Max lifted his head, focused on his coach's words.

"We need a pre-game interview subject. You're it." He smiled. "You can do this."

Max stretched again, took a breath, and headed out into the hallway where Clint Beauchamp was standing.

"Max St. Laurent, welcome back to the Empires and this big game."

He smiled back and took the hand that was extended. "Thank you so much, I am glad to be back to help my team today."

"This is a big game for the Empires. Toronto is moving up in the standings and this game might, if we're all lucky, be foreshadowing a big race in your team's future. How did you prepare for this game?"

He smiled, once again being careful with his words. "Our team is lucky...we have a pond not far from our practice space, so we had some days on the pond. It's a different game, you know, outside, so it was good for all of us to remember what it's like."

"But you, Max. You're back from a major injury, and not only back, but you're now going to play forward? On a line with M.F. Smythe and Chris Emerson. Are you intimidated?"

And that was it. This time, he had a plan, and he was ready. First he locked his *percée* down and took a breath. This was a question he'd been asked most of his hockey career, so he was ready to answer it. Even when Clint Beauchamp asked it.

"I've been playing offense and defense both since I was a kid, you know, since…juniors and all, so playing offense is…something I do," he began, deliberately referencing one of Beauchamp's favorite subjects. "And it's our team, so if they need a guy to play on that wing, who can fit that moment, and they ask me, I do. I think our coach knows our team and knows who can play where, so if he says play there, I will do my best."

When he'd finished answering the question, he opened up his *percée*, and instead of anger, there was surprise and…excited understanding. "Yeah," Beauchamp replied. "That's right. You have played both offense and defense since playing in Juniors. But that's because you had a great coach in Juniors. Marcel Voisin, has a great reputation, and for a good reason."

Max nodded, glad the reporter had taken the bait. "Yeah, Quebec has a great system…the QMJHL. So many great people, including Coach Voisin, helped at every level, you know? And my family and my team."

And after all of that, Beauchamp nodded, satisfied. "Great talking to you, Max! Good luck today."

"Thank you," he replied before heading back into the locker room to cheers from his teammates. He'd made it through the interview, but all the triumph reminded him was that Kayleigh was no longer in his life.

Kayleigh

She followed the rest of the orchestra onto the field, taking a deep breath as she walked through the tiny path the stadium crew had created. It was cold, but she'd been in worse. Unfortunately, that didn't make it any easier because her fingers were still freezing. Once again, she was grateful for the electric violin.

"Holy crap," murmured Pete, the first chair of the second violins. "It's crowded…"

She nodded, but she'd expected it. Tickets had sold out despite the dire predictions of below-zero weather. But this was New York; the two other outdoor games that had been held in the tri-state area had sold out. New Yorkers knew how to bundle up, and the other team was from Toronto. Again, no big surprise the game had sold out.

As Kayleigh sat down on top of her heated seat cushion, she looked around at the stadium. It was filled to capacity; she didn't think about where her parents and the rest of the Empires family had been assigned to sit. All she focused on was the brief sounding of a tuning note.

Finally, Arun joined the orchestra, standing on the podium provided for him. His face was serious, focused. She focused on him, setting her violin on her shoulder and placing her chin on the rest.

Finally, the downbeat.

Max

The team only had a short time to finish getting ready after Max finished his interview.

Finally, there was a knock on the locker room door. "OK, guys."

"Now remember," Coach MacArthur said. "We follow the path out of the dugout that will take us to the copy of the Kosciuszko…"

"Why did they choose that bridge?"

Max was glad someone had asked; he'd wanted to know too.

"It connects Brooklyn and Queens," the coach replied. "They wanted to have us walk into the stadium on that bridge as a symbol of the journey from where we usually play to here. Did a good job too, barely recognize that ugly bridge. Anyway, architecture aside, they'll announce us, and then we walk across that bridge. Stay together. Don't move to the music. Just follow your line mates. Defense, forward. Stick together. Right?"

"Right," the team shouted, clapping.

"We got this, boys," said Emerson. The guy who'd be playing on the center of his line. His captain.

And they lined up, leaving the locker room one by one. They stayed together in single file, waiting at the dugout, listening to the familiar PA announcer's voice.

"And your New YORK EMPIIIIIIIIIIIIIIIIIIIIIIRES!"

At the sound of the team name, they started to move across the bridge, crossing the stadium, and into the sight of the fans. It was magical.

He followed his teammates, then waited at attention and held his breath.

Kayleigh

The anthems were fast; the Canadian singer insisted she sing a capella; the American singer wanted the orchestra. They'd practiced both, but she knew it was a game-time decision.

After the anthems, the orchestra was shuttled off the ice and sent into an area where they'd be able to watch the game.

"This is exciting," she said.

Jonathan nodded as Arun sighed. "Here we go," he said and pointed out at the stadium below. "Puck drop. Game time."

Yes, Kayleigh thought. It was time to play.

First Period

Max

The puck dropped, and Max felt the exhilaration immediately. He stayed focused, watching the puck as it moved. He skated down the ice with his line mates, holding the line, and then…

There was an open side. Evans's new/old defense partner, Dobrynin, wasn't doing what he was supposed to, and there was going to be a goal scored if he wasn't careful. He felt the other players' uncertainty and so he immediately moved into position to cover the hole he saw on the left side. But it was too late.

The player he was supposed to be paying attention to had gotten past him, the defenseman he was covering, and everybody else on the ice. Now he had the kind of shot on goal that not even a perfectly executed dive in the way of the puck would stop. And Semenov, wonderful as he was, had no chance.

And then, the red light.

Tabernac.

Kayleigh

Nooooooo!

There were assorted snarls and curses that matched her own, and even a few cheers. Toronto had scored, with five minutes left

261

in the period. Damn it.

But five minutes left in the period also meant she had to start to get ready to go out and play. Layers, gloves, and deep breaths all were the order of the moment. As was the extra jersey her brother had given her.

"Kayleigh!"

Arun's voice sounded half stressed and half as if he was trying desperately to keep from losing it.

"What can I do you for?"

"They want an interview from us," he answered, sighing as he ran a hand through his hair. "They didn't say they want you, but, well…"

They didn't have to. She knew where she stood It was easy to figure out what story the reporters were searching for. "Fine," she said, sighing herself. "I'll go. I know." She reached out again, only stopping her reach inches from her conductor's perfectly shorn hair.

And so she adjusted her jersey—her brother's, of course—before heading off into the hallway. She followed Maureen, the Philharmonia's PR person, through the halls of the building.

"She's here," Maureen said.

She looked up into the eyes of Clint Fucking Beauchamp, the reporter who'd been responsible for exposing Max's linguistic difficulties to the world.

Instead of punching him in the throat, she smiled.

She behaved herself, answered the man's questions while doing her best not to strangle him on live television. After the interview was over, she headed back to where the rest of the Philharmonia was preparing to head back onto the field.

"I made it through," she told Kassie as they stood in line. "I almost killed him. But I didn't."

Kassie, the smart flautist she was, laughed.

And then the orchestra headed back onto the field.

First Intermission

Max

When the buzzer rang, signifying the end of the period, Max stood, then followed his teammates back to the locker room. Nothing was said until the large door was closed.

"All right guys. We can't afford to let their momentum take us down," the coach began. "We need to take a step back. All of us. And get back in the fucking game. Because even though it looks pretty out there, this game fucking counts. And we cannot forget that."

"Five minutes" Emerson said. "Then we go out to make my sister blush. Two lines. We sit. Got it?"

"Yes," Max said adding to the team's chorus.

He took a deep breath and stared at his locker.

"I need you guarding my ass, being my wingman," Emerson said darkly, "not being some phantom fucking defense thing out there. Get your ass together."

Max did the only thing he could. He nodded. "*Ouais*," he said.

He didn't have to look behind him to see the sudden freeze in Emerson's expression. He felt it. Didn't need his *percée* to feel it either. "Good man," Emerson replied.

Then he stood, following Emerson, past Evans, who was snarling at Dobrynin. Past Semenov who was studiously ignoring everybody, trying to get into a groove.

"St. Laurent?"

Max stopped at the sound of the Coach's voice. Then he turned on his guarded skate blade to face the man.

"You need extra time. You're not fully set on offense," the coach began. "Close. I could see sparks. You screwed up on that goal, not because you don't have sense, you're just playing with the wrong one. And you need to play with the right one…"

He didn't say anything.

"I have confidence in you, otherwise you wouldn't be here right now. And I get it's a switch, but you need to make it. Do *not* let your defensive instincts overrule your offensive ones when you're playing forward."

Max nodded.

The coach sighed. "What I'm going to do is to sit you down and make you watch this second period. You need to mentally follow the game for a period before I let you put skate one back on the ice. Right?"

"Yes, Coach."

"Offense," Coach said, before leading him back into the locker room. "Offense. You're not defense today. And we need you to be the best fucking forward you can be."

And as the coach went out to join the rest of the team, Max sat back down on the bench in front of his locker, took a breath and closed his eyes.

Kayleigh

Kayleigh knew this was going to kill her. Knew it. The song was too appropriate, the piece was too sad. And she was the one who broke up with Max, so it was her fault. Damn it.

The show must go on, as they said. And the world was watching. So she held her breath and joined the ensemble in her assigned seat. As they'd practiced, she would play with the ensemble and then stand for her solo. She was glad they'd nixed the skating idea. Even though she could have, it would have been impossible to implement.

She noticed that the Empires were there, as Chris promised, kneeling on the ice, or at least as much of the ice as they could legitimately cover. At least most of them. She didn't see Max, although he had spent the back end of the period on the bench, after the Sirens' goal. That meant he could be in Chateau Bow-wow, the coach using the time the rest of the team was watching her play to give him a blistering lecture. He also could be hurt. She knew which one she would prefer; no matter what was going on between them, she'd already seen him in the hospital. It was a nightmare she'd rather not relive.

"And now," began the public address announcer.

The rest of the words washed over her, and she closed her eyes, let go of mostly everything around her and focused on the page. Then she looked up at Arun, waiting for his signal.

And then the downbeat, and they started. In her brother's jersey, she played. The song, the lyrics broke her heart, but she held tight, held close.

"Caught in the headlights…loose this fight…lost in your arms," the singer sang plaintively."

And there it was. She stood and let the notes fly out of her instrument, the solo connecting her to the singer, the song and the moment.

She sat down, took a quick breath, the time signature counting silently in the back of her mind. Then immediately back to the music, the backing part printed on the page. Quick staccato slips of the bow on the strings. Closing her eyes. Waiting for the right moment. And then.

"Lost in your arms, baby lost in your arms…"

Once again she stood, lost in the music.

Damn it.

She had made a mess of everything. But what was she going to do to fix it?

Second Period

Max

He watched the game from the bench during that second period. Semenov stood tight, didn't let anything in. That was what saved them. They were missing something, and it was his fault. He needed to change that.

First was his mental state when he was watching the game. What was he focusing on? Right away, he noticed that the center of his attention wasn't the puck and forward momentum. It was defense. And so he forced himself to think about the offensive lines and how they played, what he'd do to retain puck possession, and forward motion if he was on the ice.

Coach was double shifting Sandberg to fill the place on Emerson's line. Which wasn't fair to his teammate. Sandberg was good, but he was used to skating with Jahr and Karpov. Emerson was good in his own way, and he had good chemistry with Smythe, but neither Emerson nor Smythe were Jahr and Karpov and everybody knew it.

Which is part of the reason he liked playing with Emerson. He was a good hockey player, but he wasn't the kind of player who demanded the spotlight unless he wanted it. And that was just fine for Max, because he liked to stay in the shadows.

"Good, Lucky Seven," the assistant coach assigned for offense said. "You're doing the right thing. Visualize yourself on that pond, and you'll be back out there in no time."

Then the older man moved down the bench to the guys who were playing, leaving Max to wonder how the man had figured out what he'd been doing.

Kayleigh

Kayleigh's heart was in her throat as she watched the second period. She was supposed to be preparing for the second intermission and the piece they'd play. Instead, she was watching the game, watching for something that wasn't there. Or, rather, someone who wasn't there.

"St. Laurent isn't playing," she said.

"They have Sandberg playing with your brother and Smythe," Jonathan said as he came over to join her. "It's problematic because he's being double shifted, being used on both of the top lines. And that can't be good for him."

"Why is the coach doing that?"

Jonathan shook his head. "Because your *Max* hasn't been playing since that incident in the first when, well."

Kayleigh nodded. "Yes. I know. When he forgot he wasn't playing defense. Common rookie mistake…"

Jonathan shrugged. "And your Max isn't a common rookie; he's a rare player who's both a winger and a defenseman. He can't afford to make that kind of screw up. Though, to be fair, he had been playing defense on that side before…"

Before. Before he was injured. Before she'd heard his truth and told him she couldn't deal with it, or him.

"I don't think it's that bad, though," Jonathan continued, oblivious to the turmoil in her head. "I mean he's there, on the bench. If there was a problem, Max would be back in that locker room or on his way to Stratford, no question. But he's in plain view of the public, freezing that tight butt off. And that tells me that he'll be on the ice during the third. Mark my words."

And as Kayleigh followed Jonathan's fingers, she saw a small, solitary figure sitting on the end of the Empires' bench. The figure was focused on the ice, not bothered by the cold, heated bench or no.

And then, she had an idea.

"Aruuuun!" she shouted. "I need something!"

Second Intermission

Max

He headed into the locker room, following the rest of his teammates in preparation for the intermission.

"Five minutes, boys," their captain shouted. "Then we go and listen to the orchestra. Make my sister blush!"

"St. Laurent!" yelled the equipment manager. "St. Laurent! We need to borrow your extra sweater. We got a request."

He blinked. "Erm…"

"C'mon," Evans said. "It's probably a kid from Make a Wish or Special Olympics."

"I…I have never…" he managed, confused at being asked for his jersey when so many other players were in the game. "Of course… erm…*absolutement*…"

"This ain't no kid," the equipment manager muttered. "It's a chick from the orchestra."

There was no air in the room, and Emerson's face was suddenly inches away. "You hurt her," his captain said, "you die. And no, I'm not exaggerating."

"*Ouais, mon chef,*" he replied as earnestly as he could. Then he turned to the equipment manager. "Where are you supposed to deliver the jersey?"

The equipment manager rolled his eyes. "I thought you'd never ask."

Kayleigh

Her heart pounded against her chest, almost through it. She took a breath, forcing herself to calm down. "You have three minutes, Kayleigh," Arun informed her as he began to prepare himself to head outside. "Make them count.

She wondered what the conductor was talking about before lifting up her head. And there he was.

"Special delivery…"

She didn't pause, didn't breathe, just ran up and kissed him. Hard. Like the world was going to end. And she let all of her thoughts, her feelings out there in the open. She gave herself in that kiss. Fully and completely.

He pulled back, stared at her, almost unruffled. His cheeks were red, his hair was in place, and yet his eyes were clear. "Are you sure? I don't want…to do this if you're not sure."

"I'm sure," she said. "Completely sure. I realized I needed you in my life, Max. Badly. I don't want to play any games. I don't want to have any more long nights by myself when the one thing that would make it better would be a conversation with you. I love you."

He kissed her then, soft, before pulling back and reaching under his jersey. She followed his fingers toward the thick material of the extra jersey he was there to bring her. She turned around, and lifted her arms up, letting him fit the material over her head. It fit perfectly over the layers of clothing she'd worn to play here, outside.

"*Je t'aime*," he whispered. "*Je t'aime*."

Fortified, she let his words envelop her, and headed toward her conductor. She was ready to play for the world, and, for him.

CHANGE IT UP

Kenzie MacLir

CHAPTER ONE

H ow are my boys doing? Empires sound off!"

A chorus of groans reached his ears, and Reiner Jahr looked around his living room, trying not to laugh at the general disarray of his teammates. Well, most of his teammates. The new kid, Max, hadn't done more than nurse a beer, and the Russians were still standing. Barely.

Stifling a chuckle, he thought, *This is what happened when you challenged a Russian to a vodka drinking challenge. There was no way in hell he was going to lose.*

The only problem, they all had to be at an event in a couple of hours.

Coach was going to be pissed.

Not that it wasn't the first time they'd all tied one on like this. However, it wasn't usually a few hours before they were supposed to be somewhere as a team. Today, they were meeting with a youth team from the local Special Olympics as part of the Winter Classic they were playing in.

Reiner didn't know about his teammates, but he was in no mood to get his butt reamed by Coach. Again. His ass still hurt from the last one.

But even though he had drunk just as much as the as everyone else he seemed to be recovering faster. Not bothering to wonder at his good fortune, he instead worried about getting his teammates back on their feet.

"Karpov! Get your ass in gear! And Emerson, you aren't captain for nothing. Pick up Sandberg and help me get him sober." Emerson hadn't spent the whole night with the team since he had the woman he loved waiting for him at home. But he'd been there for part of the drinking contest and then come back by this morning to make sure no one had died of alcohol poisoning, claiming you never knew what was going to happen with this group. Reiner was sure he was supposed to be offended, but as it was true, he'd shrugged and let Emerson in.

With a bit of a chuckle in his tone, he hollered at Brody Evans, "Oh, and Evans? By the way, you drunk dialed your girlfriend last night. Again." The snickers and groans that met his ear were followed swiftly with a "Shit," from Brody.

Ignoring calls for him to make coffee, and other comments telling him where to stick the coffee, Reiner hollered, "I'm not your mother, get your ass in gear!"

His accent was slight; after so many years in the States it only really came out when he was drinking or picking up women. American women had a thing for men with accents and he wasn't ashamed to admit he'd taken advantage of it more than once over the years.

"Fuck off."

The guys groaned and flipped him the bird, but Reiner started the coffee machine and began pulling mugs from the cupboards. Rolling his eyes, he figured he might as well be their mother, since no one else could pull it together enough to even curse at him. Mentally shrugging, Reiner figured that since a drunk team reflected poorly on them all, and he definitely didn't want to look bad this afternoon, he was really helping them for selfish reasons. Adding a little whistle to his coffee-making duty helped, too, especially once everyone started groaning for him to *shut it* and to *tone it the fuck down.*

Once he'd annoyed the guys enough with his whistling, he called, more loudly than necessary, "Coffee's ready! Come and get it, or I'm dumping your asses in the showers!"

"Can I help?" a soft-spoken voice with a heavy accent asked. Reiner knew it was the new kid, Max. French-Canadian, he thought Coach MacArthur had said. Reiner didn't care, as long as the kid could handle a puck. From what Reiner had seen, Max's stick-handling skills were top notch. They'd figure out if they held up once the pressure was on.

"You wanna help? Get Evans to quit texting his girl."

With a muttered, *"Merde,"* Max went up to one of the biggest guys on the team to try to pry his phone out of his fingers.

This wouldn't end well for the kid.

Reiner chuckled to himself. A bit of hazing the new guy and a fresh pot of coffee went a long way to improving his mood.

Surprisingly, he saw Max whistling as Brody Evans, six foot seven inches of solid muscle, looked mystified. Sure enough, Max handed Reiner the phone. But Evans noticed at the same time, and came charging at him. Oh great, he thought as Brody charged him. He grabbed one of the cups of coffee and held it up in front of him. Normally he'd welcome and be prepared for his hit, but he had zero desire to wrestle with Brody in his kitchen.

It took almost an hour before anyone was in any kind of shape to leave his place. For some reason, his apartment had become the unofficial hang-out for the team. The first time all the single guys on the team had crashed at his place after a home game, he'd been surprised.

He wasn't typically the guy people gravitated to, preferring to spend his time with a few select friends. He knew it was how he'd grown up. Life in a small village in Norway, with a population of maybe five hundred people, wasn't conducive to furthering his social butterfly status. Instead, he'd played hockey. When they had enough guys for a team, great, if not, he played alone, or with his dad. Hockey was his life.

When it had become obvious he was what some called a hockey prodigy, his parents had moved to a big city, where he could play teams more his level, a more aggressive hockey.

It had taken him years, and there were times he still struggled with large crowds, and groups of people, but for now, he loved it when they all crashed at his place. It reminded him of those times when he was just a kid playing hockey. Because, really, wasn't he just a big kid playing hockey now? He had the best job in the world. He played for a living. And he made a good living.

The New York Empires were in line for the Stanley Cup, and he was going to make sure they won it. However, challenging teammates to a drinking contest the night before a major event hadn't been the smartest thing his teammates had ever done. Now they were all dragging ass. It was a good thing they had a couple of hours before they had to be on the ice. He just hoped that they didn't embarrass themselves out there.

By the time he arrived at the rink, Reiner was ready to play some hockey. The fact he was going to be playing with kids didn't detract from the adrenaline pumping through his veins at the thought of lacing on his skates and suiting up. Just being on the ice gave him that boost. Didn't matter if he was playing with kids, in a house league, or with his teammates. Reiner never felt more alive than he did when he was on the ice.

For today, however they weren't wearing their Empires uniforms. They'd be wearing their jerseys and black pants. The improvised uniforms reminded him of the ones he wore when he played roller hockey, but these prevented the cold from seeping in. Not that he felt the cold. He could skate in his jersey and jock strap, and he had once, because you don't back down from a double dog dare! But today wasn't about him. This game wasn't even about the Empires. Today it was all about the kids.

Walking into the locker room, he smiled at the trash talking that was happening among his teammates. It didn't matter the language, and there were many in the NHL, the trash talking always sounded the same. There were even enough Norse players that if he ever wanted to speak his native tongue he could usually find someone.

"Jahr, in here now!" Coach barked at him.

He dropped his bag on the bench and followed his coach into the room he'd commandeered for the game. Sandberg and Karpov were already waiting.

Shit. This wasn't good. It wasn't as horrible as if Emmerson had been there, but it still wasn't good. He chanced a look back at his teammates and didn't see any signs of the drinking party that had happened the night before on them.

"What's up, Coach?" Karpov asked.

Coach handed each of them a piece of paper. Reiner looked at his, and saw a picture of a little boy, sitting in a wheelchair, clutching a hockey stick, and wearing his jersey. Underneath the picture was information about the child. He read his quickly. Karpov and Sandberg tilted their papers, and he saw similar images and info on theirs as well.

So they weren't in trouble. It was about the kids.

"As you know today's game is for the kids in the Special Olympics. These three love hockey, and you three are their favorite players. Your sole job today is to be the skates for the child on your paper."

Reiner could do that. Hell, he looked forward to it.

With a brisk nod, coach dismissed them, and they joined their teammates back in the locker room. Reiner toed off his shoes and slid his feet into his skates. Lacing them up, he let his mind wander to information on the paper about his fan, Kenny.

From the grin and twinkle in the kid's eye in the photo, the next couple of hours were going to be a lot of fun.

CHAPTER TWO

Emma Chase looked around the room, satisfied at how the night was going. She'd pulled it off. With a deep breath, she finally allowed herself to relax. Swiping a glass of champagne from a passing server, she sipped the bubbly liquid and began to mingle. The game that morning with the kids and the Empires had been a huge success, and now many of the hockey players were filing in. She knew most were uncomfortable in the tuxedos, but man, did they look good. Her ogling was interrupted by a colleague tapping her on the shoulder.

"Emma? I have someone I want to introduce you to."

Her friend Ruby Langley was gripping the arm of super-sexy hockey god Reiner Jahr. *Damn it, Astrid*, she swore in her mind. She knew exactly what Reiner did to Emma, and why she needed her here to be a buffer between them and let Emma embarrass herself in front of a lot of important people. The first time she'd met him, she'd been an exchange student to Norway, living in his bedroom. She'd stumbled out of it, her hair sticking up every which way, thick black eyeliner smudged on her face from the night before, and wearing holey pajama pants and T-shirt way too big for her frame. She'd yelped and ran back to her…his room.

Whenever he'd come home she'd managed to make an idiot herself, made all the more awkward due to the giant teenage crush she'd had on him.

From the moment the Empires had agreed to be a part of her event she hadn't been able to stop thinking about him and the fact they'd be working together. OK, not *together* together, but in close contact. She'd wanted to say something to him earlier at the rink, thank him for being Kenny's legs. By the time she'd finished getting the kids returned to their parents and the myriad of other things she'd needed to do, he'd already left the arena. As much as she'd love to visit the locker room, she wasn't quite ready to barge in on all the guys.

She never missed a chance to see him play hockey. She held season tickets to the Empires, not that he knew. But that was fine with her. He was beautiful to watch. No other player looked so smooth, like he'd been born on the ice, or even *of* the ice. He was like a Viking god. She chuckled to herself. What, he was the god of hockey? The thought nearly had her snorting out loud. Although it was easy to picture. The man was magic on the ice.

Watching him interact with Kenny and the other kids today had brought back the teenage crush she'd had on him. Well, she could admit to herself that it had never really gone away.

Now he was standing in front her. And her heart had decided it wanted to run the Kentucky Derby at being near him.

"Reiner, I want you to meet the woman who organized this event. Emma Chase."

"Good to see you again, Emma," he murmured. His accent was hardly there, not nearly as noticeable as his sister Astrid's was. He was eying the glass of champagne in her hand like it was a king cobra about to strike him. Not that she blamed him. The last time she'd seen him, just before she'd started working for the Special Olympics, she'd spilled wine all over him, ruining what she was certain had been a very expensive suit.

Spotting a waiter, she waved him over and placed her glass on his tray. As soon as her hands were free he took them, raising one to his lips brushing a kiss across her knuckles.

"You, too." Making banal small-talk was difficult with his light blue eyes meeting hers, and her hand engulfed in his larger one.

The rate her heart was beating, it wasn't going just after the Kentucky Derby, but the Triple Crown. *Damn it, Astrid*, she swore again.

"You look…different." There was a question in his voice. One she wasn't surprised by. She looked nothing like she had that last disastrous time they'd met.

She'd out grown the dark black pixie cut she'd worn up through college and now embraced her natural curls and color, with natural looking highlights in her red hair. She'd also ditched the lip and eyebrow piercing. She'd kept the small stud in her nose, though, liking the tiny bit of glam. It was at the point where when she looked at pictures of that time, she didn't recognize herself. She'd hidden behind her goth hair, piercings, and clothes that were three sizes too big.

Now, however, she embraced who she was and how she looked. She wasn't model thin, as was all the rage, at least according to fashion experts. She was a throwback to the Marilyn Monroe era, with curves a man could hold onto if he wanted, and she loved it. Besides, if she had to choose between running and chocolate, chocolate would win any day of the week.

"Have you spoken to Astrid lately?" he asked.

"Yeah, I talked to her last week. She couldn't make it. Something held her up back home. She was supposed to be my date for tonight."

"So you don't have a date?" When she shook her head, he held his arm out. "Then allow me."

She giggled as he whisked her away. Good crap, what the heck was that? She'd giggled. She wasn't a giggler.

It was sweet of Reiner to offer to escort her around tonight. She knew he was only doing it to be nice to his sister's friend, but to her, it was an exercise in restraint. The tingles shooting up her arm made her want to press her whole body to his and rub up against him like a cat in heat. She had it bad.

A woman would have to be dead not to be affected by him.

At six-foot three he wasn't the tallest in the NHL, but nor was he the shortest. His face was all sharp planes and angles, combined with the pure blue of his eyes, and the twin dimples in his cheeks when he smiled. The square jaw made her want to run her fingertips against it to see if it was as hard as it looked. Of course that wasn't the only thing she wanted to run her fingers across…

Oh boy. It made a girl wish she was home with her favorite toy. Imagining it was him. She'd better stop this, or she'd end up drooling on his shoes. How embarrassing.

Her gaze dropped as she took in his suit. It was so well-made, that she knew it must have been custom made. Nothing off the rack could fit him this well. She wished she could admire his ass without looking like she doing exactly that, but unless she wanted him to catch her drooling over him, she kept her eyes to the front. Why did he have to look so good?

She'd bought several copies of the ESPN Body Issue the year he'd been on the cover. Because hello, Reiner naked. How could she not?

Don't sniff him, don't sniff him, she chanted in her head. Too late.

She nearly groaned. He smelled delicious.

Down girl, she warned her inner vamp. She was working, tonight was important. Too important to screw up because she had a major case of lust for her best friend's older brother.

Especially when he was being nice enough to escort her around as a replacement for his sister.

CHAPTER THREE

Reiner couldn't stop staring. Holy shit, Emma had changed. The floor-length gown she wore skimmed her hips and hugged her ass in such a way that he'd glared at the man behind her who couldn't keep his eyes off her.

He'd never known her hair was red. The soft red curls framed her face, giving her a more glamorous quality. He'd watched her change over the years. He very much preferred this Emma to the one who'd lived with his family. That Emma had acted like he didn't exist, all sullen and full of teenage angst. At the time he'd loved the fact someone outside of this family wasn't treating him like a hockey god. Being the youngest player to win a Stanley Cup in the NHL had brought all sorts of media attention. Attention he hadn't been prepared for.

So when it had been his turn with the Cup, he'd headed home, taking it back to the small village where he'd donned his first pair of skates. That was the year Emma had been an exchange student. Whenever he'd seen her after she'd left Norway, she'd been with his little sister, Astrid, and caused something to happen to him, from spilling food and drinks all over him to walking in on him in the shower. Thank the gods she hadn't known it was him or he'd been certain something horrid would have happened.

Looking at her now, he felt certain the girl who'd caused all of it was gone, and in her place was a woman he wanted to get to know more about. Not because she was his little sister's best friend but because she was a damn sexy woman who was lighting the room up with her energy and passion. Her cheeky smile caught him off-guard. Did that mean there was no boyfriend in the picture? He was sure Astrid had mentioned Emma was dating someone. But if she wasn't...

His cock stirred at the thought of getting some action. It had been so long since he'd been attracted to a woman, he couldn't remember the last time he'd had sex. OK, he could remember, he just didn't want to.

It had been with a puck bunny, and she'd tried to tell him he didn't need to wear a condom as she was on the pill and clean. It wasn't the first time some chick had tried that with him. He hoped to the gods it would be the last. At that point he'd almost gotten up and left. But he'd needed the release, and been tired of using his hand. He should have left, as it had been a very unsatisfying interlude.

Since then, he'd taken a break from women and sex.

But now, watching the way the Emma's dress hugged her figure as she walked to join her friend Ruby, he wanted. But he only wanted her.

The question was...did she want him?

"So you going to tap that?" Sandberg asked him.

He'd been so lost in his thoughts about Emma, he hadn't heard Sandberg or Karpov come up on him. That was never a good thing. They were his best friends, and according to them, this meant they had the right and duty to give each other massive amounts of shit about everything. Especially women.

The fact they'd just caught him staring at Emma's ass, meant he could only do one thing. Go with it.

"If the gods permit, yes, I'm going to have sex with Emma. Tonight," he told them in a mixture of Norwegian and Finnish. A mixture only the three of them understood. No way did he want someone overhearing them and then telling the gossip rags about it. That's the last thing he needed.

Kyle Sandberg and Alexei Karpov had joined the team at the same time he had. Karpov had been in the States for a year, and Kyle had just moved to the U.S. like Reiner. As the only non-English-speaking players on the Empires farm team they'd bonded. The language hadn't been much of a problem, at least for Reiner; one of his aunts was from Finland, and his cousins had spoken a mixture of Norwegian and Finnish, resulting in most of the family doing the same. It had just made sense to him when he'd met Karpov to do the same thing. Kyle had added the Swedish words, leaving them having conversations that no one could understand unless they spoke all three languages.

"Does she know that?" Karpov asked, his Finnish accent thick as the day he'd come to the U.S.

"Not yet, but she will," he replied. Tossing back the rest of his beer, Reiner set it on a nearby table, preparing to go after Emma.

She looked over at him, and he caught the flare of attraction in her gaze. Emma smiled slowly. Then her gaze flicked to Sandberg and Karpov, and her eyes widened.

"Fuck, man, did you see that?" Sandberg whispered.

He had. It pissed him off. He'd shared women with both of the men at his side, and while he knew a lot of guys got off on it, he was happy to say he'd been there, done that. But with Emma, he found he didn't want to share. And he definitely didn't want her looking at his friends.

"Yeah, I did. But we all agreed…"

"We're too selfish to share the woman in our bed."

"Exactly." They'd better remember that.

Emma sauntered back to them. Fuck, she was sexy. "Wow, Renier Jahr, Kyle Sandberg, and Alexei Karpov, the fearsome threesome, right in front of me. How did I get so lucky?"

Even after years in the States, he sometimes missed nuances in the English language. Now was not one of those times. Emma was teasing him.

He liked her teasing.

Reiner smiled and noticed her breathing increased. Good. She wasn't unaffected.

"We are the lucky ones," Sandberg said raising her hand to his lips.

If it had been anyone else Reiner would have growled and told him to back the fuck off. But they had an unwritten rule of no poaching. They already knew he wanted her, so he wasn't worried. But it didn't mean he liked seeing another man's lips touching Emma. Even if Sandberg was his friend.

He bumped Sandberg out of the way, and placed his own lips to the center of her palm, his tongue lightly touching her skin before pulling away.

Her skin flushed, and he wanted to see that flush over her entire body. He had every intention of ending the night buried so deep inside of Miss Emma Chase that she'd wonder where she ended and he began.

CHAPTER FOUR

Emma ushered the last person out of the ballroom and heaved a giant sigh of relief. It was over. The day and night and been a huge success. Now she could take a break and breathe before she started working on the next event.

"You all done here?"

Slowly she turned to the voice behind her. Reiner was leaning against the bar, his bowtie undone and hanging around his neck, the top two buttons open on his shirt. His hands were shoved into his pants pockets, stretching the material across his package. *Er, pelvis, I totally meant pelvis*. Because she didn't ogle men's crotches. Ever.

Oh, man. She nearly pressed her hands to her cheeks, but instead forced her fingers to clench together.

Swallowing she answered him, "Yeah. The hotel and caterers will take care of clean-up."

He straightened and started walking toward her.

Beneath her dress her nipples pebbled, and she clenched her thighs together.

Not even in her wildest teenage…and, OK, even her adult dreams, had she ever imagined that hockey god Reiner Jahr would ever look at her like that. Her sexual experience could be chalked up to some not bad, but mostly mediocre, partners.

Something she would bet her Empires season tickets Reiner wasn't. Sometimes a woman could look at a man and just *know* that he was amazing in bed. Reiner would be a god in bed.

She was so out of her depth…and comfort zone.

She really liked her comfort zone when it came to men. Hence the term *comfort zone*. Oh Lord she was babbling in her head now. Again.

The only daring thing she'd ever done in her life was that year she'd been an exchange student. That had really only been to escape her parents' divorce. Living halfway around the world meant she'd been able to escape all the drama of being put in the middle of two people she loved. Mentally shaking her head, she focused back on the here and now, the here and Reiner. Emma watched him stalk closer.

He stopped inches from her, and she got another whiff of him. Holy moly, he still smelled good. How was it possible?

Reiner stretched out an arm, wrapping it around her waist, he drew her into his body. His very hard body. There was no give in is his muscular form, forcing hers to melt into him. Or maybe that was just her body instinctually surrendering to the inevitable.

"What are you doing?" she murmured, knowing full well what would happen.

"What I've wanted to do all night."

His head descended, slowly, giving her plenty of time to say no. There was no way on God's green earth she was saying no to a kiss from Reiner Jahr. Did she have stupid written all over her face?

His lips brushed hers gently, but it wasn't enough. She wanted more. His mouth nipped and teased, never pushing her, but not taking the invitation her parted lips offered.

Warm lips pressed against the corner of her mouth, drifted down her jawline, never coming back to her lips, instead settling against her pulse. When his teeth scraped her throat, she gasped. Emma pressed her body even more fully against his, fitting herself into him, damn near wanting to climb him. Reiner dragged his tongue up to her earlobe and nipped her.

Her hips shifted against his, and Reiner fisted her hair, dragged his mouth back to hers, and kissed her. Kiss was too tame a word. He plundered. He devoured. He conquered.

Her mind blanked, and all she could do was clench her fists in his jacket and hold on. Kissing Reiner was better than a molten lava chocolate cake topped with ice cream. Better than…

With one hand still gripping her hair, his slid the other down to her ass, palming it, pulling her tighter into him. She felt his erection, his very impressive erection. Good God, did she want him.

Reiner lifted his head, breathing hard. His blue eyes branded her with their intensity.

"Where do you live?" he asked.

"Red Hook. You?"

"Park Slope."

So they were both in Brooklyn.

"Your place or mine?"

It took her a moment to wrap her tongue around the word, "Mine." He nodded, looking pleased, but what he didn't know was that she was claiming him with that one word as well. Once she got him in her bed, she wasn't letting him out.

Her grandma had told her once, that she'd known she wasn't just in lust with her grandpa, but in love with him after their first kiss. Emma had scoffed at the idea of knowing you were in love with someone by a kiss.

Having just been kissed stupid by Reiner, she wondered if her grandma hadn't been right.

"Do you need to get anything?"

"My coat," she rasped.

He nodded and followed her to the coat room, never letting go of her. With his hand trailing down her arm to brush against her breast, he pulled her in tightly. She'd never had a man do that, and had wondered how it would feel to have one hold her like that. It was fan-freaking-tastic, and she wanted more of it.

They walked together to the coat check, and found the person who'd been checking the coats was gone. Emma walked into the room and found her own coat. She checked the pockets and found her phone, cash for a cab, and keys were right where she'd left them. Reiner took the coat from her and held it up so she could slip into it. Once she had it on, he took her hand once more, and they stepped out into the cold New York night.

Whoever said having a man be chivalrous was archaic had never had a man be that way with them. It wasn't archaic, it was…she didn't know what it was, but she knew she wanted more of it.

The temperatures had dipped into the low twenties, and she should have been freezing, but the heat coming off of Reiner, and the low burn in her system about the fact that she was about to have sex with Reiner, had her warm from the inside out.

Reiner held out a hand, and a cab stopped in front of them. He opened the door and waited for her to climb in and then slid in next to her. She gave her address to the driver and settled back into Reiner's arms. His hands came around her, but they didn't settle in. It started with small, light touches. His thumbs rubbed softly back and forth against her rib cage, never quite brushing her breasts, but hinting at it.

Reiner didn't have to lean down much to meet her for the kiss. Their lips brushed, tongues met, and with a gasp, that simple sound,

Emma was lost. Deepening the kiss, their mouths fused. With no space between them, their tongues twined and tangled, never pausing, never taking a breath, this kiss consumed him.

"All right lovebirds, out you go." The cabbie's voice had her jumping a bit.

This time of night, it hadn't taken long for them to get to her place. Reiner paid the cabbie, and then they were inside her apartment.

She took her coat off, tossed it on the couch, and turned to Reiner.

He was leaning against the door, his hands in his pockets, legs crossed at the ankles. It should be a sin to look that good. He could have picked any woman to be with tonight, and yet he was here, in her apartment, with her, about to get very naked.

Oh, crap. That meant she was going to get naked as well. Maybe she should have thought about this some more. She'd seen the women he'd usually dated. Tall, beautiful, and skinny. Petite, beautiful, skinny. Like super skinny. Something she very much wasn't. Even as a teenager she'd never been the super skinny type.

She had curves.

It didn't matter how many miles she ran, or how much Zumba she did, those curves weren't going anywhere. Plus, she loved chocolate. And ice cream.

She'd made peace with her curves. Or so she'd thought until Reiner had stepped into her apartment.

"What are you thinking?"

"That I look nothing like the women you normally go out with." *Stupid. Stupid.* Why had she blurted that out?

He straightened away from the door and moved—no, stalked— across the room to her. "No, you don't." She inhaled, pretty offended, until he continued, "and thank the gods for that." His hands framed her hips, pulling her flush with his body. "If you looked like them, you wouldn't be you. And I very much want you, not someone else."

"I have lots of curves." Her voice was breathy. She was never breathy, she was always in control and self-assured. She didn't care. All she cared about was this moment. This night. Reiner seemed happy with her figure; there was no mistaking his very impressive erection.

His hand palmed her ass, slid up along her hips back to her waist, pulled her in close. "Oh, yeah, you do." The words were nearly growled, and his erection wouldn't let her mistake his intention. He turned her around so her back was to his chest, and since she was still in heels, his erection pressed against her ass, nestling between her cheeks, through her dress. His hands met on her waist, and slowly slid up the curve of her belly, past her ribcage, to cup her full breasts. His cock twitched against her, making its presence known. As if she could forget.

With both of his hands on her breasts, his thumbs began slow circles against her pebbled nipples. Her head fell back to his shoulder, and his mouth began a trail from her cheek, to her earlobe, on down. His tongue laved her, his lips left fire in their wake, and when he sucked none too gently on her throat, moisture pooled between her legs.

Pressing her thighs together, she wanted more, needed more. More of everything. More of him. She turned to face him, but his hands gripped her even tighter, never leaving her breasts, his thumbs never stopping their torturous assault on her nipples. He wouldn't let her turn around.

"Let me make you feel good." Reiner's accented words were felt, rather than heard. He didn't bother to lift his head from her neck.

Her breath hitched as one hand made a slow journey down. By the time he passed her hip, he began pulling her gown up, handful after handful, until he brushed skin. She had thigh highs on.

Noting his surprise, she breathed out, "I hate pantyhose. I feel like

I'm squished into them. I wear these so I feel like I can breathe."

His growl of approval made her thighs tighten even more. She needed his hand there now.

"Don't take them off."

She wasn't doing anything. Not with him pressed up against her, his hands on her naked thighs. She was terrified if she moved, she'd wake up, and this would all have been a dream. A very dirty, very erotic dream.

Reiner spun her around and took her mouth in a blistering kiss, one that had her on the verge of another orgasm.

Placing her hands on his chest, she slipped them under his jacket and pushed it off him. He lifted one hand off her and shrugged that arm out of the jacket before returning the hand to her waist, and then doing the same thing with the other arm.

Emma slowly undid his tie and then slipped the buttons on his shirt out of each buttonhole. She wasn't going slowly on purpose, but her fingers trembled, and she had to concentrate.

Reiner's hands had been busy brushing up and down her body. "I like your curves."

Her hands froze on him, as his started moving up her ribs. His hands stopped beneath her breasts, not touching them. Not yet. Her eyes flicked up to look at his face. He was looking not at her face, but at her chest.

She hadn't been sure about the bodice of her dress, as it was strapless and barely contained her girls, but seeing the way Reiner was looking at them, she was glad she'd gone with it.

His fingers found the zipper hidden in the side of her dress, and pulled it down slowly. His eyes moved to hers, and she felt singed by the fire in them. She felt the heat all the way to her core. It wasn't going to take much to send her over the edge with him.

All he had to do was look at her, and she was ready. For anything.

With the zipper all the way down, he stepped back, and took his hands off her. The material clung for a heartbeat to her breasts then slid to the floor, leaving her standing there in nothing but her thigh highs and heels.

With any other man she'd have felt vulnerable and tried to cover something. As it was, her hands fluttered as if to hide her from his gaze. But the way he was looking at her. Like she was his favorite meal—or because this was Reiner Jahr, hockey god, like she was the Stanley Cup—she cocked her hip and thrust out her breasts in her best Marilyn Monroe sex kitten pose. She felt ridiculous.

Granted she'd only ever done the pose in her bathroom, with the door closed.

But by the way Reiner's eyes dilated and his nostrils flared, he liked it.

"You were naked under that dress?" He growled, a hint of his Norwegian accent came through.

God, she loved his accent.

"Lines," she breathed out.

He stepped back into her personal space and backed her up until her legs hit the back of her couch.

"I'm not going to be able to go slow this first time. I'm going to fuck you, and it's going to be fast, hard, and dirty. You good with that?" He growled, actually growled at her.

She hadn't thought it was possible for her nipples to get any harder, yet they did, while she grew ever wetter at his words.

She nodded, unable to form coherent thoughts.

It was all he needed. His mouth descended on hers, taking, demanding, consuming her.

His hands were on her breasts, her hips, her thighs, everywhere.

She squirmed in his hands, needing more. Her fingers slid to his shirt and plucked at the buttons. She got one unhooked before he gripped her thigh, hooking her leg around his hip.

She no longer had the patience to mess with his shirt and grasped the already partially open ends and pulled. Buttons popped and pinged as they hit the floor, and she shoved his shirt off his shoulders and ran her hands all over his naked chest, discovering all the grooves in his rock hard abdomen and chest.

She'd known there was ink on his chest and arms, she'd seen them in an underwear ad he'd done, and in that Body issue spread. She couldn't wait to run her tongue all over his tattoos.

He moved his mouth to her jaw and skimmed it, then her throat, moving down her body. He bent her back over the couch, giving him easier access to her openness. His mouth latched onto one of her breasts, she tightened her fingers in his hair, holding him there.

She needed more.

She found his belt and tried to unbuckle it. Her fingers had barely touched the leather before his hands brushed hers away, making quick work of the belt, and then he was falling into her hands. Her grip was sure, even though she felt anything but.

Reiner made her feel bold.

"Protection?" He growled against her hot skin.

"Pill," she got out. She never had sex without a condom, but if Reiner wasn't inside of her soon she was going to go up in flames. "I'm good," she whispered.

"Me, too," he said into her neck.

His hand at her leg lifted her higher, opening her to his invasion. The plump head of his cock brushed at her entrance, eliciting a moan from her. But he wasn't in yet. She needed him. "Now," she ordered against his lips.

"As my lady commands."

She could feel his smile against her lips. Her smart-ass remark was lost when Reiner pushed all the way in, feeding her inch after inch until he was seated to the hilt.

She wrapped her other leg around his waist and hooked her ankles, holding him inside and tightening her muscles. He felt so good, she never wanted him to leave her.

"Emma," he groaned, not moving, not yet. He pressed his forehead to hers, resting for a moment. Did he need to gather his breath? Was it possible that Reiner was as affected by this as she was?

He walked them until her back hit a wall, and then he was moving inside of her.

"Just like that Em, don't fucking move." His hands were under her ass, her legs were gripping his hips, and she was crashing over the edge.

Reiner chuckled. "Oh, Emma, I'm nowhere near done with you." He lifted her higher, changed his angle, and she gasped. Her eyes flew open, and she looked down to where they were joined. She'd never looked when she had sex, preferring to keep her eyes closed. She could admit now, as Reiner moved inside of her, his hands gripping her thighs, holding her in place, that it was because she'd been imagining it was him in her bed, instead of the men she'd been with at the time. Her imagination had nothing on the real thing.

His mouth was back on her breasts, sucking and driving her insane. His hips pistoned against her until she couldn't take any more. She screamed his name as she came, but still he didn't let up. While she wanted nothing more than to melt into the floor and lay in a boneless heap, he worked her body. Within seconds she was climbing again. Reiner pressed a finger against her clit, and she screamed her orgasm to the room. Her throat was hoarse, but still he kept his promise. He wasn't finished with her.

Reiner slid her legs to the floor, but she couldn't hold herself up. Didn't matter, he turned her and bent her over the arm of the sofa and entered her again. His fingers bit into her hips as he slammed into her again and again.

The new position and deeper angle had Emma close again. He leaned across her back, and bit her neck, soothing it with his tongue. Emma lost it. She bucked against him, unable to do much more than lay there and take it. She chanted his name over and over until he stiffened against her and found his release. She felt him come inside of her. Something she'd never felt before, and something she wanted more of. Oh, yeah, when she'd claimed him, she'd meant it. Reiner wasn't going to get away from her. He was hers.

CHAPTER FIVE

Reiner rested his head against her back, and struggled to breathe. He'd just taken Emma against her wall. And her couch. It was the hottest fucking sex he'd ever had. Without a condom at that. By the gods, the woman got inside his head. He'd never gone bareback, but now he never wanted to go back to condoms. Shit, he never wanted sex with anyone else. It was just Emma. She was it for him.

He couldn't wait for more.

Already he could feel himself hardening inside of her.

Stepping back, he slid from her, and smiled when he noticed she was still contracting around him. Oh yeah. Emma wanted more as well. First, though, he needed to ditch the rest of his clothes, and hers.

As hot she'd been with those heels on as he fucked her, they'd been digging into his back. Reiner watched her back rise and fall with her uneven breathing, her skin a rosy hue he found sexy as hell, her lips swollen from his, her hair in a wild disarray, and her eyes half closed, Reiner knew he'd barely scratched the surface of all the things he wanted to do to the lovely Emma Chase.

He toed off his shoes, stepped out of the pants that were caught around his ankles, and shrugged out of his shirt.

He contemplated Emma. He could either take off her hose and shoes now…or carry her to her bed and do it there.

If he removed them while she was laying down, he could…bed it was.

Reiner swung her up into his arms, and carried her to her bedroom. He placed her on the bed and went to the bathroom. He cleaned himself and took a warm washcloth back to the bedroom.

Emma hadn't moved since he'd placed her on the bed. "You still with me, Em?"

"Mmpf. Brain shut off."

She hummed when he pressed the warm cloth to her. He'd never had the urge to clean a woman before, but it was strangely intimate.

"You like that?"

"Um-hmm."

Done cleaning her he tossed the cloth over his shoulder and grabbed one of her legs. He started rolling down her hose, kissing her skin as he revealed it. It was silky smooth.

"Reiner, again?" He smiled at the shock in her voice.

"Unless you're too tired…"

He laughed when she pushed him back and straddled him, one stocking still on. He'd never laughed during sex before. In fact, he'd never had so much fun with sex before. Emma was really something special.

"What's so funny, Reiner?"

"Nothing," he leaned up and wrapped his arms around her, reversing their positions. No way was he letting those wandering fingers of hers play. This was still his turn. He wanted his mouth on every inch of her silky skin. He wanted this to be perfect for her. Normally, he couldn't wait to leave after he was done with his bedmates, but this was different. This was Emma.

He relished her hoarse cries as he put his mouth on her, and swore he'd spend the rest of the night making her scream. She'd never want to leave. And Reiner didn't find that scary at all. Instead, he found himself looking forward to the next day with her. When he was finished with her, Emma wouldn't be able to move. Deciding this was a good goal, Reiner added his fingers into play, and brought her to climax before climbing up her body, and worshipping her lips with his own.

He was ready to go, and he had all night with Emma's lush body.

Settling his hips in between her legs, he pushed his cock in, slowly, not allowing for a break from her last orgasm, and began to gently rock into her. He could still feel her contracting around him, and his balls drew up, tight and full. By the gods he was ready, but this was for Emma. He'd hold on until she came again.

And she did. As soon as he heard her breath hitch, he pumped once, twice more and shouted his release to the ceiling. He was dead. Sex had killed him, and he was OK with that. Being inside Emma was where he wanted to be.

Her hand fluttered to his face and dropped back to the bed. "You OK?"

He chuckled. "Em, I'm so much better than OK." He kissed the tip of her nose. "Sleep. I'll be right here." He rolled over and held her, realizing that while he'd never liked to cuddle women before, but he could hold Emma forever.

By the time she fell into a sated sleep, the sun was lightening the sky and he had to get up for practice. He hated to sneak out, but he had to go.

He wanted to see her again. Maybe he'd cook for her tonight, something special. Something that they could eat quickly so they could fall into bed right after. His dick hardened in his suit pants. He couldn't help it. He thought about Emma, and he wanted. He didn't even mind the walk of shame in last night's suit. By the gods, he had it bad.

CHAPTER SIX

Emma rolled over and reached for Reiner. Her fingers trailed across the pillow to find not his warm body, but paper. A note? Emma sat up in bed, shoved her hair out of the way, and opened the note.

Early practice. Dinner tonight. My place.

He hadn't signed it, but had left his number.

Normally a girl didn't want to wake to an empty bed and a note, but in this case, she'd let it pass. Biting her thumbnail, she leaned back against her pillows and reread the note. He wanted to see her again. Dinner, he'd written. At his place. That had to mean something, right? Slapping her hand across her eyes, she groaned. This was just sex. Nothing more. She smiled against her hand. For now.

Pushing off the bed, she headed to the kitchen where the dark aroma of freshly brewed coffee teased her nose. *Oh yeah*, she thought. She was keeping him. Pouring a cup, she went over the events of the night before.

If she'd told her teenage self that the cause of most of her angst would one day spend the night giving her orgasm after orgasm, she'd have thought herself insane.

But he had, and it had been wonderful.

Bonus: he wanted to see her again.

Blowing steam across the top of her coffee, she walked through her small apartment to the table and chair she'd set up next to the window. Her view wasn't the greatest, but it was hers.

The door opened, and Ray and Kevin, her next door neighbors, walked in. They never knocked. It didn't bother her anymore, but it had taken some getting used to.

"So who was he?" Ray asked as he helped himself to a cup of coffee.

Kevin put a box of pastries from the shop next door on the table. "Details, girl. We want details."

She studied Ray and Kevin as she took her first sip of coffee. They were polar opposites. Ray was solid, contained, and a cop. Kevin was drama personified. Ray wore jeans and T-shirt when he wasn't on the job, and Kevin dressed like he was going on a job interview all the time. They shouldn't work, and yet they did.

"Remember my friend Astrid?"

"Who can forget Astrid? That girl has flare," Kevin said around a croissant.

"Right, well, it was her older brother."

Ray spewed coffee across her tiny kitchen. "That was Reiner Jahr?"

Emma smiled. "I thought you were a Yankees fan?"

Kevin waved his croissant at them. "He's a sports fan. Doesn't matter if it's baseball, football, hockey, basketball, rugby, lacrosse. Hell, he even watches bowling. Who watches bowling? I mean, why do you think our cable bill is so high? It isn't because of porn, let me tell you."

"Back up." Ray was still sputtering. "Can we get back to the fact that Reiner Jahr, the youngest player ever to win a Stanley Cup, was here? Reiner Jahr who makes the NHL player of the week at least twice a month. Reiner Jahr, was here, in this very apartment, and *I didn't get to meet him?*"

Sipping her coffee, she hid her grin and nodded.

"You need to give me details. Now." Ray moved Kevin out of his way and took the only other seat at her table.

"I'm pretty sure you heard all the details last night."

If they hadn't, she'd be surprised. Heaven knows she heard everything they did. Not that she was complaining. The things they did sounded pretty hot. She'd always wondered what being the focus of all that attention would be like.

Granted she'd probably have had a coronary if it came to actually doing it. Because what woman didn't fantasize about two men seeing to her pleasure. So that one would stay firmly in fantasize-but-never-actually-do box. Besides, after last night, she realized what she really wanted was to be the focus of Reiner's attention.

"Yes, we did. But while my love here wants to know all about sex with Reiner, I want to know how you're doing? Because honey, having sex with your best friend's sibling is never something you do lightly. Unless you're both drunk off your asses. And neither of you sounded drunk last night," Kevin said, wagging is eyebrows at her over his coffee cup.

Just how thin were these walls?

She thought about her answer. "I'm OK."

"Really, because I can tell you I wasn't OK when it happened to me." Kevin told her, taking a sip from Ray's coffee. "In fact it messed me up a lot."

"I remember." Boy did she remember. Kevin had been a stressed-out wreck for weeks after he'd slept with Ray. Though Ray hadn't been that much better. He'd still been in the closet to his family. "But I really am OK. He wants to have dinner at his place tonight."

"How do you think Astrid is going to react?"

She didn't have to think, she knew. Astrid would be happy for her. Unless she'd been lying to her about wanting to hook her up with Reiner. In fact, she wondered if Astrid hadn't been able to meet her at the benefit in order to force the two of them together?

"Trust me, I've got this."

She did. It shocked her how well she was handling everything. Normally interactions with the opposite sex left her a mess in the first couple of weeks of a new relationship, but there was something about being with Reiner…and yes, she knew it had been less than twenty-four hours since they'd met, reconnected, whatever. It didn't matter. It felt right. That's what mattered.

Her grandma had been right. Sometimes you just know from the beginning.

CHAPTER SEVEN

G et your head in the game, Jahr!"
With his coach's shout ringing in his ears, Reiner forced his attention off the warm and willing woman he'd left sleeping in bed, and tried to get his ass in gear.

There was too much riding on tomorrow night's game for him to be obsessing over a woman. He banished all thoughts of how warm and luscious she'd looked when he'd left her place that morning, and skated to center ice.

Coach dropped the puck and he battled Emmerson for it. He won the battle and skated around the lineman. He flew down the ice, passing the puck back and forth between him and Kyle seamlessly. There were times when he was on the ice when he bought into his parent's belief that he'd been blessed by the Goddess Skaldi.

He's family still believed in the old gods and goddesses. Along with Christianity. He'd thought it was weird, until Astrid had told him a lot of people believed in the gods and goddesses of their forefathers and in Christ. He didn't care where his talent came from, all he cared about was being able to play, and play well.

There was no one between him and net. The goalie was weaker on his left side, so Reiner flicked a wrist shot toward the upper left. He took the shot. The puck hit the post and came flying back at him. He ducked and skated out of the way and ran into Max. His skates went out from underneath him, and he fell backward.

Reiner found Emma standing in front of their bedroom window. The view overlooked a small neighborhood park. It wasn't big like the ones in the city, but was perfect for them. They hadn't planned on buying a house, content to stay in his apartment. It was big enough for them and the baby. but when they'd seen the for sale sign on one of their nightly walks around the neighborhood they hadn't been able to resist buying.

He'd been anxious to have them moved in and unpacked before the baby came and his season got crazy.

He came up behind her, resting his head on hers, and his hands on her rounded stomach. "How are you feeling?"

"Tired. From the way Thor here is kicking, soccer, not hockey, is going to be in our future."

"Thor?"

"You don't like it? How about Loki?"

"What if he's a she?"

"She can be Thoretta. Besides, Thoretta sounds like an awesome name for a soccer star."

He smiled. The teasing was part of them. He'd never been so happy. And as for soccer? He didn't mind. But while the baby might kick now, hockey was in his blood. He'd play for the pure sport of it, because hockey was fun.

Reiner breathed in the scent of Emma's hair. Rosemary and mint. Until Emma, he'd never cared about scents...unless it was the scent of ice. He inhaled deeper, wanting her scent inside of him. He would never forget how she smelled right now. He wanted to keep this memory, the anticipation, and when she tipped her head back to look at him, all of the love she felt for him shining in her eyes, he'd never felt more at peace in his life.

"Jahr, open your eyes."

Blinking Reiner opened his eyes. What the fuck? He was laying on the ice, coach and the trainer were leaning over him. Where was Emma?

"What happened?"

"You tell us. One second you're skating away from the puck, and the next your head hit the ice."

He moved to sit up but was stopped by the trainer. "Hold on, I need to check you over."

"How long was I out?"

"Couple of minutes, three tops."

"Where's my lid?"

"Your helmet came off when your head hit the ice. I've never seen one break like that before. You must have a hard head."

Ignoring the bad jokes, the trainer made, Reiner couldn't get his mind off what he'd just seen. What in the hell had happened to him? And what was up with the dream of him and Emma?

"I'm fine," he assured the trainer. He'd never had a concussion; hell, he'd never been hurt, which was unusual for an athlete. He'd figured it was because he was just that good. This was odd. Something didn't feel right.

"Humor me then," the trainer said.

He lay there while the trainer flashed a light in his eyes and had him follow his finger. Determining he was well enough to move him off the ice, the trainer told him to sit up. With the help of coach and the trainer he got to his feet.

His team was standing around watching him. He could feel their anxiety while they waited to find out how he was. As much as it chafed, he understood their concern. They were all still dealing with one of their teammates being out for the season due to injury, and the new guy Max, taking his spot.

The last thing they needed was another major injury.

"I'm fine," he assured them again. He really was.

An hour and what felt like a thousand questions later he left the practice rink.

"Care to explain what happened on the ice today?" Kyle asked, wearing one of his signature shirts. Today's said, "Keep a dentist in business. Play hockey."

Fuck a duck. He should have known they wouldn't leave without demanding answers.

Kyle and Alexei were leaning against the doors to the rink, just out of sight. Their bags at their feet, they crossed their sticks preventing Reiner from leaving. He would have done the same if it had been either of them being knocked out, even if it was only for a second. But there was no way in hell he was going to tell them what had happened while he was out.

"Not really, no."

He still wasn't sure what had happened, and he wasn't about to dwell on it either. Not when he had a gorgeous woman coming over in a couple of hours for dinner.

"How about what happened after we left the party last night?"

"Not that either."

"He's hiding something."

Ignoring his friends, he pushed through their sticks and makeshift blockade, and made his way to the subway station. The only downside to living in Brooklyn was the long commute to the practice facilities on the other side of New York City. Which he normally didn't mind.

Today, however, was one of those days he wished he lived closer.

"You know you want to tell us." Kyle cajoled.

"*Nie*," he said, reverting to his native tongue.

Kyle and Alexei pestered him until they reached their stops, and then he had the subway to himself.

There was something about Emma that had him not wanting to share her with even his best friends. It wasn't just that; he never invited women to his place. It was his sanctuary, the one place in the world where no one expected him to be a hockey superstar or aware of what was going on around him.

The only women who'd been inside of it were either related to him or his housekeeper, who came in once a month to do a major cleaning of his apartment.

But he wanted Emma in his space.

More so after that dream, whatever it was after his head hit the ice. More than the fact that Emma had been pregnant and there were rings on their fingers, what struck him most, had him anxious to see her again, was he could feel like love he had for her pulsing in his veins. Love? Shaking his head, he realized that he did love Emma. So much. He really wanted that dream to come true.

It scared him how much he wanted that…he was going to go with dream. Yesterday he'd been happy in his life; with the choices he'd made; today he wanted more.

No, he wanted Emma.

Now he just needed to figure out how to get and keep her. Dinner tonight was a great place to start. Maybe she'd go with him to the Family Skate coming up for the team.

He left the subway and pulled out his phone. First order of business was making something besides steak or fish and veggies. Which meant he needed to talk to someone who knew Emma.

His finger hovered over his mom and his sister's contact icons. If he called his mom and asked her what Emma's favorite food was, she'd ask a million questions about why he wanted to know. On the other hand, Astrid would only ask a thousand. But Astrid would ask if was planning on sleeping with her, whereas his mom wouldn't, and he could play it off that he'd reconnected with her a charity event and was treating her to a thank you for a great event dinner.

Mom it was.

He calculated the time difference, it was coming up on nine in Setså his mom was still up. He pressed her icon and waited. He didn't have to wait long.

"Reiner, this is a nice surprise."

He couldn't help but smile at her greeting. She said it every time he called. Considering he called her at least once a week, and she had caller ID, it cracked him up.

"*Hei, mor*. Do you have a minute?"

"For you my son, I have more than one."

The only downside to being in the NHL was the fact his parents lived in another country. He'd offered to move them to the U.S. after Astrid had graduated from college, but they'd said no. Norway was their home, and while it pained them that their children had left it, they took comfort in the fact that both he and Astrid went home every chance they got. There would always be room for them in his parents' home.

"What's Emma's favorite food?"

There was a pause and he wondered if he'd dropped the call. "*Mor*?"

"Do you mean Astrid's Emma?"

"*Ja*. Astrid's Emma. I ran into her last night at a charity event she was putting on. I gave her a ride home, and I want to make her something as a thank you for an amazing day and night."

"Chocolate, and ice cream. Oh she loves your *bestemor's pinnekjøtt*."

He defied anyone to not love his grandma's *pinnekjøtt*. "I don't have time to make *pinnekjøtt*." But he could do something similar. He had time for that. "Thanks, *mor*. I know what I'm going to do."

"Good. Now catch me up on everything else. We caught the game the other night. Is Dobrynin OK?"

That was one of the many things he loved about his parents. They might choose to remain in Norway, but they knew each one of this teammates and their families, and cared about them. He got her up to date, and she regaled him with the goings on from the neighborhood and his family back home.

By the time he hung up with her, he was at his favorite neighborhood market. In the three years he'd lived in the neighborhood, he'd never not found what he was looking for there. Moving through the market, he picked up the items he needed, plus a few he didn't typically buy. This would go well; it had to. Tonight mattered.

He was putting the finishing touches on dinner when a buzzer sounded. He hit the open button and forced himself to wait for her to knock instead of waiting for her in the hallway. Opening the door at her first knock, he was floored once again by his reaction to Emma. "Hi."

"Hi."

"Come in," he stepped back so she could enter.

"Something smells good."

He took her coat and hung it up. "Thanks. I made lamb chops with grilled vegetables."

"Yum. I love lamb. Though no one makes it as well as your grandma."

"Hopefully you'll like mine as much as hers. But first, this."

Pulling her into his arms, he tipped her head back, and kissed her. Fuck, he loved her mouth. He could spend hours kissing her.

Reiner pulled the lamb from the oven and plated it along with the vegetables and directed her to the side of the counter where he'd put out placemats.

"I'm sure I'll love it."

"What do you want to drink? I have beer, wine, water."

"Water is perfect."

Grabbing a couple of bottles of water from the fridge, he joined her at the counter. They ate in silence, but it wasn't awkward, it felt... natural.

"How was your day?" he asked as they were cleaning up.

"Good, I was able to get caught up on all the paperwork I'd pushed aside while I was working on the event for last night. It went over well, and I had a good time, but I'm glad it's over. Thanks again for what you did for Kenny. His mom called and told me he hasn't stopped talking about you."

"He's a great kid."

"Yeah, he is. The first time I met him he told me, just because his body doesn't work doesn't mean his mind is broken."

Reiner laughed, "He said the same thing to me. What's his family's situation?"

He couldn't imagine it was cheap to have a kid with the amount of medical issues that Kenny had.

"It could be better. Most families who have severe needs kids are on a lot of assistance."

Reiner considered himself one of the lucky ones when it came to contracts and had already made more money between his contract with the Empires and his endorsement deals that his great-grandchildren wouldn't have to worry, unless someone mismanaged his money. He could more than afford to help a family like Kenny's.

"Can you get me a list of what their immediate needs are?"

Emma paused, her water bottle halfway to her mouth. "Excuse me?"

"I want to help them. So can you get me the information?"

"Um, yeah. I think so."

"Good."

"You're a good man, Reiner Jahr."

They finished eating, and Emma helped him clean up, and then they were settled in his living room on the couch.

"How was your day?" she asked.

He'd never shared his day with a woman not his mom or sister, but the compulsion to share what had happened to him at the rink was overwhelming.

When he was done talking, she was staring at him like he had three heads. She was probably freaked out about his vision. "What?"

"You didn't get hurt? At all? Like not even a headache?"

"Nope."

"That's like freaky crazy. Have you ever had that happen before?"

"All the time. I've never so much as gotten a scratch."

He waited for her to freak out about his dream, vision, whatever the fuck it was.

"Must be nice. I'm a grade-A klutz, as you well know."

Fucking A, he was going to have to bring it up. "What about my dream-slash-vision?"

"What about it? Have you talked to your parents about it? Or your grandma. I'm convinced that woman knows everything."

"No, why would I?"

"You might not be the only one in your family who has this."

He was floored. She wasn't freaked out about this at all. "Why aren't you?"

"Freaked out?"

"Yeah." He was.

"I don't know. I guess I've always wondered, hoped, that the stories about people who had these things happen to them were real."

She didn't really believe that did she? From the look on her face she did. He said, "So you think I…"

"Should talk to your parents. Or your grandma. Go call them now. If you're like Astrid, you won't be able to relax till you know what's going on."

He really didn't want to go call his parents or his grandma, but Emma was right. He wouldn't be able to relax and enjoy Emma unless he knew what was going on. It irked him more than a little that it hadn't occurred to him to ask his mom when he'd had her on the phone earlier too.

He left her to go to the bedroom and called his parents. When they didn't pick up any of their phones, he called his grandma.

"My, Reiner, what has you so upset?" she said instead of a greeting.

Emma was right, she did know everything. For the first time in his life, he wondered how she always knew what everyone was feeling, and if maybe what was happening to him came from the same place.

"How do you always know?"

She was quiet for so long he didn't think she'd answer when she finally spoke.

"Why do you want to know?"

He told her about what had happened at practice, leaving nothing out.

"Did he contact you?"

More confused than ever he asked, "Did who contact me?"

"Your birth father. He swore an oath to never contact you unless you asked him to."

"My what?" he forced out.

His dad wasn't his dad? No, he wouldn't believe it. There was no way his mom would have cheated on him.

"Oh, dear." His grandma sighed. "Listen to me, Reiner, you need to contact your parents now. It isn't what you might be thinking."

Yeah, because thinking your mom had had an affair and you were a product of it wasn't what he was thinking.

"Grandma, I need to go." He didn't give her a chance to respond before he hung up and walked back out to the living room where Emma was waiting for him.

"Did you find out anything?"

"Yes and no."

Before he could say anything else. his phone rang. Glancing at it, he saw his mom's name. He ignored it.

"I know we were supposed to have…" At this point he didn't know what they were supposed to have, all he knew was that he needed to be alone. To deal with everything that had happened, was happening.

He felt like a complete ass kicking her out, especially when a quick look outside showed the snow storm they'd been predicting all day had started.

His phone started ringing again.

Fuck, fuck, fuckity fuck.

This wasn't how tonight was supposed to have gone.

"I think you need to leave."

CHAPTER EIGHT

Emma slammed the cab door closed and pulled out her phone. Opening her favorite contacts, she tapped Astrid's number. *Come on, pick up*, she chanted to herself.

Astrid didn't pick up.

Emma called again. On the fifth ring, just when she was sure it was going to roll over to voice mail again, Astrid's voice came on the line.

"Do you have any fucking clue what time it is here?"

"Yeah, yeah, middle of the night, sorry and all that, but this is important." She took a breath. "I think I fucked something up with Reiner," she told her.

There was a pause and shuffling on the other end, Emma forced herself to breathe while she waited for Astrid to say something. Patience was never her strong suit.

"Say something."

"First, what where you doing with Reiner, and are we talking about my Reiner?"

"Yes, we're talking about your brother, and we hooked up last night

320

at the event you were supposed to come to."

"Define 'hooked up' for me?"

Emma slunk down in the seat, her head resting against the back of cab. She'd been hoping by the time she told Astrid about her and Reiner, it would be in the form of asking her to be maid of honor. Not telling her she'd just had a one-nighter with him, and well, screwed up any chance of anything ever happening long-term.

"He came to the charity event I put on last night, we connected, or reconnected, however you want to put it, he hit on me, I hit back, and then he came home with me."

"Yes!"

She pulled the phone away from her ear, staring at her phone screen, wishing they'd been on video chat. She would have loved to see Astrid's face. Instead, she waited for Astrid to calm down.

"Don't celebrate too soon. I messed up already, and he told me he needed to be alone."

"What? Really? That doesn't sound like him. OK, what happened?"

She recounted the events of the last hour, leaving nothing out. Paying the cabbie, she climbed out and trekked inside her building and up the stairs to her apartment.

"Oh, holy mother of fucking god! Of all the gods, for that matter!" Astrid exclaimed.

"What, Astrid?" The fact that Astrid was freaking out more than she was told Emma more than anything that whatever was going on was bigger than she thought.

"When I went home a couple of summers ago, I was helping my parents clean out their office. I found a file with Reiner's name on it. I thought it was like mine, you know, school papers, awards, things like that. I opened it, not thinking twice. Instead of finding a bunch of old schoolwork, I found the adoption paperwork and a letter stating he was never to know."

"Oh, shit," Emma muttered. "So when I told him to call your parents or grandma…"

"Pretty much. I don't know what's going to happen now, but the impression I got from the letter was it would be bad for him to know his birth family."

Emma headed straight for her bed, flopping down on it. Running her hand across her eyes, she moaned, "You should have seen his face when he walked out after talking to your grandma. He looked like his world had just ended."

The silence on the other side of the call spoke volumes.

"I'll call him and see how he's doing. I know my brother, though, and I have a feeling that once he's adjusted to this, he'll come looking for you. Oh, shit, that's Mom calling me now. Em, I have to go. I'll call you back when I can."

Astrid hung up before Emma could say goodbye, and Emma stayed in her bed with her hand over her eyes, her mind reeling with everything. She wanted to be there for Reiner; gods, how she wanted to be there for him. He didn't want her there though. And even with Astrid's reassurance she was sure he would come looking for her, what they had was too new.

That didn't mean she couldn't be there for him though. She just needed to figure how.

But first she needed a shower and wine. Lots of wine.

Thank God tomorrow was Saturday, and she didn't have to work. Because she was fairly certain she was going to have a hangover and be unable to concentrate on anything but Reiner and what he was going through.

Tossing her phone on the bed she rolled off it and stripped down to her bare skin, ignoring the sexy underwear she'd put on for Reiner. She walked into her bathroom and turned the shower on to blistering hot. She was cold inside and out. Gathering her hair, she piled it on top of her head and stepped into the steaming water.

Thirty minutes later Emma was curled up on her couch, a glass of wine next to her as she contemplated her binge watching choices. *True Blood, Game of Thrones*, or *Thor*. All three had hot Scandinavian men, and yes, she was fully aware that Chris Hemsworth wasn't actually Norwegian, but he played the Norse god Thor so he counted.

She was hoping that watching them would give her inspiration for how to undo the mess she'd made with Reiner.

Before she could choose, her front door opened, and Kevin walked in. He took in the shows up on her TV for her to choose from, the wine, and joined her on the couch.

"What happened?"

Bursting into tears she told him everything.

By the time she was done, she was emotionally wrung out. It hadn't hurt this much when she'd talked to Astrid.

"Have you tried calling him?"

"No. He said he wanted to be alone."

Kevin patted her knee. "Honey, that's what all men say when they've taken an emotional hit. That doesn't mean that he doesn't want to hear from you."

"You sure?"

His left eyebrow lifted into his hair. "Yes I'm sure. Now call him."

She wasn't convinced this was the right decision, but as Kevin and Ray were the only men she was friends with…no, they weren't friends, they were family, and she was going to do what he said.

Emma picked up her phone and scrolled through her messages until she found his number and pressed call. She held her breath while she waited for him to pick up. After the fifth ring it went straight to voicemail.

"Reiner, this is Emma. I…" She trailed off. She wasn't sure what to say. Kevin nodded encouragingly at her, so she continued, "I'm sorry about tonight. Call me please."

"Good, now let's watch *Thor*."

"No *Game of Thrones*?"

Ray hated the show, so the only time Kevin got to watch it was with her. They were binge-watching Season Four, and Season Five would be loaded up in her instant queue by the time they were done.

"As much as I want to know what's going on with Jon Snow, you're in no condition to watch it with me."

He was right, but she couldn't resist teasing him, "You know if you read the books you'd know what was going on with him."

He threw the remote at her, "I've still not forgiven you for not telling me about the Red Wedding."

She caught it and turned on *Thor*.

Hopefully by the end of the movie Reiner would call her back.

CHAPTER NINE

Reiner was speechless. His mom was crying, his dad was trying to console her, and Reiner felt like an ass. Apparently his parents *had* found him on their doorstep. He'd been tucked into a basket, like some damn cliché, with a note saying he was the son of Ull and that he needed a stable and loving home. His parents had always told him that he was a gift from the gods. He'd thought it was just his folks' way of saying they were proud of him. But if he could believe them now, he was literally a gift from the gods.

His father was a god, and his mother had been a human woman who didn't know how to care for a demigod. She'd kept in contact with his parents until she died, but she was afraid for both Reiner and herself. She didn't want the gods to harm him, so she'd found his grandmother, a woman renowned for honoring the old traditions. His grandmother had helped hide him with a mortal family. Her own.

Reiner couldn't have asked for a better family, but damn it, this was something he'd had a right to know about! Was this why he'd gotten a vision? He was part god?

This was crazy. He knew shit like this didn't exist. Yet, he couldn't discount that vision. Or his abilities. More than never having been sick, or never having gotten injured, Reiner had a connection to the ice. When he took the ice, his skates became one with the ice. *He* became one with the ice. He was fast. Faster than any other player. So, what, his dad was the god of hockey? This was bullshit.

He started pacing again. He had to get his head on straight before the game tomorrow. Finding out his whole life was a lie, and he was only good at hockey because he was a god, was not OK with him. This sort of thing only happened in the movies. He was a normal guy; he was a hockey player. He wasn't the bastard son of a god. Because that shit wasn't real.

It couldn't be.

The phone ringing shook him out of his thoughts, but when he saw who it was, he didn't pick up. Emma. After sending her to voicemail, it rang again. And again. And again. Finally, he picked up and snarled into the phone, "What?"

"*Hei, bror*. What kind of greeting is that for your sister?"

"Astrid."

"*Ja.*"

"I thought you were Emma."

"Well, that's a horrible way to greet Emma."

"You don't know what my day's been like."

"Actually, I think I do. And I'd like to talk to you about it."

"Not tonight, Astrid."

"Yes. Tonight. I know you're pissed, and you have every right to be."

"Jesus, does everyone know but me? What the hell, Astrid. Who else knows?"

326

"No one! I swear! I wasn't even supposed to know. I found out by accident!"

"And what, decided I didn't need to know?"

"Reiner, please."

"I gotta go, Astrid. I've got a game tomorrow."

"No, don't hang up…"

But he did.

The urge to throw his phone across the room was immense, but that'd only mean he'd have to hit a phone store in the morning before skate time. Something he didn't have the time nor inclination to do.

Instead he grabbed the bottle of pure Russian vodka one of his teammates had left at his place and poured himself a drink. Maybe he could find oblivion at the bottom of the bottle.

After a sleepless night full of restless thoughts, Reiner took to the ice no closer to sorting his life out than he had been the night before. He missed Emma. But he couldn't bring himself to talk to her yet. It was too soon, and this was all too new. It hadn't helped he'd had the family skate that morning with everyone bringing their significant others and various other family members. He'd always liked the event, but not today. Not when everywhere he'd looked he'd seen Emma. He had a game to play. The Empires needed this win, and he'd do his part to make sure they got it.

Knock, knock. Alexei was tapping on his helmet.

"Cut it out," Reiner snarled. They were sitting on the benches, waiting for the line change. The game was going well. The team they were playing was good. But so were they. And now was the time to prove it.

"OK, OK." Alexei held his hands up in surrender. "We're cool. But where were you? You weren't in the game, that's for sure."

"Don't worry about it." Reiner didn't want to talk about it. Not now, that's for sure. Maybe not ever.

"Change it up," Coach's voice sounded.

"We're up."

Alexei stared at him, knowing Reiner was blowing him off, and knowing he couldn't do anything about it. Reiner mentally shrugged him off. It was time to play. For the next two hours he was determined to not think about the past couple of days, and to do what he did best. Play hockey.

Climbing over the boards, his skates hit the ice, and Reiner was home. He let the rest melt away, keeping his eye on the other team's offense. They had a good lineup, and Reiner knew they were going to play it man on man, so he watched the guy he was on and skated after him.

The next thirty minutes passed in a blur, until he was sitting back on the benches pounding water, wiping sweat out of his eyes. His eyes cleared, and he looked toward the action and swore long and low.

The new kid was stuck against the boards with a big guy from the other team. Reiner had gone up against him several times in the past, as had the rest of his teammates. This wasn't going to end well. The guy had a reputation in the league of being beyond brutal on the newbies. When the hit came, and Max started to fall toward the ice, Reiner hoped it cushioned him much like it had when he'd taken the hit the day before.

He glanced around the rink; his teammates were furious. The fans were screaming obscenities at the player. When the refs didn't call for a penalty, he, along with all of this teammates, voiced their anger.

His eyes found Brody, their enforcer, on the ice, who was staring at the player who'd started it all. He knew that look.

The entire team was on their feet in an instant, shouting at the ref, at the other team, at anyone within earshot. Max was flat on the ice, and the medical team was bringing out a stretcher. Once the ice was cleared, and no penalty was called, the guys lined up for a new play.

The second the puck hit the ice, their enforcer was on him. Brody was pounding the other player. It had been a dirty hit, and Brody showed his displeasure by rearranging the opposing guy's face, which got him thrown off the ice and out of the game. His muttered, "Worth it," earned him a couple pats on the back, but really it meant they were down another good player right when it counted.

Coach threw Reiner and Kyle in, double shifting them, and they jumped over the boards. Reiner's skates never hit the ice, though. One minute he was in the game, the next he was standing in the middle of a blizzard.

Putting his hand up to shield his eyes from the stinging wind and snow, he squinted against the blinding white snowscape. And then it was gone. Calm descended, and Reiner dropped his hand to his side, looking around. There was nothing but ice and snow. What the fuck? Gone was his gear, and in its place was the suit the he'd worn the night he'd met Emma.

"Hello, Reiner."

He spun around and gaped. The man standing before him looked exactly like he did. At least the parts of him he could see.

"Who are you? Where am I? How did I get here?"

"You know who I am. As for where you are, you are near my home, your home. Look?" He pointed behind him. Reiner turned and squinted. There in the distance he could see the E6 train. He looked around him again, recognizing the area. He was near his grandparents' farm.

"How did I get here?" More importantly, how could he get back?

"I brought you here, and don't worry I'll have you back in the game, before the medics are done with your teammate."

That made about as much sense as anything had in the past day. "Why did you bring me here?"

"Because you were told about your adoption. If you'd never been told, what's about to happen never would."

"What's about to happen?"

"You, my son, are going to come into your powers."

His what?

"You want to run that past me again."

"If you'd never found out about who you really were, you'd would have gone through life as a mortal with a little extra to him. Now that you know, however, while you're still mortal, you'll have powers."

"I thought I already had my powers. The whole bonding with ice and hockey thing." Just thinking about the fact his hockey skills weren't because of his talent and hard work still pissed him off. It felt his daddy had paid off all the coaches to get him on every team he'd ever played on instead of earning his spot.

"No, those aren't your powers, at least not completely. If you'd been born to two mortals, you'd still have those for the most part. Some people are like that. Think about some of the great athletes in the world, it was all them. Just like your talent on the ice is all you. Yes, being my son helps a little, but what you've achieved on the ice is solely you."

The polar bear that had been sitting on his shoulders since his conversation with this parents was gone. "What, no, who exactly are you?" While his grandma was a devout follower of the old gods, he only knew of Odin, Thor, and Loki, and that was more because of the movies than anything he'd ever been taught.

"I'm Ull, the god of ice and snow, the son of Sif."

He'd heard of Sif...once again thanks to the movies.

"So what does that make me?" He really had zero desire to be anything other than a hockey player and…the vision he'd had of Emma flashed in his mind. The emotions in it overwhelmed him.

"That makes you Reiner Jahr, the son of Lars and Stella Jahr. It also makes you Reiner Jahr, the son of Ull and grandson of Sif. You are both the same and different."

Reiner was glad Ull had listed his human parents first, because regardless of where his genes came from, they were his parents. And standing here in the presence of Ull, he could admit to himself he'd have made the same decision his parents and grandparents had made.

"So do I have to do anything?" Please tell him he didn't, he prayed. He wasn't sure to who he was praying to at this point.

"Just win the Stanley Cup. I've got a million bucks on your team winning it in a four game sweep."

"Nice."

"What, a god can't have a little fun every now and then?"

"What about my powers?" Not that he wanted them, he just wanted to be prepared.

"I don't know. It's different for all of my children."

All of his children? "Just how many siblings do I have?"

Ull smiled, "At the present I have six children living, the youngest is six months old."

"And do they all know you?"

"Yes. You were the only one adopted by a mortal family. Your birth mother couldn't handle who I was and who you would be. You and one of your brothers are the only ones not from my wife. Now that you know about where you come from and about me, she will expect you to come to our family events, and on our annual family vacation. We have T-shirts and everything."

This was too surreal. He already had a family, and Astrid was the only sibling he wanted or needed. Finding out there were five more and that he was expected to be a part of their lives, that was going to take time to adjust to.

Something Ull—Reiner would never refer to him as Dad, he already had one of those—said had him pausing. "Wait a minute you said I only got my powers when I was told about who my birth parents are. But I've always had little things that don't make any sense happen to me. I've never been injured when I should have been, or been sick. I can drink anyone under the table and have no hangover, and I had a vision yesterday."

Ull shrugged. "Well, your full powers, we'll say. You're the son of a god. Of course you have a few…*extras*, we'll call them. The son of a god would have good genes." The *duh* was implied. "And as for what happened yesterday, that was me. You're welcome."

"What do you mean that was you? The dream? Was it really my future?" If so he needed to talk to Em, and fast. He hoped he hadn't screwed things up with her.

"I was at your practice yesterday and saw you take that hit. I cushioned your head. As for the vision, that must have come from your mother's side, as no one in my family tree has prophecies or visions. That's an ancient trait that goes back to when humans first walked upright. Why do you think gods always needed an oracle? My guess is someone in your family tree had that gift. Odin knows your grandmother does, which is why your birth mother went to her in the first place."

He could handle this. He was part god, but his hockey abilities were his own. Deep breaths, right? He could do this. So he healed faster than others, that wasn't a huge deal. He understood the ice. He felt the ice. But he wasn't superhuman and using his strengths to cheat or anything. He blew out a breath. OK. This was manageable.

"This has been great and all but…"

"You have a game to win."

Reiner blinked, and he was back on the ice with his teammates, watching as the trainers worked on the new kid, Max. He glanced up at the glass and met a pair of brown eyes. Emma. There was concern there. Concern and something else. That something else gave him hope. But he couldn't think about that at the moment. He needed to get his head back in the game.

The trainers helped Max off the ice, and Dobrynin took his spot. The ref blew the whistle and everyone took their positions. The puck dropped and the game was back on.

A last minute goal by Alexei won them the game. Reiner was anxious to shower and go find Emma. He had some serious apologizing to do.

In the locker room, the captain's voice carried as he stomped over to the new kid, Max.

"I saw what happened at the family skate."

What the hell? Reiner had put in an appearance at the Family Skate, but only long enough to be seen by his coach and those who cared about that shit. He glanced at Kyle and Alexei, who shrugged their shoulders, not knowing what was going on either. The new kid finished lacing up his skates and looked up at Emerson. Reiner knew the kid's English wasn't very good. He'd been taking lessons from their captain's sister. In fact, it looked like that wasn't all that was happening between them.

"You need to stay away from my sister. I don't give two shits that you're helping her or she's helping you. This helping shit needs to stop. You're too young and too fucking immature to treat her like she wants to be treated."

Max didn't say anything. He just looked at Emerson.

Someone muttered, "Oh shit," just as Emerson got in the kid's face.

"You're not saying anything. Open your fucking mouth and

goddamn promise me you're not going to touch her again."

There was about half a beat before, like an arrow honed in to its target, their captain threw a punch. While Emerson had power, the new kid had speed and agility.

At the last second, he ducked, pivoted and lightly grabbed Emerson's arms mid-punch. "You don't need this," he whispered. Clear, soft, and sure. "Not now. Not *avant*..." Reiner heard this clear as a bell, but he knew no one else had. This must have been what Ull was talking about and enhanced powers. Yay him.

Except Emerson was a hockey player, and brawls were nothing new. He threw an elbow, hard, slamming into the center of the kid's chest. Max caught himself right before he hit the ground.

The look on Emerson's face was beyond angry. And as the rest of the team came in, Reiner and Alexei grabbed Emerson to keep their captain from tearing into him, while a few others held back the kid based on some mistaken belief that he had any desire to punch the captain. Reiner knew Max wouldn't throw a punch.

Once they cooled Emerson down, and Max left, Reiner double-timed it to the showers. This was important, and he wouldn't go to Emma smelling of hockey.

Chapter Ten

Emma waited near the locker room where all the fans were congregating to catch their favorite players and get autographs. She'd debated with herself all through the third period on whether or not she should come down here, but that look he'd given her when they were working on his teammate had seared her.

She had to see him.

The locker room door finally opened and some of the players started coming out. All of them stopped and signed autographs and took selfies.

Having worked for the Special Olympics for years, she'd been around a lot of athletes, and her favorite when it came to fan interaction were the hockey players. Several of them nodded as they walked past her. While she appreciated it, they weren't the player she wanted to see.

The door opened, letting out Alexei and Kyle, wearing a shirt that said Go Puck Yourself, closely followed by Reiner. None of them looked happy. Neither did the players who came after them. Whatever had happened between the time they'd left the ice and now wasn't good. She just hoped it wasn't so bad that he'd walk past her.

All of them stopped and did their duty with the fans, and then he was there in front of her. She tipped her head back to meet his gaze, and the fire in his eyes seared her. She opened her mouth to say something when he crushed his lips to hers. This was no gentle kiss. This was a claiming. One hand gripped the back of her neck, the other her hip. She'd have bruises by the end of this kiss, but she didn't care. She'd missed him. And something had changed with him.

Her fingers curled into his slightly damp hair, and she opened for him. She let him take. Emma was planning on taking plenty once they were alone, so he could plunder her mouth, claim her in front of the press, because tonight, he was hers.

Lifting his head, he didn't say anything, he just held out his hand. Taking it she followed him out of the stadium to the parking lot. He stopped next to a sleek two-door sports car that looked incredibly fast and opened the passenger side door for her. Climbing in, she tried to look at his face to gauge what his mood was.

Before she could get a good look, he closed the door and walked around to the driver's side and climbed in.

The drive across town should have been full of tension considering how they'd left things the night before and the way he'd come out of the locker room, but it wasn't. She studied him as he drove through the late night traffic. There wasn't much of it at this time of night, unlike during the day when it took forever to go five blocks.

Before she knew it they were pulling up in front Reiner's apartment. That she hadn't been expecting. She'd thought for sure they'd go to her place; that way he could leave at any time. Not that she was trapped there either. She'd just have to call for a cab and wait. Not something she necessarily wanted to do in the middle of the night in December.

But that kiss left her with the feeling that she wouldn't be leaving any time soon.

Neither one of them said anything as they made their way to his apartment. He was deep in thought, and she did not want to disturb his mood. He obviously had something on his mind, and she wanted to hear it.

Reiner tossed his keys onto a table next to the door and made his way to the kitchen, where he pulled open the freezer and pulled out a clear bottle. Still not speaking, he tilted the bottle toward her in silent invitation. Emma shook her head.

Someone needed to break the silence, and it looked like it was going to her after all. "Are you OK?"

He took a deep swig from the bottle, and barked out a laugh. "Yes and no." Running his fingers through his hair, he took another pull from the bottle.

"Why yes and no?"

"Let's see, last night I found out my parents aren't really my parents." Emma winced, knowing that had been her fault. "Then I made my mom cry when I called her in the middle of the night pissed off. I hung up on my sister. Then I met my biological father, who by the way is one of the old gods, and wasn't that a trip?" He took another drink, his eyes never leaving hers. "And I hurt you."

He had, and as much as she wanted to focus on that, this wasn't about her. She'd known about his folks being upset, and about how he'd hung up on Astrid. After all, she'd talked to Astrid before she'd left for the game.

"You met your biological father?"

He took another long drink. "That's what you focus on?" He laughed, although she knew he didn't find anything funny. "Yep, and you'll never guess who he is and where I met him."

Emma pulled out one of the stools at his counter. "Tell me."

"Fuck, let me get you something to drink." He opened the fridge and pulled out the bottle of wine that had been on the table last night. Grabbing one of the wine glasses sitting on the counter he poured her a glass.

She took a small sip, wanting to keep her head clear, and then gestured for him to tell her about his biological father.

By the time he was done telling about the visit, she was tempted to exchange the glass of wine he'd poured her for the bottle. While she'd told him things like that made sense, finding out the guy you were in love with was actually a demigod was going to take some getting used to. "What are you going to do?"

"What can I do? Take it one day at a time."

"But something else is bothering you."

"Yeah, some shit that went down between Max, the new kid from the farm team, and Chris."

"What's going on between them? And why do you call him the new kid? He's been on the team for a couple of months, hasn't he?"

"He'll be the new kid until someone else is. And maybe not even then. He's only twenty, for Christ's sake. And Emerson's sister…is more than twenty."

"So? Good for her! Who cares how old they are?"

"Chris."

Emma was gob smacked over everything that had happened in the last couple of days. It was a lot for anyone to take in, and she felt for him. But she needed to know about the kiss.

"What about…"

"Us?" he finished.

"Yeah."

He moved around the counter and took her hands, pulling her to her feet. His hands slipped up her arms, over her shoulders, cupping her neck, his thumbs tipped her head back and his mouth took hers in a kiss.

There were kisses, and then there were *kisses*. This was one of the latter. This was the kind of kiss people dreamed about getting their whole lives. She'd been dreaming about this kind of kiss her whole life. If the other kiss had been a claiming, this kiss was a promise.

Growing up with parents who fought more than they showed affection, her only examples of love had been in the romance novels she'd sneaked and the movies she'd watched. Having Reiner kiss her like she was his very breath was everything she wanted and then some.

She broke away from him, gasping for her own breath, "I don't understand."

She really didn't.

"Let's just say I realized that there is a lot I don't know and can't control about my future, but there are two things I can."

"What are those two things?"

"Hockey," he replied instantly. But he took a deep breath before finishing. "And how I feel about you."

Emma was fairly certain that her heart was beating so fast it was going to jump out of her chest at his words. "How do you feel about me?"

"For years I've heard about this amazing woman who was best friends with my sister and loved my crazy family. She was kind, generous with her time, and more importantly not impressed with the fact that I was a hockey player. She never asked my sister for tickets to a game or to meet me or any of my friends. Then I met her again. She didn't approach me; I doubt she even noticed me until I went to her."

Oh, she'd noticed him. Not that she'd be stopping what he was saying at any time soon.

"Then I went home with her. The truth is I've been falling in love with you for years, and had no clue. It wasn't until tonight that I realized it."

Emma was fairly certain that if Reiner hadn't been holding her up she would be a pile of goo on his floor.

"You love me?"

No one outside those she considered family had ever told her they loved her. Not even her past boyfriends. She couldn't believe until she heard it again.

He brushed a kiss across her lips, "*Ja.*"

"But we just…"

"Emma, time doesn't matter when you know it's right. And this is right."

His thumbs brushed across her cheeks and she realized she was crying. This wasn't how she'd expected the night going, it was so much better.

"I love you, too. I have for years. I just always assumed it would be an unrequited love, something I told my grandchildren about."

"You still can." He brushed a kiss across her lips. "But they'll be *our* grandchildren, and our memories, and *our* love story," he told her just before he kissed her again.

This time the kiss was full of passion, and when she closed her eyes, she saw the future. *Their* future.

EPILOGUE

Reiner looked around the locker room at his teammates, his brothers. This season had been one for the record books. To say that it had had its ups and downs was an understatement. Not only had he reconnected with Emma, but they'd also gotten married and discovered that she was pregnant. His vision had come true, and he couldn't be more excited. And scared. And excited some more.

His gaze touched on each of his teammates. The guys were celebrating. They'd just won the Stanley Cup. Hard work paid off, and now they could relax and enjoy the fruit of their labor. At the moment, Kyle, in a T-shirt that said, *Education is Important, but Hockey is Importanter*, was trying to convince their captain to let him sleep with the Cup. Surprisingly, Cap looked like he'd give in. If he did it would the perfect time to test out his new god powers by turning the Cup to ice when Kyle took it home.

Yet for Reiner, even though he'd just realized a lifelong dream, he wanted nothing more than a shower and to find his wife. *His wife.* Those were words he'd never tire of hearing.

But tonight they'd join the guys.

His mates, his new friends, and now his wife, all held a spot in his life, in his soul. He had the rest of his life to spend with Emma. But tonight was for hockey. Tonight was for celebrating.

Tomorrow was for Emma. And every tomorrow after that.

If you've enjoyed

ICING THE PUCK

Don't miss

Book 3 in the New York Empires Series

Coming Soon!

ABOUT THE AUTHORS

Isabo Kelly

Isabo Kelly is the award-winning author of numerous science fiction, fantasy, and paranormal romances. She also writes best-selling paranormal romance under the name Kat Simons. Her life has taken her from Las Vegas to Hawaii, where she got her BA in Zoology, back to Vegas where she looked after sharks, then on to Germany and Ireland where she got her Ph.D. in Animal Behavior. Now Isabo focuses on writing. She lives in New York with her Irish husband and two beautiful boys, working as a full time writer and stay-at-home mom. For more on Isabo, visit her at her website http://www.isabokelly.com.

Stacey Agdern

Stacey Agdern is an award winning former bookseller who has reviewed romance novels in multiple formats and given talks about various aspects of the romance genre. She's also a romance writer. You can find her on twitter at @nystacey. She's a proud member of both LIRW and RWA NYC. She lives in New York, not far from her favorite hockey team's practice facility. Website: https://staceyagdern.wordpress.com/

Kenzie MacLir

Kenzie MacLir is the writing duo of contemporary romance author Heather Lire, and Scottish Romance author Laura Hunsaker. One night they decided to pool their creativity and start writing together. They spend their days chauffeuring their kids to all of their various activities and their nights plotting how to torture their characters. Between Highlanders and hockey players, there's a story for everyone. Enjoy the Romance, and for upcoming events and news, subscribe to our newsletter (http://www.kenziemaclir.com/).

www.ingramcontent.com/pod-product-compliance
Lightning Source LLC
Chambersburg PA
CBHW050916250626
47155CB00001B/260